MORSEL

AUDREY RUSH

Morsel: An Erotic Horror Novel by Audrey Rush

Independently Published

Copyright © 2024 Audrey Rush

Cover Photography from DepositPhotos.com
Cover Design by Kai & Audrey Rush

Amazon Paperback ISBN: 9798329360783
Barnes & Noble Paperback ISBN: 9798331416386

This is a work of fiction. Names, characters, places, and incidents either are the product of the author's imagination or are used fictitiously. Any persons appearing on the cover image of this book are models and do not have any connection to the contents of this book. This book is intended for mature audiences only. Any activities represented in this book are fictional fantasies only.

*for the horror readers who dream of
being hunted and eaten*

Author's Note

This content notification contains spoilers.

This is a *horror* novel. The violence in this book builds slowly to an extremely intense conclusion. As such, this book contains graphic violence, animal death, and flashbacks of child abuse. Furthermore, it also contains disturbing content including but not limited to rape, cannibalism, and the defilement of animal corpses. A detailed list of content can be found on the author's website.

Reader discretion is advised.

MORSEL

PART ONE

FINGERTIPS

CHAPTER 1

THE BUTCHER SLAMS THE CLEAVER INTO THE MEAT, AND MY PULSE races at the familiar thud. Instead of raw beef, I imagine a woman's head as it rolls off the red-stained counter and drops onto the rubber mat-lined floor. *Thump*, like a sack of garbage slung into a bin. *Thump*, like my heart when it knows how close release is. My mouth dries, and I close my eyes, imagining my fingers twisting through its tangled hair as I lift the head from the floor.

The paper crinkles around the filet, and I'm back to reality. I glimpse at the door, pretending I'm in a hurry like everyone else. I used to buy two filets—one for me, one for whomever I was paying that night—then I realized they didn't give a shit about steak. They were with me solely for the money.

There is always something better about vegetarians anyway.

"Sixty-five dollars," the butcher says.

My jaw ticks. Sixty-five dollars? That's five dollars up from last time. I tap my boot, holding back the urge to rip the meat from his fucking hands.

"I need a damn loyalty punch card," I mutter.

"Do you want it or not?"

My skull tingles as I hand over the cash. I save money and live a meager lifestyle to pay for indulgences like this. The price for organic, free range, grass-fed meat can get outrageous—sixty-five dollars for one fucking filet—but in the end, it's worth it. The savory undertones are richer than you'd expect, layered with the healthy, green life each animal had, and those flavors build on your taste buds with every bite. Sometimes, I even ask the escort services for vegetarians. Not because I'm going to eat them—I'm not a cannibal—but because of the *idea* of it.

If grass-fed meat tastes better, vegetarian women must taste better too.

A hollowness flutters in my stomach, the need inching to the surface. I collect my treat and clutch the brown paper sack. The butcher scowls at me. I keep gawking at the cold display cases anyway, taking my time. I've practically memorized it all, and yet I marvel at a perfectly marbled sirloin like it's a slice of a woman's back.

The door chime jingles; another customer has arrived. I take that as my cue. The butcher is distracted for now.

The butcher shop is in the middle of a strip mall. A narrow alleyway is in the back, which is where the mall's garbage bins are smashed between the stores and a row of trees. I head directly to the butcher's bins.

My fingers vibrate with nerves as I jab at the waste. I need to finish shopping for very specific extras before the butcher notices me back here. When it comes to what I need, turkey is pointless; it's too fibrous, and the follicles are annoying. Chicken will do in a pinch, but I can get that kind of meat at work. The best choices are pork and beef: their flesh is textured, yet strong enough to stay intact.

And near the top of the first bin, there's a thin, black slab covered with a scaly green membrane. Thick, pink liquid drips down the sides, like blood and saliva sliding down a woman's breast. I smile to myself. You can't tell someone what they should or shouldn't throw away, but you *can* do something with their leftovers.

And I can't pass up a rotten beef tongue.

I open the second bin. As I reach for a piece of lightly used butcher paper, my fingers skim the hard surface of flesh. I freeze.

4

Don't look, I tell myself. *You already have a good piece, and you're too curious for your own good. You need to be quick so that they don't catch you—*

My dick twitches. I can't help myself. I pick through the debris until I see it.

A beef heart, the fat tinted bluish green.

Warnings ring in my ears, but I'm alone, and I *want* this. I pry a ventricle open wide enough for my dick, then I unzip and unbuckle my pants and slide my cock inside. It doesn't fit right, but that's why I like it; the muscle squeezes the head of my dick, forcing pleasure up my spine. I close my eyes and let the ambient-temperature flesh soothe me. A woman's heart—carved from her chest—would feel like this. A final fuck before eating her most vital organ.

A car honks, and I startle, dropping the heart on the pavement.

"Damn it," I say.

I quickly wrap the beef heart and tongue into the brown paper I pull from the bin, then stow them under one arm, my bagged filet in the other. It's not really stealing if it's garbage. And it's not really animal cruelty if it's already dead.

MY VAN COASTS DOWN THE STREET. IN THE DISTANCE, BROWN hills circle each side of the road, and dull green trees speckle their terrain. In the bottom layer, unremarkable stores sandwich the asphalt, and people march around like ants.

Then the street becomes a two-lane road that pounds through the farmland. Corn fields. Sunflower stalks. And tall, tall grass. I pass the local dump—the high sides of the pit piled with waste and backed by dead grass. The stink clears, the asphalt ends, and the path shifts to a dirt lane, which ends at my home.

Although the mobile home is in decent shape, what I like most are the grassy fields surrounding it. We're off the grid. There's enough space that I built a platform for my industrial meat grinder, *and* I dug a large offal pit for any extra meat I collect. Offal pits aren't something you usually find in California, but a week after I moved here, I began digging. Pork spleens, lamb brains, beef hearts and tongues, any organs or scraps discarded and left to rot get added to the six-foot-deep hole. Depending on the weather, the odor can get worse than the dump, and sometimes the larvae and the odd wild animal get to the meat. But if you add enough salt, they stay away.

When I get time, I grind and freeze the salted meat for further preservation; I even custom ordered an oversized hopper to chop up the biggest chunks of meat. And when the urges come, I always have the offal pit to come back to. Rotting meat, salted or not, feels better than a silicone sleeve. It feels *real*, and with the gamey stench in my nose, I can almost pretend it's a dead woman.

That's part of why I like living alone. You can't predict if your housemate will appreciate your conservation efforts or your sexual needs. You also can't know if they'll hate what you're doing and report it, or worse, if they'll leave you.

Still, I dream of having a woman here.

A rabbit bounces across the dirt driveway. I imagine a predator somewhere, a wolf maybe, stalking it. Waiting for the right moment to strike. A feast waiting to be devoured.

The cool wind whips past my cheek. The landfill's compactor shudders on, the engine's whine reminiscent of a semi truck; it's one of the only reminders of civilization out here. Unless you invite someone to these fields, cars don't come down this way. And as there's no reason for the power lines out here, I keep a generator at the back of the mobile home. I switch it on, and it powers the house. I also have a small one inside for my fridge and freezer. You can never be too careful with food.

I toss the beef tongue and heart into the offal pit. The organs slop on top of the pink and green sea, and flies buzz out of the hole to greet me. I smack them away, then grab a sack of salt and pour some over the top of the pit. Then, after shoveling some salted organs into a wheelbarrow, I take one scoop at a time up the steps to the industrial grinder. The meat slops into the giant hopper. I power on the grinder, and it rattles away. The raw flesh sloshes into the oversized funnel, and the metal blades chirp like a million dying birds. Not many people would appreciate my hobby, but it gives me a sense of control and reassurance that I'll never be left unsatisfied.

As I'm storing the first batch of ground meat in a plastic container, the low rumble of a car cuts through the metallic grinding. I turn off the machine.

A car is parked in the driveway, and at the front of the home, a brunette with light skin beams at me.

No makeup. That's good.

I clutch my filet mignon to my side and wave with my free hand.

"Sorry I'm late," she says. "I had an emergency."

"No big deal. Let's eat."

I open the front door, and she enters the home before me. She studies the dried hydrangea wreath clinging to the door hook. Pink rose wallpaper peels in sections of the home, and an old box TV sits on the floor of the living room. I don't use it much. There's not much I'm invested in updating out here, unless it has to do with meat.

The brunette points at an old circular photograph. "Is that your mother? She's gorgeous."

I peek at the brunette's bare legs: skinny, scrawny little things. Nothing more than chicken thighs. Not that I mind. You can enjoy a lean thigh every now and then, especially with the right preparation.

"She is pretty," I say.

I head to the kitchen and unwrap the butcher paper. Even with the hint of sulfur and iron wafting up from the meat, I can smell something else. Something synthetic. I wrinkle my nose. Perfume. The brunette's perfume. Honeysuckle, maybe.

A headache blooms across my forehead. I grit my teeth and shove it all down. This escort service is new to my patronage, but I told them to keep her as natural as possible. Honeysuckle is technically a natural scent, but it's too floral for me.

I'm already irritated.

She's not wearing makeup though. I have to give them credit for that. Besides, I *need* this to work. Tomorrow, I'll meet Mona for

AUDREY RUSH

the first time, and I don't want to blow my load the second I shake hands with my dream girl.

I gesture toward the bathroom. "Help yourself," I say to the escort. "Lay on the dining table when you're ready."

"Thanks, baby." She disappears behind the closed door.

My groin tingles as I listen: the faucet runs, the toilet flushes, and fabric swishes against skin. There's still hope. Even if she's wearing perfume, she has to be enough to satiate my needs tonight. I have to give her a fair shot.

The bathroom door opens. The dining table creaks. I lick my lips and head toward my meal.

The brunette lies on the teal-painted table. Black silk covers her breasts and cunt.

My back pinches, the strain aching through my body. I had specifically asked the manager for a woman who would be naked on my dinner table, as close to a basic, quiet woman as possible. No makeup. No jewelry. No perfume. No fucking lingerie. It's not hard. My only special request—the reason the last escort company refused my continued business—was the willingness to do knife play.

The table's teal paint is cracked underneath her, and it exposes splotches of the brown wood. Almost like her. An unnecessary blotch on my plate.

I blink and center myself. Perhaps she's the *only* one willing to participate in knife play.

I can make this work.

I have to give her a chance.

It's just a fantasy, I remind myself. *It's not like I'm actually going to eat her.*

I slap the piece of raw meat on her stomach—one of the only places that's completely bare—and she wiggles, her lips coiling into a smile.

"So cool," she coos. "It feels good."

My jaw clenches. I don't engage. I avoid her eyes as I use the steak knife on the meat. Translucent red juices run down her skin. The serrated edge of the blade cuts through the filet, hitting her

8

stomach, and she jolts and moans like she's performing for a camera.

"Hurt me," she whimpers.

My upper lip curls. It's a line meant for a stage show. Is she making fun of me?

"Has your food ever made a noise like that?" I ask flatly.

"I'm just having so much fun, baby." She giggles. Fury clouds my vision, and she licks her lips. "Come on, baby. Eat me. Eat me like you're the big bad wolf."

I drop the knife, then rub my forehead so hard that I see stars. Meat doesn't speak. Meat doesn't respond like it's a joke to them. Meat doesn't act like I'm some kind of freak to be laughed at in the middle of a circus.

Meat simply exists. Meat is ready to provide for you. Meat *gives*.

Most escorts are like this though. They indulge through theatrics. Sometimes, I can get past the obnoxious acting; today, when I'm so close to meeting my dream girl, my patience is thin. I just need this to satiate me until tomorrow.

This bitch can't even do that.

"What?" the brunette asks, suddenly aware that I'm upset. "What is it?"

I take several hundred-dollar bills out of my wallet, exactly what I owe her. I can't tell her what to do, but I can end this exchange before my temper gets out of control. I'm not an animal, and I refuse to let my anger control me.

They always bolt anyway.

"I asked for someone who wouldn't mock me," I say, a hard edge to my tone.

She sits up and clutches the filet to her stomach like she can salvage this. "You really just wanted me to pretend to be dead?"

I hand her the money. "Lie there. Don't speak. It's not hard."

Thoughts ricochet behind her eyes as she processes my words. I shouldn't have said anything. They always get offended. But for fuck's sake, *she's* the one who doesn't understand simple directions. The fucking idiot.

She snatches the money, and the steak slaps onto the table. She rolls her eyes.

"If you wanted someone to play dead, it'd be cheaper to fuck a piece of raw meat," she scoffs.

I glance in the direction of the industrial meat grinder. I suppose that's true. It's my go-to when the daydreams are too hard to contain.

I wanted someone *alive* tonight, a woman with a beating heart. Like Mona.

The brunette pulls her dress over her head. The meat juices soak into the fabric. She stomps to the front door.

"I'm a sex worker," she says. "I'm good at playing pretend, but I'm not a piece of meat."

I shake my head. "Good for you."

The door slams shut behind her. Within a few seconds, her car's engine dissipates, and then there's only the hum of the generator and the soft cries of the insects outside.

She wouldn't understand my fantasies. Practically no one can.

But there's a chance Mona will.

CHAPTER 2

I EAT MY RAW STEAK WITH ONE HAND WHILE I JACK OFF WITH THE other. When I was a kid, I used to get sick from consuming raw meat, mostly chicken, but it hasn't bothered me in years. I guess I've built up a tolerance for it, just like I'm numb to the ridiculously fake sex workers out there.

Now that it's just me and my meat, I watch computer-generated cartoon videos of a Tyrannosaurus rex eating a naked woman. My dick stays limp. The cartoon is no better than the sex worker, and it's like the creators used a dinosaur to show me how pathetic I am. *You're not a dinosaur,* they say. *You're not even a predator. You're a pathetic little man who is so desperate for a woman's touch that you want to eat her.*

It's not like that though. I swear it's not. I know who I am, and this fascination—eating a woman—has been with me since I was a teenager. I used to try to get off to spanking videos like normal people. It's not enough though, and I can't just clap my hands and make this obsession disappear. I have the offal pit and the sex workers to keep me busy. Maybe after Mona, I won't need the pit or the escorts anymore.

Eventually, I give up and drive about an hour away to a wealthy neighborhood in Sacramento. Lush green lawns—real grass—decorate the properties, a lofty display of wealth. Even if the drought has been over for ages, the state loves clinging to its conservation laws. It's one of the shitty things about being in a blue state.

I'm not here for the environment though. I'm in California because the women are more open here, more willing to explore. And if I'm right about Mona, I won't need anyone else. One day, we can move somewhere else together. Maybe Florida.

I park my car around the block, then walk to Mona's house and let myself into her backyard.

Her house has six rooms, a library, a bar, a massive kitchen, and a formal dining room. Even her backyard is massive, stacked with patio furniture, a spa, a firepit, and a garden. The land-scaping is garnished with sculptures that I assume are hers. Being a successful artist means you're rich, I guess.

Mona, the artist who lives here, posted an anonymous personal ad on a local website with a few faceless nude pictures. *I'm tired of not having my needs met,* her ad said. *I want a man to eat me like a piece of meat. Serious inquiries only.*

I had never stumbled on an ad like that before. I'd been hunting for a new escort service that would actually fulfill my needs and send me a sex worker with a brain for once, and instead, I found something better.

Mona Milk.

In the first picture, she's on her knees, her legs spread wide, her face shadowed inside of a large dog kennel, with chains wrapped around her shoulders and wrists. In another picture, her back is to the camera lens, and a metal collar encircles her neck, and that collar is attached to a bulky chain leash. A distinct tattoo stays visible on her neck: charcoal-like strokes of a snake eating its own tail.

I used reverse-image searching to find a full picture of her. Long black hair. Black eyes, seated in hollow sockets, rimmed with thick black eyeliner. Light pink lips.

That's when I found out that the little meat hole creates art *and* is a celebrity icon in the art world. She even teaches at the university. It didn't take long to find her home address.

All men can eat pussy, but I want to eat your flesh, I replied.

Immediately, she responded: *Meet me in the bathroom at the Sway Gallery on Thursday, nine p.m.*

I found the woman of my dreams, and she lives close to me. And Thursday is less than twenty-four hours away now.

I'm so lucky.

A figure appears in the master bedroom window. Mona's naked breasts push against the glass as a man fucks her from behind. My dick spasms. Smashed up like that, she reminds me of ground meat, slung from the styrofoam tray into the frying pan.

If she's got someone there, I can't go in tonight.

I find a hiding place in the corner of the garden, behind the giant leaves of an elephant ear plant. I crouch down, keeping myself out of view. I'm not a stalker. A stalker is a threat, and to Mona, I'm merely an admirer. A soon-to-be friend eager to make her acquaintance. Besides, she knows we're meeting at the gallery soon, and we both want the same thing: a serious connection where one eats the other, even if it is just fantasy. It's rare to find a shared fetish like ours.

I pull a small plastic bag with a reddish-brown tampon out of my pocket. A pubic hair sticks to the string. I dug it out of her bathroom last week, the night after I found her personal ad. She was going to throw it out anyway. It reeks like a dead animal, the blood sour and putrid. I stuff the whole thing in my mouth, my appetizer, groaning as the cold, metallic blood squishes over my tongue. I pretend it's a blood popsicle. Between my gnawing teeth and my fierce suckling, soon my mouth is coated in her delicious essence.

There's a chance Mona will accept me for who I am. Not just pretend like it. Not just appease me so I shut up. There's a chance Mona Milk is real. A real person who wants to be consumed by me, just as much as I want to consume her.

One day, when I find the right woman and confirm she's as obsessed and dedicated to sexual cannibalism as I am, I will take her to my fields. I'll treat her right. She can roam freely, and I'll be there, raising her to be the best piece of meat anyone can ask for. A steak so good, she can only be truly appreciated if fully consumed. Money can't buy meat like that.

It's a daydream though. I would never jeopardize a genuine relationship by becoming a threat.

Mona's face twists in orgasm, pain and pleasure mixed into one haunting scream. I heard that the French word for orgasm means "little death," and when you think about it, it's difficult to tell the difference between a face distorted by orgasm and one wracked with gut-wrenching pain.

Is that the look Mona will give when she dies?

I imagine thrusting into her as I eat a hunk of her breast, and hearing her moan in pain as she bleeds out. I give the cotton popsicle a hard, final suck and savor the last hints of her menstrual blood. A curl of pubic hair hooks onto one of my taste buds, a little hand clawing its way out of my mouth. I instinctively gag, then swallow it down too. I press the plastic bag to my mouth and lick the insides as I pretend her pussy is clenching around me one last time.

My cock bursts.

My cum drips down my palm as I stare up at her bedroom window. Condensation clings to the glass where her breasts were, the heat of her body causing me to salivate again. I exhale slowly, letting my mind coast back into reality. It's not like I'll actually eat her, nor will I kill her. I would never hurt someone like that. Our shared interest is unusual, and after years of yearning for someone like her, I can't ruin it by taking things too far.

It's only a daydream. A fetish. An idea that makes me come.

I know that.

CHAPTER 3

I WRING MY FINGERS TOGETHER, NUMBING MY NERVES. SWAY Gallery sits like a birthday cake, the windows brightly-lit candles, people happily gathering inside to celebrate Mona's art.

I keep the street between us, my body hidden in the shadows. My stiff button-up shirt itches my neck, and I run my fingers around the collar in an attempt to loosen it. Mona made me come here. I'm uneasy, and yet, I'm ready for her.

I cross the street and reach for the door handle, but then I freeze. A small paper sign is taped next to the door in bold type-writer letters, the edge of the last word smeared with a fingerprint: *Enter At Your Discretion.* A red umbrella is painted above the words, the tool shielding the ominous warning. It reminds me of a road-block outside of a haunted house: *Enter if you dare.*

"You going in, man?" a male voice asks just as a cloying waft of perfume registers. I don't turn around to look at the man and woman I know are behind me. A feminine chuckle flutters nervously in the air, and I sigh heavily. I'm already irritated by the crowd here.

It will be worth it though. It *has* to be worth it.

Mona is worth it.

I hold my breath and shove myself inside.

Spotlights illuminate each piece of art. In the far corner, a wheel of white bras and blood-dripped dollar bills spins, and in the back, there's some sort of circle, a wreath maybe. I inch closer and realize that the wreath is made of mannequin limbs. On the walls, there are monochrome photographs of dismembered mannequin pieces too: dull lips sawed from a face; a plastic hand in the shape of a circle; a head with a gaping hole in the mouth.

My heart races. This is good. Maybe she destroyed the mannequin limbs because she wanted more from them.

Maybe she is *exactly* what I want.

The onlookers hold their wine glasses and whisper to each other, pointing dainty fingers at each piece. A sticky film of sweat covers me. I don't like people. Being at a party or in a group feels like being outside of my own skin. Even if I tell myself that Mona's art is a sign that we're meant for each other, it doesn't change the fact I don't belong here.

"Wine, sir? Or perhaps a craft beer?" a server asks. I examine his drink tray. "May I interest you in the open bar next to—"

Mona told me to meet her in the bathroom.

"Where's the toilet?" I ask.

"The Elimination Craftsmanship is in the hallway," he says. "The only door. You can't miss it."

Elimination Craftsmanship? What the fuck?

I walk rapidly to the back of the gallery. I stomp down the hallway, and I see the only door. It's comically huge, like the gallery owner—or Mona, I guess—made it big just so the user would feel smaller.

A sign is posted next to the door handle: *Occupied.*

"Great," I mutter.

I tap my thumbs on my side. I pace back and forth in front of the door. A few gallery visitors gawk at me with upturned noses like I'm going to piss or shit myself. I don't care though; let them think that. You can't change the way a person feels about you, but you can wait for the perfect woman to meet you in the bathroom.

Ten minutes pass. I don't hear anything through the bathroom door.

She said to meet her here, didn't she?

I check my screenshot of her personal ad again: *Serious inquiries only.*

I'm deadly serious. I'm here, aren't I?

I knock, my knuckles pounding into the wood.

Nothing.

"Fuck it," I say. I twist the handle, and the door swings open.

Shadows. A large sink. A toilet. The counter is covered in tealight candles, melted wax shimmering in the small metal cups, each flame's light dancing on the walls, and it reminds me of a primitive gathering.

"Come in," a woman's voice says.

I close the door behind me. The noise from the gallery dulls into a murmur. Water drips. A clawfoot tub, filled almost to the top, is situated in the corner of the room, next to the toilet. A woman's neck arches out of the water, her hair pulled into a messy bun on top of her head.

"Sorry," I murmur. "I was looking for the bathroom."

She tilts her head toward the toilet. "Help yourself."

I raise a brow. Is she serious? It's dark, and my eyes haven't adjusted yet; I can't see her face. I'm not sure if she's Mona.

This woman told me to "help yourself," so why shouldn't I take a leak?

I unzip my pants as I skim her. Closer now, I can see that her lips are painted the color of a purple cherry.

I face the toilet. I don't want to stare too much. I piss, and my stream is loud, drowning out the dripping water and the gallery's white noise.

"The door said *occupied*," she says.

I shake my dick until the piss drips are gone. "I knocked. You didn't answer."

"But I told you to meet me here, didn't I?"

My mouth drops open. Under the water, the shadow of her legs part, and I lick my lips. The hot water steams, and it reminds me of a hearty stew. Her legs are the main protein, a meal mouth-watering and rich.

"It's you," I say.

Fire twinkles in her round pupils, a predator waiting inside of a cave. Reading me. Drawing me in. Tempting me into her darkness. The hairs stand on the back of my neck, and I gulp down extra saliva. It's like she's hunting me.

My jaw flexes. No. *I'm* the predator here.

Even if she thinks she's capturing me, I don't want to stop her. I want to see what happens. I want to see how this ends.

Mona pulls herself up, her small breasts exposed above the water as she reaches over the tub. Water sloshes over the side and splashes on my boots. I'm hypnotized by her every move, like a lion tracing the edge of its cage. *She's just a woman,* I remind myself. *A woman who may casually like the idea of being eaten. She may be a scam. She may want nothing to do with you.*

She grabs a bottle of wine off of the floor. I hadn't noticed it before. She sinks back into the water and lifts the bottle. The cork is halfway out of the neck.

"Drink with me," she says.

I perch on the edge of the tub. My pants soak up some water.

"No wine glasses?" I ask.

She pulls the cork with her teeth, spits it out over the edge of the tub, then drinks straight from the bottle. A subtle moan drifts from her lips.

She hands the bottle to me. Restless energy prickles over my skin. I tell myself it's like drinking blood—her blood—to form a pact.

No. It's just wine, I think. *Just wine. There's nothing wrong with drinking wine.*

I bring the bottle to my lips. The spicy liquid runs over my tongue, and I pretend it's her blood. Blood tastes metallic—like pennies—but with her, I'd imagine there'd be more spice. Perhaps black pepper and cinnamon.

The crevices around her mouth deepen in a smile. I hand her back the bottle, and she dangles it by the neck, a pendulum swinging closer to the pit.

"Why are you here?" she asks.

My heart beats in my chest, a drum drowning everything else out. It's a real conversation. We aren't anonymous strangers on the internet with weird needs and fetishes anymore; we're two actual people right now.

This question may be a trap.

Warning bells blare in my mind. There could be a recording device under the toilet. A hidden camera waiting to catch me in the act. For all I know, there is a plain-clothed officer waiting right outside of the bathroom to arrest me for even *thinking* about eating her.

Okay. Maybe that's far-fetched, but she could be planning to use my words and actions against me, some sort of blackmail to help her pay for her art materials. Even if she is rich, people are weird. I couldn't put it past her.

Calm down, my brain argues. *She's just a woman, and this is only a hookup. She just wants to make sure you are who she thinks you are before she reveals herself.*

"I came to see you," I say.

Her sharp words slice through the air. "Try again."

I grit my teeth. "I came to see your art."

"That's nice. It's not *real* though, is it?"

She sits up, and more water splashes onto the tile, splattering over my boots. A few loose tendrils of wet, black hair crawl over her shoulders, and her bun is a crown on top of her head. Her eyes are hollow, endless caves carved into the side of a mountain. She's surprisingly small. Even in the bathtub, you can tell she's short. A bite-sized woman. Something I can carry with a single hand.

Her small breasts rise into the cool air, the fatty tissue pooling at the ends in tear drops. Her pert nipples pucker, and fuck me, my dick stretches in my pants, ready to suck and bite those pink knobs off until she's a bleeding faucet.

She tilts the wine bottle, and the red liquid races over her neck and down her shoulders. It fills the divots of her collarbones, then travels down her breasts. The wine is like red rain, mixing with the warm bathwater, and it reminds me of thick, meaty blood mixing with boiling water.

"Be honest this time," she says. A smirk dances on her lips; she obviously knows what pouring wine over her body does to me, and she *likes* it. "Why are you here? I want to hear you say it."

She pours more wine over her body, and each drop is another layer, a marinade caressing her skin, another flavor to unlock against my tongue. I'm falling deeper into her trap.

"To taste you," I murmur.

"Give me more than that."

Irritation and lust grow in my chest like a bonfire. This isn't a trap then; it's a *test*. She wants me to prove that I came here for her and our mutual, fucked-up desires. *Serious inquiries only.* Being here isn't enough.

"To devour you," I growl.

"Then eat me."

I yank off my dress shirt. Buttons rip from the fabric and tap the floor. I stumble out of my jeans and kick off my soggy boots like an eager schoolboy, then I crawl into the bath on top of her. I'm a big man; my body displaces so much water, it splashes on the floor like a waterfall.

Mona grins at me, her teeth sharp and white, as if I'm the one who is going to be eaten alive.

"That's it," she says. She grabs the back of my neck. "Now drink me."

I press my lips to her skin, tasting the wine and salt. Berries and musk and smoke and everything I've ever wanted in each of her salty pores. She arches her spine, her cunt pushing into my stomach.

"Bite me," she commands.

My teeth knick her shoulder, and she squirms.

"Harder," she demands.

My dick lurches at the command, both aroused by the action and annoyed by her dominance. I bite her until I hear her skin crunch and pop, harder than I've ever bitten someone before, and she moans with delight.

"Drink every drop," she whispers, her voice raspy with desire.

She reaches for my cock in the water. My body heats. Everything under my skin crawls to the surface.

This is it. My first chance with my dream girl.

I can't fuck this up.

She cocoons me in her limbs, an arachnid about to suck my blood. I'm pulled deeper into the water.

Her words set me on fire. "Eat every piece of me until there's nothing left—"

A groan, deep and guttural, tears through me. My cock gushes in the water.

As the orgasm subsides, my breathing remains heavy. She scoops up my winey, watery cum, and her plump tongue writhes over her palm. Her eyes are animated, watching me watch her, as if to make sure I know she's eating a part of me too.

A stinging sensation skims my scalp, needles stabbing down my neck and shoulders, forcing me back into the present moment.

I'm in a bathtub with a stranger. A famous artist who has her own gallery. A woman who teaches art at the university. A cannibal lover who sent out an anonymous advertisement to fulfill her fetishistic needs.

I'm into sexual cannibalism too, but I don't know much about her besides where she lives and what her period blood tastes like. She's technically a stranger, and this is a bad idea.

She points to the side.

"There are towels under the sink." She lifts herself out of the water and steps over me. And it's dismissive. Like her conquered prey is no longer necessary to her long-term goals. Like I'm one of her completed sculptures, and now that I've been sold, she no longer needs to pay attention to me.

Anger creeps under my fingertips as she rubs the towel over her body. I let that frustration dissipate. A minute passes.

Then I dry my body too.

"Was that performance art?" I ask.

"What do you want it to be?"

Her vague answer seeps under my skin, flooding me with irritation. That's what an arrogant artist would say, isn't it? It's like she takes herself way too seriously to give me a direct answer.

I curl my fist, imagining a knife in my hand, ready to stab her in the neck. *Now give me a straight fucking answer,* I'd say.

No. Stop that, I think. I can't let the fantasies change into that. Not with her.

I finish drying off as quickly as I can and pull on my tattered clothes while she side-eyes me. *Control yourself,* I chant in my mind. *Control yourself, and you'll get what you want.*

As I exit the bathroom, I turn over my shoulder and attempt the same dismissive attitude as her. "Thanks for the good time," I say.

"Of course, love," she says, and I swear, I can hear her winking like it's a game to her, and that rage bubbles to the surface again, the need to wring her neck like a chicken filling my fingertips.

Even if my heart bleeds angrily at the loss of my dream girl, she's just a woman, and this is only a hookup.

CHAPTER 4

I CLOSE THE BATHROOM DOOR, THEN NOTICE A NEW SIGN NEXT TO the handle. *Do Not Enter*, it says. Like someone waited for me to go inside, then switched the sign once the door was shut.

Our bathtub hand job had to be a piece of performance art. That's the only way to explain it. She posted a personal ad and used me like another sculpture in her gallery. It was only a stage show where I had no idea I was a prop.

My facial muscles twitch. The little bitch played with me like I was *her* food.

I rub the back of my neck before digging my nails into my own flesh. That wasn't what I wanted. I'm a stupid, stupid idiot for letting her use me like that.

Tsk tsk, Mona's imaginary voice coos. *You were willing. You wanted me.*

"Fuck this," I growl.

I stomp toward the gallery exit. There are probably double-sided mirrors in that bathroom and a stadium full of her pretentious fans on the other side, laughing at me. My gut churns like I'm nine years old again with a bowl of cereal and spoiled milk, hoping that if I eat it, my mother will be happy.

Mona is dismissive like my mother, isn't she?

Despite those threatening thoughts, I stop in front of the exit door.

There's a chance I will *never* find a woman who shares interests again. And I can't fuck that up for some ego-driven tantrum.

Fine. I can do this.

I whip around and head to the open bar. I grab a beer off of the countertop and chug it like it's the last swigs of expired protein shakes in the pantry, the last chance I have at a meal for the unforeseen future. I signal the bartender for another, then I grab the second bottle.

The gallery is full of people who know art. Who care about art. Who don't have to worry about where their next meal is coming from, or whether or not they'll find a true connection with another human being. I'm not like these people. I don't belong here. I know that.

I also know that I need to calm down.

Control yourself, I repeat internally. A woman like Mona is a once-in-a-lifetime opportunity. Even if she was using me for her performance art, there aren't many people who would even *pretend* to indulge in something like sexual cannibalism. For fuck's sake, she told me to eat every last bite of her. And with the way I ran out of there like a scared little boy who came too fast, I probably ruined my chances already. She probably thinks I'm a little bitch or something.

"'Thanks for a good time'," I mock myself. "How stupid can you be?"

I take a long swig of the second beer, then ponder my next move. The art pieces blur around me, and it's like being in the middle of a grocery store, except instead of branded product boxes, you're left trying to guess what's inside. Eat blue. Eat red. Eat green. Eat white. The colors swirl until my mind can't stop fixating on that word: *Eat. Eat. Eat.*

Eat me, she said. *Eat every piece of me until there's nothing left.*

I can't let this be a one-time thing.

"Marvelous, isn't it?" a male voice asks.

In my periphery, a man with long hair stands next to me. His dark gray ponytail trails down his back.

"Violence," the man says.

My nostrils flare. Shallow wrinkles crowd his temples. He's older than me, maybe in his mid-to-late forties. A leather jacket dominates his thin frame, making him look like a half-starved rooster. I recognize him, though I'm not sure why. Maybe when I was researching Mona, he was in the background of one of the pictures. A loyal super fan or something.

I turn back to the "marvelous" art in front of me. I don't really see it.

"The devastating hunger for total power that lurks within all of us," he continues. "The need and desire to conquer the weak through sex."

I grunt, my only attempt at conversation. He angles himself toward me.

I don't face him this time. I don't want to.

"What do you see?" he asks.

Jagged mirrors cover the surface of a dog kennel and a twin bed. Puzzle pieces of my reflection stare back at me: my strong jaw, my clean-shaven cheeks and chin, my muscular neck and shoulders, my dark blue eyes. A tan wallet covered in the same mirror scraps lies on top of the structure.

It's a bunch of junkyard scraps.

I don't see the same things other people see. Art is supposed to represent emotion and deep, intellectual thought; I don't have the patience for that. Art is just colors and textures. Or garbage, I guess.

I don't say any of that out loud. The man seems like the kind of person who would repeat my words to Mona, and even though I don't like being used in her little bathtub show, I find myself desperately wanting for a second chance with her. I don't want her to hate me yet.

"I see mirrors," I say.

"No, my friend. Look beyond that," the man says. "Look *inside* the cage."

Cage? Not a dog kennel?

I crouch down and peer inside. Another mannequin, this time with a faceless expression, is positioned in a crawl. Dirt paints the plastic in wide strokes, and chains wrap around the object's neck and body.

Mona wore a metal leash like that in her personal ad, and there are so many possibilities for human food preparation with strong chains, like hanging the carcass in a walk-in freezer. I can't say that out loud though. This man doesn't need to know about Mona's and my sexual interests.

"It's just mirrors, man," I say.

He chuckles like I said something funny, and a gnawing irritation creeps in my jaw, itching to slit his throat on the broken glass and see how much he likes eating those fucking mirrors.

"That's the interesting thing about it. We see what we want to see," he says. He scrutinizes the sculpture like it's that one asshole's painting of the Last Supper. "You see mirrors. I see the lines," he continues. "The cuts. The spiteful layers. The way our own image slices through reality and creates something new. Something chaotic and frightening. Something we must keep inside."

"Arty!" a woman shouts.

Though the voice is too low to be Mona's, I swing around like she'll be there with wet hair and pink bath water pooling on the floor beneath her.

Brown hair. Brown eyes. Not Mona. Someone forgettable.

They kiss each other's cheeks. "Gorgeous as ever," the man says. His name is Arty, I guess.

"Mona is doing so well, isn't she?" the woman says.

"Surpasses every bar, every time."

"Agreed."

The woman glimpses in my direction, a coyish smile aimed at me. I smile back. I often have that effect on women. They want me.

Then she steps closer to Arty, like she doesn't want me to hear their conversation, and I get the sense that even if I'm attractive, she's *afraid* of offending me. Like she's scared. I narrow my eyes, heightening that primal power over her, pride flooding my veins in an overwhelming heat.

Suddenly, I break myself away from them. If she's one of Mona's friends and she wants privacy, I'll give it to her.

"I hate to do this to you, but can you walk me to my car?" she whispers. "After seeing this—what these women go through—I don't want to walk alone. I figure the boogeyman inspiration can scare away any creepy jerk."

"Boogeyman *creator*," the man corrects her. "Of course, I'll protect you. You don't have to ask me twice." He turns to me and shakes my hand with a surprisingly firm grip. "It was nice speaking with you."

I grip his hand back harder. His posture never changes, as if my show of dominance doesn't bother him.

He links arms with the woman, and as they walk away, her words repeat in my mind: *what they go through.*

Who was she talking about?

There's probably a plaque explaining the exhibit somewhere. I don't care enough to ask. Instead, I stare at the mirrors again. The junkyard scraps. The pieces of trash. There must've been a mirror in the bathroom too. I don't remember seeing it though. As soon as I stepped past that oversized door, I was fixated on Mona.

Her body. Her flesh.

I'm not a cannibal. It's wrong to eat people, and I know that. If anyone finds out you ate *any* part of a human, you'll live your life in jail. You can't eat other people in prison for long before they put you in solitary. Anyway, eating other men doesn't interest me; their meat is too firm, and I've never been into autocannibalism.

But there's a part of me that's always been fascinated by the idea of eating a woman. As haunting as she may seem, a woman like Mona is attractive, and that makes her meat even better.

I stop by the bathroom. The sign has been replaced with one that reads, *Vacant.* Inside, the candles are blown out. The tub is empty. The floor is dry.

She's done, then. She's not waiting for anyone else who answered her ad.

It was all for me.

Me.

27

Warmth dances in my lower stomach. I don't know why I like that. After years of solitude, I guess it's comforting to know that even if it was an art performance, she did it for me. And that lets me entertain the idea that my little meat hole wants to be eaten by me. Only me.

I finish the beer, then take a final scan around the gallery to search for her. A crowd surrounds her like pillars guarding a prized treasure. She tells them an animated tale. Her cheeks are flushed, still cooling from the bath.

She locks eyes with me and lifts her hand, her fingers rippling slightly. A wave. An acknowledgement. I nod back as warmth blooms in my chest.

I...want...more.

I motion her over, and like a good pet, she comes to me. That inner heat settles firmly within my torso. I take a deep breath, and the inhalation draws her into my very soul, a boiling scalding essence which is as much a part of me as my cum is now a part of her.

"Did you enjoy the show?" she asks.

Old bath water, wine, and sweat waft from her skin, and I want to lick every inch of her. Drink every drop. Eat every bite until there's nothing left.

I want to devour her.

"You're even more handsome in the light," she purrs.

My jaw tightens. My mother may not have given me much, but I've got her dark blue eyes, clear skin, and tall height, and that means I'm attractive to most women. On top of that, I've got short, golden-brown hair women seem to like running their fingers through. I'm muscular too; men think twice about fighting me, and sexually submissive women like Mona find my physical power appealing. It helps that I keep my carbs down, concentrate on protein, and workout in the field whenever I have extra energy. I've never been more grateful for my appearance than right now, and if that's what draws Mona to me, then I'll have to thank my dead mother later.

"I have to see you again," I say. "Where can I find you?"

She smirks, and that sly expression guts me, like I'm the pig and she's the butcher in charge of my carcass. I want to smash into her body, my dick like a knife, killing her and fucking her at the same time.

No—I want to fuck her vagina *with* a knife until it's pulp, then eat it like it's a bolognese.

"Come to my office tomorrow," she says.

Not her studio. Her office. That means at the university. Earlier this week, I sat in on one of her lectures and kept myself hidden in the back row. I can't tell her that though. I don't want to scare her.

"Where's your office?" I ask.

She laughs, then brushes my shoulder with her fingertips.

"You'll find me," she says. "Won't you, love?"

My body flames. She passes me, her ass shimmying with each step, and I lick my lips. Her rump is round, bigger than her breasts are, and I have this gut instinct that her ass will taste like a honey-glazed ham.

She returns to her adoring fans, and it isn't lost on me that she dismissed me again. This time though, I asked for a second chance.

And she granted it.

CHAPTER 5

GIANT OAK TREES STRETCH ACROSS THE QUAD, AND THE OUTER RIM is lined with departmental buildings. A lion's roar blasts with a gust of wind, the ever-present reminder that the university neighbors the city zoo. I head across the green lawn, past a quiet yoga class, past a guitar player strumming an irritating folk song, and past a survey table. I don't need a campus guide. I know where she is.

Mona Milk's office is on the fourth floor of the arts building, in the luxury corner office saved for visiting faculty.

Before I can knock on the double doors, they swing open. A young woman—the edges of her large areolas poking out of her cleavage, too exposed to be a college student—zips past me, rank of perfume. Jasmine. It's an organic scent, but it's too strong, covering up a woman's natural, savory undertones. It isn't appetizing.

Then Mona catches my eye, and everything else disappears.

A tight, black dress with peek-a-boo cutouts clings to Mona's body. A portion of her stomach is exposed, her innie belly button like a giant pore waiting to be filled with truffle oil. Her straight, black hair frames her face, and dark makeup circles her eyes. I don't mind the makeup with Mona. Since we have the same interests, I can let that slide.

She appraises me, her tongue snaking across her bottom lip.

Desire pulses in my fingers. I want to squeeze her soft flesh so fucking bad.

"So you're *hungry* for another treat," she says.

She winks at me, and my jaw strains. Is she mocking me? It's not like I'm the only one who is into cannibalism roleplay. She is too. *She's* the one who put up the ad in the first fucking place.

I start to shake my head, contempt swimming in my head. But Mona steps to the side so I can enter her office, and I force myself to relax. I need to take this one step at a time. I can't be too careful with Mona.

A floor-to-ceiling window overlooks the quad, and because of the office's high position, there's a view between the buildings straight to the lion's den at the zoo. I squint; I see trees and metal bars, but I can't see any lions.

In the natural light from the windows, Mona glides toward her desk. Her skin is pale, almost translucent, like a ghost that could evaporate at any moment. Haunting, yet beautiful.

I rub a hand across my jaw. Stubble pricks across my chin—I must've missed a spot—and under her eyes, I'm very aware of it.

Despite my flaws, her smile stays. I force my shoulders to loosen. *She invited me here,* I remind myself. *If she doesn't like the haggard look, then she can go fuck herself.*

I take the seat in front of her desk. The office is filled with cameras: vintage models and the newest editions, some of them for pictures and others for recording. She must be constantly cataloging her life.

"You found my personal ad," she says.

I peer at the zoo's metal fences off in the distance and gauge how to play my cards right. Mona may be testing me again like she did with the wine bath, and that irritates me.

I also know I can't scare her. I can't let her know the personal ad was only the beginning of my infatuation with her.

"I did," I say.

"And my art didn't anger or scare you?"

I laugh. "Scare me? I'm not scared of art."

She presses her lips together, reading me. My chest compresses under her scrutinization. Is she fishing for a compliment, then? Is that what she meant when she asked if I was scared of her art?

Her art confused me. Though judging by her fans last night, she probably wouldn't like hearing that. I can't risk pissing her off, not when I'm *this* close to getting what I want.

"Your art intrigued me," I lie.

Her grin loosens, and she reveals her white teeth, almost the same color as her skin. Even though she's short, she peers down at me from her chair like she's a giant. She must have risers under the furniture to give herself a bigger presence, an arrangement created to make her students feel small. To make *me* feel small. Like prey.

Why does it seem like she's the one hunting *me?*

"Cannibalism is more common than we think," she says. "In the animal world, a mother may eat the weakest infant in the hope that she lives to take care of the other babies. Or perhaps it's too crowded and the only logical option is to eat whoever is beside you. There's scavenging too. Some mates even consume each other to increase the chances that they'll successfully procreate."

I blink rapidly. I don't think much about the animal world. At least, not the living ones. I can't say that out loud though, because while her art doesn't scare me, I don't know how she would feel about my animal meat sleeves.

"But humans?" Mona laughs. "Cannibalism is far too taboo for *them*, but not us." She leans forward on the desk, her small breasts smashed against the wooden surface, plump and meaty and juicy, begging me to consume them. "What's your name?"

"Kent."

"Tell me, Kent"—her voice lowers—"did your mother try to eat you, or do you want to consume me because you're a predator? Why are you so drawn to eating women?"

Heaviness lurks in my body, my muscles tense. She's trying to psychoanalyze me. As if my cannibalistic interests can be summed up by a few moments in my childhood. As if it all leads back to my mother.

I drop my gaze to my hands, my fingers fidgeting with energy.

I can't get mad at Mona. She's the only woman I've ever met who may actually like this as much as I do. I *have* to play along.

"It's not my mother," I say calmly. "It's always been about eating a beautiful woman." I lift my eyes, meeting Mona's. "Like you."

Then I stare down at my hands again.

My mother wasn't beautiful. She was lifeless.

Mona is different from her. Mona is like the *darkness* at the end of a tunnel. Like hope. And at the same time, she's worse. A bittersweet poison.

Even if my instincts say she's dangerous, I have to do this.

She smirks. "You're perfect, and you don't even know it."

I pull back slightly, a blood vessel on my eyelid twitching. I'm perfect? What does that mean? What is she hiding? It's like she's inviting me into a game. Like she's confident she can successfully execute an ambush. Like she knows she'll eventually kill me.

Mona's delighted coo fills the air, causing my mind to go blank.

"There's a private screening I'd like for you to attend," she says. "I put together a film collage. I think you'll like it."

She licks her lips, and I salivate at the thought of that flickering muscle. It's not big enough to match the beef tongue in the offal pit, and yet it's *meaty*, like a medallion of steak. Her tongue would work well in a taco, seasoned with oregano and marjoram.

"A movie?" I ask. "You filmed it?"

"It's a work-in-progress for my next exhibition." She scans me with a vacant expression. "You're in my art criticism and theory lecture, aren't you?"

She recognizes me then, even if it's only been one class. After I figured out who she was in the personal ad, I sat in the back of her lecture and listened to her speak, hoping that a clue might slip out of her mouth and reveal the true nature of her desires. A sign that she wasn't faking it like everyone else.

"Auditing," I say.

"I always like a curious student."

Before I can get pissed off at being at the bottom end of the teacher/student power dynamic, she places a large stack of papers in front of me. The stark white papers contrast against the dark wood. I stop on the title of the first page: *Non-Disclosure Agreement.*

"An NDA just to see a movie you're working on?" I ask.

"It's more than that," she says. "I have a reputation to protect. You understand, of course?"

Stiffness rolls through me. I've never liked contracts. Legal forms tend to lead back to the government, and I avoid them as much as I can. That way, it's easier for everyone.

Mona looks down at me. A pale vein dances down the fleshy column of her neck. The rhythm of her blood thumping through that vessel captivates me, a clock ticking its way back to the top, marking the final beats of a dying heart.

Everything about her is hypnotizing.

"I'll have to think about it," I say. I shuffle through the papers and try to read quickly, but there's more than forty pages, and after a few seconds, the words blend together. "I need to go through this."

"Good." She clasps her hands together, then stands. "Read it thoroughly. Every last page, love. Don't miss a thing. Please keep in mind the private screening starts this evening at five, not a second later."

I flip through the pages again, adrenaline smothering my chest. "I have work today."

"Where do you work?"

"At the chicken processing plant."

"How lovely. An intellectual worker," she says.

I furrow my brows, unsure of what she means by that. Is it an insult?

"I'm afraid the offer ends once the screening begins," she continues. "After that, I'll move on to another subject. You know how the muses control an artist." She tilts her head. "For now, I have to prepare for my next appointment, but remember, love: five o'clock. I'll be waiting for you."

Before I can say another word, she pushes me out of her office. The double doors close behind me, and the metal lock clicks shut.

I glare at the papers. My nostrils flare, and I swear I can still smell the sweat coming off of her skin, that salty *need* oozing out of her pores and yearning for me.

I need to think, and I can't think here. Not with her right behind the doors.

CHAPTER 6

AT THE PROCESSING PLANT, I GLANCE AT THE ANALOG CLOCK ON the break room wall. My skin is flushed, and my hands are trembling with nerves. I meant to check behind the student union to see if the food court had any leftover meat, but Mona took over my brain, and I forgot what I was supposed to do before my shift.

If Mona has a forty-page contract she wants me to sign before we even watch a movie together, then there's something wrong with her. A secret she's hiding. A trap she's set that I'm *willingly* walking into. A corral at the end of the barn, leading me to the slaughterhouse.

She gave me until five o'clock. I've only got an hour or so left until I need to take the commute back to the university.

If I sign those papers.

The supervisor adjusts his glasses. The plastic frame slides down his nose.

"And so, please remember that we have cameras everywhere," he says, his voice monotonous. "Even if it isn't being sold under our company's brand, taking organs from the rendering packages is stealing." His eyes narrow in on me. "Let me repeat: there are cameras *everywhere*. It doesn't matter how good of an employee you are. It doesn't matter if it's a handful of intestines or a few livers. We know how much we should be exporting from the plant each day. If you take the rendering shipments, it will be considered stealing, and I will be forced to fire you."

I huff. He's acting as if I'm the only one who takes meat. For fuck's sake, that's how Jerry lost his finger. I saw him digging around the buckets and accidentally startled him. His hand slipped against the cutting machine, and there went his pinky.

The contract pages flutter under the ceiling fan. As the supervisor continues lecturing, I subtly pick through the contract. I catch different phrases.

The subject agrees to participate—
…an art series dedicated to the topic of cannibalism—
By signing here, I give up all claims to my photographs—
I understand my likeness will be used—
…series shall explore humans eating humans.

My pulse quickens as I continue scanning. This isn't just an NDA to watch a movie together; this is about being a part of her next project.

An art project on cannibalism.

I flatten my lips, keeping my simultaneous desire *and* irritation at bay. Mona wants to use me for her art. In a way, creating art on human cannibalism is putting people like me behind a fence and gawking. My mother's words echo in my mind: *You little freak.*

I grind my teeth and chew over the printed words. Mona will probably depict me as a cannibal that must be kept in a cage. Her fans will laugh at me. Judge me. Think of me as less than them. And I hate it, hate it, fucking hate it, and hate *her* for doing this to me. To *us.*

"It's not like corporate needs the profit from a few ounces of meat," Jerry whispers.

"Seriously. The fuck is their problem?" I mutter.

We bump fists, then pretend to listen to the supervisor again, and I find myself staring at Jerry's missing pinky. On the day of the amputation, the supervisor was pissed; we had to toss the entire bucket Jerry was working on, and to spread out the blame, I pretended to be working on it too. The supervisor and a few other workers helped sift through the bin, but no one could find the rest of Jerry's finger to reattach it.

It was in my jumper pocket. I had stuffed it in there before anyone even thought about searching for his severed finger. Instead of wasting his flesh with reattachment, I got to confirm my suspicions about men's meat. I ate it in the bathroom stall as soon as I got a second alone.

It was too tough to truly enjoy though. I spit it out and added it to the furnace. Besides, there's a good chance he never would've recovered the full sensation in his finger anyway.

When the supervisor asked why we were monitoring that part of the cutting machine *together*, I didn't mention seeing Jerry put chicken breasts in a separate container; Jerry appreciated that. Now, he even eats the specialty ground meat I prepare at home.

In the end, that amputated finger started our friendship.

I haven't tried Mona's meat yet, but I'm certain her flesh will be softer than Jerry's. Tender. Sweet and savory. Delicious in every possible way.

I'm not a cannibal though. Jerry's pinky was only a sample, and to be honest, the texture was disgusting, like the gristle from a turkey leg.

Jerry gestures at the contract. "What is that?"

"This woman I'm dating wants me to sign it," I say. "She needs privacy or something."

"You'd do that for pussy?"

"If it's a guaranteed premium cut, then fuck yeah."

He stifles his chuckle behind his hand. I want to enjoy the joke too, but I grit my teeth.

The problem is that I don't know if Mona is a prime slice. Is Mona my dream girl, or is she going to end up leaving me like everyone else?

The supervisor keeps yapping about the newest safety protocol, undisturbed by our quiet conversation, so I pull out my phone and flip to a picture of Mona from the personal ad, the one where she's halfway inside of a large dog kennel.

"Here," I say as I hand my device to Jerry. "Check it out. She's an artist."

Jerry's eyes widen as he glimpses at the image. He squeezes my shoulder. "She's kinky too? I didn't think you'd be into that shit!"

He must think the chains around her shoulders mean we're into sadomasochism or pet play. I guess in some aspects, sexual cannibalism *is* about pain and caging the livestock.

Not that I want to hurt her.

Not that I'm actually a cannibal.

I wink at Jerry. "I'd do anything with her," I whisper.

"Even sign a contract?"

I inhale sharply. "I don't know, man. This is intense, right?"

"The crazy bitches always are." He lifts his shoulders. "Does she put out?"

I pinch my lips together. Even if I came too fast, the hand job in the wine bath definitely counts.

I bob my head. "No complaints so far."

"Who cares what you have to do to get your dick wet, right?" He wipes his nose on the back of his hand. "I dated an artist once, and she never even let me *smell* her. You know what I'm saying?" I laugh quietly, and he puts a hand on my shoulder. "Pussy is always a feast or a fucking empty plate."

Jerry is always talking about women like that, and though I know he's talking about licking pussy and eating ass, he still treats women like objects, something to be fucked and consumed. And I like that. They aren't objects, of course, but that isn't the point; I like how the objectifying camaraderie binds us. Besides, I don't actually want to eat a woman; I simply like the idea of it.

Tension rolls through my groin as I reflect on the fact that Jerry is probably right: Mona may be truly crazy. If she's willing to be eaten, then she's also probably willing to chop off my dick and feed it to me.

But the bottom line is that she's insane enough to actually indulge her cannibalistic fantasies for her art instead of hiding them in her mind. It's her choice to go public with her fantasies, to put them out in the open, to force others to witness her desires.

Our desires.

If I get to eat a part of her, does it matter if it's forced out of some artistic bullshit?

I can inspire her.

I can eat her too.

No, no, no, my brain argues. *You can't actually eat her. It may be tempting to take a small bite, but you can't fuck a woman who wants to be eaten. You'll take one little nibble, and that will turn into more, and before you know it, you'll be fucking her battered pussy and eating her tongue like she's a fucking buffet. You can't be a monster. You can't. Control yourself, Kent. Control yourself, and you'll get what you want.*

I flip through the pages again, this time stopping on a new line: *I understand that no compensation, including payment from art buyers, will be given to my benefit.*

A headache blooms across my temple. I don't need to read through the rest of it; I've gathered enough. First off, I don't care if I get paid for this; I have my job here at the processing plant. And secondly, is it really that bad to be a part of her art show if there's a chance I'll get to eat a piece of her too?

I check the clock again. It's getting dangerously close to when I need to decide.

Do you want to consume me because you're a predator? Mona had asked, and it was like her voice was made of honey. Her throat and tongue braised in sweet water for so long, she would melt on my fork. *You're a predator,* she had said, as if she saw the animal inside of me and wanted more, as if she knew my sharp teeth were longing to be tainted with her blood.

I can't let this opportunity go to waste.

I keep my voice low. "Fuck the empty plate," I say to Jerry. "If she's a buffet, then I'm in."

His laughter booms. "That's what I'm talking about!"

A throat clears.

Jerry and I startle, then straighten in our seats.

"Can I help you, gentlemen?" the supervisor asks.

The whole room is staring at us, judging us like we're big cats caged behind thick glass, and for a split second, I imagine snapping everyone's neck in my jaws like a fucking lion.

"We're good," Jerry says.

"Well, then." The supervisor angles toward the door. "Let's get back to work."

The workers shuffle out of the break room, and I shake hands with Jerry. I nod toward the back exit, then lift the stack of papers.

"I'm going to clock out early and take care of some important *business*," I joke.

"Signing your life away for pussy, then?" Jerry smacks my back. "Get it, my man. And thanks for the ground meat. I'm going to grill some burgers tomorrow."

"Fuck yeah," I say. "Eat up!"

"And you *eat* too!"

He wiggles his tongue like he's licking an ice cream cone. I laugh, then head to the supervisor. I fumble an excuse about indigestion, and though his shoulders flinch like he doesn't believe me, he lets me go. Health code rules come in handy in situations like this. I change into a button-up shirt and get in my cargo van.

I may not be *eating* Mona, but I am serious about this. I'm even willing to sign a contract. And if I drive fast enough, I'll be the first one in the movie theater, ready to watch her creation and become a part of her art.

CHAPTER 7

When I step through the office doors, Mona stands. A wide grin stretches across her face. She takes the papers from me, then scans for my initials and signatures.

"Good," she says. "Everything looks perfect. Do you want a copy?"

I shake my head. She grabs my hand. A chill runs through me at the physical contact, a mix of nauseous dread and excitement brewing in my veins. This isn't a hookup anymore. This is a *commitment* to her art and to our shared sexual interest. This may be the best thing that's ever happened to me, or it may be my worst mistake. The adrenaline spikes in my veins, pushing me to keep going.

We're doing this.

I have to do this.

"Follow me," she says.

Mona strides across campus, and I follow after her, my fingers tingling with numbness. This is a trap. Even now, she's leading *me*, not the other way around, and it's another red flag that I should listen to.

I ignore those warnings. I focus on her. This is what I've been yearning for, the chance to have a connection with someone who understands me. So what if it's a trap? Something real may come out of it.

In another building, Mona leads me down the stairs to a dark theater. Multiple rows of tiered seating face black velvet curtains. She pulls the cord at the side, and the fabric opens, then frames a dim screen.

No one else is in the theater.

"Get comfortable," she says. Another order.

My stomach hardens as she runs up the aisle to the projector and clicks through the buttons. Those warning bells keep chiming, the volume increasing as each second passes. If someone comes in here, and it's just us, what will they think? Will they know she invited me, or will they think I'm preying on her? Is this a trap to make it seem like I'm her abuser?

Why does she keep telling me what to do?

Why do I keep obeying her?

"I thought there would be more students," I say.

"Private screening."

Sourness coats my tongue. I rub my forehead. If it seems too good to be true, it probably is.

Even though I signed those papers, I don't have to do this. I decide my place in this world.

And yet I can't make myself exit the building.

"Sit," she says.

Like a stupid little dog, I find a seat in the middle row, in the direct center of the theater. Black-and-white images flicker across the screen. Once I see Mona slinking down the aisle, I lose focus on the film.

She points at the screen. "Watch."

I clench my jaw, but I do as I'm told.

The projector plays a video of a group of people walking in a single file line. All of them help carry a long stick with a woman attached to it. My balls tense, pressure swelling in my groin.

"What is this?" I ask.

Mona shushes me, and before I know it, she's on her knees in front of me. She reaches for my belt buckle.

My shoulders stiffen. "What are you—"

"Relax." She pushes on my thighs and spreads my legs apart.

"Enjoy yourself for once. It's not every day you get to indulge, right?"

She reaches for my belt again. I stay still as she undoes my pants. Her cold hands touch my cock, and warmth pulsates through me.

"Keep your eyes on the screen," she says.

The images switch every three seconds, giving me just enough time to get the briefest grasp of what I'm seeing. A giant breast being severed from a body. *Switch.* A close-up of meat strings caught in a person's teeth. *Switch.* A man with long hair laughing so hard that his uvula convulses. *Switch.* Slender fingers peeling a prosthetic from skin.

Mona's breath, hot and wet, fogs around the head of my cock. Her plump lips tease my tip, the barest hint of her tongue snaking across my skin. She swallows me whole, her mouth bobbing up and down, her throat constricting around me. The hairs lift on the back of my neck, the tingling sensation spreading across my shoulders.

I'm supposed to eat her.

Why is she the one swallowing me?

"You aren't going to bite me, are you?" I ask.

"Not unless you want me to."

The sharp ends of her teeth scrape against my shaft, and I grip her hair and grunt with violence, reminding her that *I'm* the predator. I move her skull up and down until she's at the rhythm I want. A groan threatens to escape me, but a thought cuts through my pleasure.

What if she's only doing this for me? What if she doesn't actually want to give me a blow job?

Do I even deserve this?

I let go of her head. "Are you sure about—"

"Look at the screen and think of eating me," she demands.

On the screen, a man snatches a handful of meat and *eats* it. Blood dribbles down his chin. The video switches again, and though I stare at the screen, I don't fully see anything, and then the clips morph until it's her every time. Mona's long hair. Mona's uvula. Mona's chopped breast. Mona eating a handful of meat.

The colorless visuals on the screen help me get there, only because I think of her. Her throat squeezes my dick, her tongue reaching out and licking my balls, and it's like my head has detached from my body. I haven't gotten a blow job in years, not since I realized it doesn't do much for me. When a woman sucks your dick, you're the submissive bitch. She can bite your dick off at any moment. I don't like that loss of control.

With Mona, it's like someone actually sees *me* for once. I have to let her do this if I want something real with her.

A longer clip unfolds: a woman impaled on a spit roast, the wooden rod going through her asshole and out of her mouth, her trussed body rotating over a fire. The camera zooms in, and the spit-roasted woman's eyes squirm with panic.

No one would live through that. It's computer-generated. Special effects. Not real.

I imagine Mona in her place. Blood rushes to the tip of my cock.

"This is yours?" I ask. Mona keeps her mouth on me and moans, her vibrations tickling my balls. "You made this?"

She jerks me off with her hands. "It looks real, doesn't it?" she says. "We can make it look more real, can't we, love?"

She swallows me again, and I groan until the vibrations rumble in my toes. My dick is so hard, it's painful, and I'm trying hard not to blow my load right now. Her nails dig into my thighs, and her words repeat in my mind, fragments that burrow into my primal drives.

We can make it real.

Eat me.

Eat me until there's nothing left.

My cum blasts her throat. Each squirt pummels through me, a full-body orgasm, sweat covering every inch of me, and my eyes burn with the overwhelming need to let go of everything. To be myself for once. To stop holding back.

That's what this is right now: *me holding back.*

I can be good though. I don't have to hurt anyone to be fulfilled. I can cherish Mona.

"Did you enjoy that?" she whispers.

I ease back into reality. She sits back on her haunches, an artist kneeling before her inspiration, as if I'm a god to her.

I'm tired as fuck, but I nod. She chuckles, then prances to the back of the theater. The screen goes dark. I adjust my pants and stand.

"You really are into this kind of thing, aren't you?" I ask.

Her eyes harden as she keeps her attention on the projector. That's when I realize the hope that she's *the one*—the person I can share my life with—is threading itself into my nervous system. Love is never that simple though. I can't assume she'll satisfy me, nor can I assume I'll be able to make her dreams come true.

Besides, I can't actually eat her. That would be wrong. For this to work, both of us will have to live and love like this. Empty stomachs. Semi-full hearts.

But I know I can take care of her.

A dull ache radiates through my neck, and I scratch the back of my head. I need to slow down. My feelings aren't a big deal right now. As far as Mona's concerned, we're just hooking up for her art. Obviously it will be my job to convince her to commit to something other than her work, to commit to me, to commit to us.

"I don't question my sexuality. You shouldn't either," she says. She grabs her purse. "Walk me to my car."

Outside, it's cold, and it's dark early. It should irritate me that I'm following her, letting *her* lead us again, but I push those thoughts down. She's indulging our mutual interests; that's what's important.

The exotic birds from the nearby zoo chirp into the night. Newly installed blue-lit phones sparkle across the quad, and a security guard walks between the buildings. A group of female students huddle together and whisper to each other. A recent news article crosses my mind. Rape and assault cases went up in the last decade, and the student council pressured the dean to do something about it. *We can't stop the rapists, but we can give students more resources,* the dean had said. *This way, they can feel empowered. They'll have more chances to take control of their academic lives.*

I spare the group an extra glance. It's good that the students get additional campus resources, but it doesn't apply to Mona or me, because I'm not a rapist. I may enjoy my predatorial roleplaying, but I'm not a cannibal. I'm not going to *actually* eat Mona. I wouldn't ruin a potential relationship with someone by eating them.

The thought of eating her though? Pure bliss.

In the parking lot, we stop by an expensive SUV. I rub my chin. It seems too big for her. She must need the extra space for her sculptures.

"Thank you for tonight," she says.

A vivid vision fills my mind: my dick in her cunt as I chew the taste buds off of her tongue.

I'm not a cannibal though. I'm not. *I'm not.* I know better than that.

But *if* I was, I would bite a chunk out of her and savor every raw flavor.

"No," I say. "Thank you—"

I cut myself off. This is another abrupt ending, and each time I see Mona—whether it's in her bedroom window, in a bathtub, or kneeling on the ground in a movie theater—I need *more* of her. In my late teens and early twenties, the women I dated were shy, and I always got frustrated with that. I gave them warnings, but they still didn't like the way I treated them in the bedroom. It's not my fault they didn't listen to me.

Mona is different though. She's not appeasing me *just* to get me to come. She's actually invested in this too.

I can't let this be the end.

"Let's go out," I say. "Let me pay you back for today."

She grins. "Pay me back how?"

"Dinner."

No, no, no, my brain screams. *Don't do this. This isn't right. Taking a woman out to dinner is a date, and you can't date a woman who fantasizes about being eaten. You know what will happen. You'll get carried away—*

But I can't let go now. Not when I'm this close.

"You know the steakhouse a few blocks over?" I ask. She tilts her head, her lips pursed. I clarify, "The chain restaurant with the cow statue out front?"

"Oh, sure," she says.

A lightness fills my chest. Maybe she doesn't know which restaurant I'm talking about because she's a vegetarian.

That would be perfect.

I lick my lips, and this time, Mona is the one glued to my tongue.

"I want to feed you," I say.

Damn it. That sounds like I want her to eat *me*. I'm probably turning her off right now.

I ball my fists. Why am I so stupid?

"You have my university email, right?" she asks. "Send me your address. I'll come pick you up."

I furrow my brows. "I live an hour away."

"I like driving."

This isn't right. She's leading me again, and I fucking hate it, but I can't leave—I can't make my mouth or my feet move to change my position.

She waves and jumps into her SUV with ease, then pulls out of the parking space.

There's no second thought. No choice. It's simply a demand. She *will* be the one picking me up. I don't have a say in that.

Irritation blooms across my skin, hot like the outside of a boiling pot. Inviting her out should be an opportunity to show her what I'm capable of, but it's like she's already taken that away from me, simply by telling me *she's* going to pick me up.

Or maybe she wants to fuck in the back of her car after she watches me eat a steak.

Sure, my brain argues. *Tell yourself she wants to fuck a creep like you after eating steak. You fucking freak.*

As her SUV disappears on the main road, the cold air and post-orgasm oxytocin numb me. I breathe slowly, glued to the same spot.

I should be grateful. Mona is out of this world. She's everything I've ever wanted. Even if I feel like I'm a toy to her right now, that won't last forever. I'll make sure of that.

CHAPTER 8

A FEW DAYS HAVE PASSED SINCE WE MADE OUR DINNER PLANS, AND since then, I've been counting down the days until I get to see Mona again. Eating a steak with her won't be like how it is with the sex workers; she'll take my foreplay seriously.

I peer out of the window. Her headlights beam down the road. Our date is only minutes away now.

My stomach churns. I have this gut instinct she would understand the offal pit and the mixed ground meat. It makes me nervous to think of her in *my* space though.

I turn off the main generator, then meet her in the driveway. When I think about it, she's like an unattainable goddess, and I'm the weak mortal who has built an entire altar of animal sacrifices for her. Meat. Flesh. Blood.

No, I think. *If anything, I am the god who eats her.*

Mona's SUV stops beside me. I swallow my nerves, replacing it with broadened, confident shoulders. She leans over and opens the passenger door for me.

"I'm excited," she says. "I've never been to this steakhouse. I hear it's good."

I sit and buckle up. "It is—"

She puts her hand in my lap and squeezes my dick and balls like she's already got me by them.

A sharp tension cuts inside of me, my vision blurring with need.

I am the god who eats her, I remind myself.

She winks. "Let's eat some meat."

Classical music plays from the car's speakers. With every passing mile, I relax. This is a simple dinner date, and it's the obvious next step in connecting with someone who shares the same interests. And that's what I've always wanted.

The restaurant bustles with noise. Mona tugs me past tables filled with diners. The server gestures to our booth, and we settle into opposite sides.

I pick up my menu. Mona fiddles with a camera.

"What do you usually get here?" she asks.

That's right—if she is a vegetarian, then she probably doesn't have many options here. I should have suggested a different restaurant, but I didn't, because I need the steak to show her what I want from her body.

"The filet mignon," I say. "Rare. You're a vegetarian, right?"

She laughs, then places the camera on top of the table.

"I eat meat," she says. "I don't usually go to chain restaurants though. I'll get the filet too."

My spine stiffens. It seems like a jab at my economic status. I don't let those insecurities surface though. Even if she usually only eats at exclusive restaurants, she agreed to dinner with *me.* She asked *me* to be in her art.

The server returns, and Mona orders. "Two rare filet mignons. Oh, and a glass of cabernet for me."

I rub my chin. I don't say anything though. I like saving money, but if Mona wants wine, then we'll get wine. Besides, they say that a glass of red wine every now and then is good for the heart. The better her organs are working, the better she'll taste. Hypothetically speaking, that is.

Forks and knives ding against dinner plates. Children whine. Men lecture.

I should say something, shouldn't I?

"How long have you been doing art?" I ask.

My cheeks redden. *Doing art?* What the fuck is wrong with me? No one *does* art. She probably thinks I'm a total idiot now.

I correct myself. "Creating art, I mean?"

She lifts her nose slightly, a flash of condescension in her expression. Then she smiles.

"My whole life," she says. "It's a part of me."

My shoulders strain as I mull over those words. If art is a part of her, then maybe cannibalism is a part of me too. My interest started young. No matter how hard I try or how many therapists I go to, I can't get rid of the urge. It's been this way since I can remember.

This time, I don't meet her eyes. In a low voice, I ask, "Why are you doing this?"

In my periphery, I see her straighten, giving me her full attention. "What do you mean?"

"This art project on cannibalism." I shrug, finally glancing at her. "Your art is always controversial, right? But why this? Why cannibalism?"

She chuckles, each note low and cutting, like there's a joke that I'm not aware of, and I'm the punchline. The hairs on the back of my neck stand, and I push back in my seat.

I don't leave though.

Control yourself, I think, *and you'll get what you want.*

"As you may have gathered by my last exhibition, I'm always interested in the objectification of human beings. Cannibalism is obviously the next step," she says. "Think about it: cannibalism is the actual consumption of a human as an object."

That's where people are too narrow-minded though.

"Cannibalism doesn't have to be about eating people like a roast beef dinner," I say. "It can be about the ultimate form of love or sexual exploration and trust. Being there for someone, even nutritionally providing for them."

She takes a long sip of wine. The silence eats away at me, judging me for being such a needy little boy.

"I'm sure survival cannibalism exists," she says. She dangles her glass by the neck. "Most cannibalism falls into survival *or* predatorial, but I'm not interested in the art of survival."

My throat dries. She's dismissing the providing love of cannibalism, and yet she's teasing me too, playing with her words. Coaxing me in. *She's not interested in survival.*

My brain imagines Mona with her limbs removed. Her torso roasted. The muscles pulled from her bones until she's nothing, not even a cadaver. An ending where she's my favorite meal.

But I'm not a real cannibal. This is pretend.

I clear my throat. "I don't want to hurt anyone. I just want to know that someone would be there for me if I needed them—"

She cuts me off. "But have you forced anyone before?"

I blink rapidly at her. *Forced anyone?* "What?"

"Rape," she says. "It's simple. You take what you want, don't you, love?"

My gut twists as I stumble over her words. *Rape?* I may have done some things that my sexual partners didn't like, but I never went into it without telling them what I was going to do. They *knew* what I wanted and what I was like. I can't control how they react to me.

My mind glimmers with a memory: a woman is chained to my oven. Tears coat her face, and her mouth opens in a blood-curdling scream. I don't hear anything though; I simply see. Red liquid drips down her chest. The knife is in my hand. Her blood dribbles on my chin and lips. It's not like she was *that* hurt. For fuck's sake, the incision was basically a paper cut.

The point is I told her what I was planning to do. She agreed.

And she got her fucking money.

"No," I say. "I'm not a rapist."

"Of course you're not a *rapist*," Mona says, exaggerating the last word. A disconcerting sensation washes over my chest and down to my groin. She continues: "Have you ever fantasized about rape though?" She licks her lips. "I have."

Romantic cannibalism has always been about digestion, when my soul mate becomes a literal part of me. There isn't anything more meaningful than that. When I think about my actual fantasies though, those sexual dreams that I can't stop, the idea of a woman's face bending in agony as I cut off a sliver of her tit has always made me hard. Licking her tears. Eating delicate chunks of her labia. Her cunt constricting around my cock as her legless and armless torso fights me.

I don't know if I consider that rape, though. I'm not hurting anyone if I'm only imagining it.

"I guess," I say. "I can see why the power in doing something like that is appealing."

"Exactly. It's just like cannibalism, isn't it?" I open my mouth to disagree. She keeps talking. "When was the first time you considered cannibalism?"

I'm instantly transported to another memory. I was too dizzy to get up, so I stayed in my sleeping bag, unable to move and being forced to watch as my mother and her boyfriend fucked. His jaws latched onto her breast, and her skin crunched in his teeth like tendons being ripped apart. She screamed, but her lips reached for his, and it didn't seem like pain anymore. It seemed as if she wanted more.

Then I see my mother lying on the kitchen table, her mouth pried open so far her jaw looks unhinged. The frayed edges of her chapped lips like a wreath around her empty, cavernous mouth. The raw muscle of her tongue warmed my palm, and I found it comforting. It was like she was finally there for me. Like she wanted to talk to me for once.

I shake those memories away. Those weren't the first times I thought about cannibalism, but Mona doesn't need to know the details of my pathetic childhood. The highlights are enough.

"Camping," I say. She wrinkles her nose. I increase my bravado to not seem so childish. "I saw some weird shit as a kid. My mother was crazy." I laugh loudly. "What about you? When did you first think about being eaten?"

"My pet rabbit ate her baby."

She angles her head and studies her wine glass, almost like she's lost in a memory. A mother eating a child, even if it is a small-brained creature, must be a shocking event to witness. It's hard to think of any mother or father eating their child.

The server presents our matching dishes: two filet mignons with smashed garlic potatoes and caramelized Brussels sprouts.

Mona squeals, and though it bothers me that she's eating meat, her excitement makes me lighter and heightens my arousal.

Now, I get to show her what I'm capable of.

I cut into my rare steak, and the watery blood oozes onto the plate. I stab the bite, mentally skimming through my filthy speech.

"Do you know how I would—"

My jaw drops.

Mona clutches the steak in her bare hands. The red drips flow down her wrists like oil in a marinade.

I look around nervously; the far tables are busy with their meals, and our neighboring booths can't see us, but there are at least two nearby tables watching us. Watching *her*. A little girl gawks, and her mother shakes her head. *Don't pay attention to them*, the mother mouths. Her actual whispers are inaudible from this distance, so I imagine her next words: *They're embarrassing themselves.*

Mona doesn't notice. She bites the meat, then closes her eyes and moans as she savors the taste. Her body shifts, her hips wriggling, and I get the sense that underneath the table, she's spreading her legs.

When her eyes open again, she glances at the camera. The red light blinks. She's recording, then. She must always be recording.

She locks onto my gaze.

"Try it," she says. "Forget about the forks and knives. Eat with your hands, like we were meant to."

A primal feast. My mind is a mess, and my cock bulges.

Every eye in the restaurant sears into us. We're going to get kicked out. I should tell Mona to stop.

The words don't form. Besides, even if I tell her what to do, she may not listen. Instead, I wait for the server to ask us to leave.

I simply can't look away.

My dick presses against my metal zipper. There's an animalistic nature to Mona, a quality I want to hold on to, and the back of my neck tingles with warning *and* thrill. She's doing this for me, isn't she? She's putting on another show to turn *me* on.

She's not going to play into your fantasies, my brain warns. *Look at how she's eating the steak. She's the one who's going to eat you alive, you pathetic little freak.*

That can't be true, though. She may like teasing cannibalism from both ends—consumer and consumed—but her personal ad asked for someone to *eat her*.

As she licks the blood off of her fingers, I realize she's finished her steak. Her Brussels sprouts and the potatoes are completely untouched.

Mona is a carnivore, then. At least for now. I'm sure I can convince her to experiment with other diets, even if it's only while we're roleplaying.

"I love a good steak," she says. "Don't you?"

I stare down at my plate. The meat has cooled, and the puddle of red blood creates an unappetizing sludge with the butter sauce.

This was supposed to be *my* turn, where I showed Mona how I can fulfill her darkest fantasies too. Instead, she took over again. Pushing me aside. Ignoring me.

My scalp prickles, and my dick is flaccid again.

I'm not hungry. Not anymore.

Not for that.

"Some people say I come on too strong," Mona says. Her teeth click, then she wiggles her fingers at the little girl watching her. The mother scowls. Mona wipes her lips with her napkin, her smug expression taunting the mother. Then Mona faces me, still clinging to that pompous attitude. "Am I too much for you, Kent?"

I grit my teeth. Another taunt. Another tease. Another way to mess with me.

I can see why most people would think Mona is too much. She's pale, like she does her art in a basement without any light, and her eyes are so dark with makeup, it's like she's got two shadowed holes for eyes. And with her short height, you'd think she'd be easily overlooked, but her personality is too big to be dismissed. Her willingness to indulge in wine baths, cannibalistic movies, and eating food with her hands in the middle of a crowded restaurant is completely out of the ordinary. I wouldn't be surprised if she hasn't had many relationships either, like me.

Even if she is too demanding, there are things we have in

common. Things I'm willing to sacrifice myself for. I'll let her have the upper hand for now, if it means I'll get what I want later.

"No," I say. "You know what you want. It's not everyday you meet someone like that."

A high-pitched voice breaks in. "I see you liked your steak." The server pauses, then subtly grimaces at me. "Do you want to take that home, sir?" I nod, and she hands me a foam box. "I brought some dessert menus."

"You're a doll," Mona says. She happily takes the menus, and the server disappears. Mona shows me a picture of a dessert. "They have bread pudding. Do you want some dessert?"

Underneath the table, Mona is probably spread out. Pantiless. Her pussy flaps hot and sweaty. Her skin moist with the animal proteins digesting in her stomach. Her fleshy meat rubbing against the seat cushions.

After eating that steak, she'll have a metallic taste, and even though she's not premium meat right now, I still want to taste her.

My head spins with lust. Maybe I am hungry after all, but not for sugar.

"I want *you*," I growl.

Her eyes glitter. "Let me go pay, then."

I grind my teeth, my erection softening once again. The fuck is she trying to do now?

"Wait," I say. "I'm supposed to—"

"Oh, love," she coos. I swallow hard and ignore the warning bells screeching in my skull. She strokes my arm. "You're the one indulging me, remember?"

My stomach flops, turbulence rising to the surface. Mona isn't supposed to be the dominant one, and yet she's paying for our meal. She leads the way every fucking time.

Then she grabs my hand, and I let go of those thoughts. I can do this. I can be the man she wants me to be, as long as she's my meat.

I tuck my boxed steak under my arm as I follow my human steak to her car.

CHAPTER 9

THE SUV CRUNCHES OVER THE DIRT, EACH BUMP IS LIKE A HOOK lodging into my lungs. My throat constricts, but I need this. Even if she thinks she's in charge, I need a sexual connection with someone for once.

We both do.

Mona parks, then grabs her purse and camera. I hold up my hand.

"Wait here," I say.

For once, she obeys.

I stuff the foam box in the fridge, saving it for later, then I run to the generator at the back of the home and flip it on. The flies buzz from the pit and whine for more flesh. I swat a hand at them. They dance around me, a mob chanting for a feast. They're more active than usual tonight. It's almost like a sign they like her too. She won't be coming to the backyard though. The flies would probably scare her away.

I run back to her car and open her door. "Welcome."

She beams at me. "Such a gentleman."

I open the front door of the house too, then usher her inside. Right across from the entrance, the grandfather clock ticks.

"The time is off," Mona says. "Is that on purpose?"

I lift my shoulders. I don't use the clock to tell time. I keep it there because of the noise. It reminds me of the clock my mother used to keep in the kitchen. It's there to keep me company, like a beating heart.

I don't tell Mona that. I pull her deeper into the house, and she runs her hands over the frayed edges of the floral wallpaper. Her garlic-pepper breath mingles with the stale air, as if she's already seasoned for me.

My tongue thickens. I'm eager, so fucking eager, that if I'm not careful, I may burst with hunger.

I can't let that happen.

Mona readies her camera. Each click of the shutter rings through the house, another mechanical heart beating with the grandfather clock.

"It looks like you haven't done any renovations in years," she says. "Is there a reason you're keeping it locked in this condition? Did someone die here?"

The mobile home holds up in the rare desert storm, and if a fire comes and swallows it, I won't lose anything of sentimental value. The flames would even potentially cook the offal pit, and I could eat that later.

"Probably," I say.

I find Mona squinting at a black-and-white photograph on the wall. It's an older image of a young woman, framed by a bulky silver frame. Now that I think of it, that picture frame is probably worth a lot of money. I can sell it and use the money for a premium cut of grass-fed beef.

"Is that your mother?" she asks, her voice quiet. She raises the camera and takes a shot of the picture. "You must've been close."

"That woman wasn't my mother," I say.

I lick my lips and stare at Mona's mouth.

"Why do you like cannibalism?" she asks.

I lower my eyes, humiliated under the weight of the question. Somehow, this question is different. Pointed. Ready to gut me. She's asking *why*, as if there's an easy answer. At the same time, I know I could probably say it's hot, and that wouldn't be a good enough explanation for her.

I swallow a lump in my throat. I know it's more complicated

than sexual desire. Mona is probably comfortable answering questions like this because she's constantly interrogated about her art, but I haven't been questioned like this since the last time I spoke with a therapist, and even back then, I didn't like answering those questions.

"Why do you care?" I mumble.

"Because I'm interested in you, love. The real you." She leans forward. "You inspire me."

My head fills with hopeful ideas, and that dissolves the humiliation.

Her art. She means her art. The contract we signed. Her next project is about cannibalism.

Even still, someone may care about me for once. Me, the little boy who was left alone.

The cannibal fantasizer. The loner. *Me.*

"You're not going to psychoanalyze my answer?" I ask.

"Why would I?"

Her tone is so matter-of-fact my chest swells. She doesn't want to fix me then. She doesn't want to try and change my sexuality. She's actually interested in me.

I try to find the words and give her the answer she deserves. My mouth fills with sand, and that frustration seeps to the surface.

For the first time in my life, someone wants to know more about the real me, and I clam up like this?

"I don't know," I finally say.

"Try." She pets my arm. "Is it the power? Perhaps the forbidden nature of it? The dominance?"

All of it, I think. I'm not sure if that's true, but it feels right though. Dominance, like conquering prey. Forbidden, like a secret I can keep to myself. Power, the act of knowing that she can never leave me again because she'll be *inside* of me. I'll always have control of her.

The camera shutter clicks, knocking me back to the present.

I bare my teeth at her. "I wasn't ready."

"That's the beauty of art." She pinches my cheek. "The best art is when the subjects aren't expecting to be captured."

My upper lip curls. Why does that response irk me? Is it the "captured" part? Is it because she's treating me like her prey?

"Here," she says. She waves for me to follow her. "Let's do a hands-on study."

I let the anger go for now, and I don't give myself time to think. Mona's hips sway into the kitchen, and she flips on the lights, comfortable in my space. The electricity hums from the fluorescent strips in the ceiling. Mona slides a hand across the countertop and moves a few utensils out of the way. She sets up the camera on the opposite side, then connects a wireless remote to it.

She wants to take pictures of us right now?

She climbs onto the empty countertop. Her dress hikes up around her hips, exposing her bare ass. I was right; she's not wearing any panties. I salivate over those pink pussy lips speckled with coarse hairs, imagining the taste of her flesh. Tangy. Sweet. Decadent. She crawls along the counter and looks over her shoulder at me seductively, before she finally flips over and lies down. Like *she's* been captured.

I snap my teeth shut. She bites her lip.

"Fuck me like I'm your meat," she moans.

Those words enter through my bloodstream, and my dick grows to its full potential. A sex worker can say the same words, and it irritates me to no end. With Mona, everything is different. There may be red flags everywhere, and a camera ready to snap your picture, but when a woman like Mona tells you to fuck her like she's your meat, you fucking do it.

Besides, she's interested in the real *me*. Why shouldn't I show her a peek of who I am inside?

I lean over the counter, kiss her neck, and suck in her scent. The faint odor of candied salt fills my nostrils. I pull down the strap of her dress.

"Tell me how you'd do it," she breathes.

I lick her collarbone. Sweat beads on my forehead, the tension of nerves and desire fighting inside of me. I want her to want me, and I don't want to mess this up. I don't want her to leave me.

"You won't freak out?" I ask. "You won't—"

"Stop being scared and tell me what you'd do to me," she hisses.

My stomach roils as I try to think straight and concentrate on the good, on the fact that my dream girl is lying on the counter asking me to fuck her like she's meat. I can't squash the inner questions though.

She expects my obedience, doesn't she?

Does she think I'm a little bitch?

Am I not man enough for her?

I shake my head. It's not like that. Mona is simply frustrated with me, like I get irritated with the escorts. She doesn't want me to perform; she wants reality.

I can tell her something easy, something she probably wants to hear. I can tell her I'd chase her, fuck her, then eat her until there's nothing left.

I'll do all of that one day. But right now, I'm starving, and it's blurring my common sense.

My heart rate increases as I hold down her wrists. She licks her lips.

"I'd chain you to a bed," I say in a low voice. I squeeze her wrists until her skin thins, and the coarse texture of her bone rubs against my fingertips. Then I bite her wrist. Her veins slide under my teeth, and she yelps, then pulls my head closer to her, desperate for more.

"I'll feed you only vegetables and fruits and leaves," I continue. "I'll make sure you never move, so your meat will stay tender. You want your meat to melt in my mouth, don't you?"

"Uh huh," she purrs.

The camera shutter clicks right as she moans. Energy fills me. If she's taking pictures now, then this is what she wants.

"I'll roast your abdomen," I say. "But first, I'll peel the skin from your leg and season you like a real leg of lamb." I bite her inner thigh, and she flinches slightly. The camera clicks. I bare my teeth, embracing the predator inside of me, and a smile crawls over my lips. She's not running away. She's here. She's listening to me.

"You'd taste so good, baby," I whisper. "And without your leg, you won't be able to run away from me."

She shivers. "You'd do that to me?"

"Of course I will," I murmur. I bend down to her thighs and bite again. "I'll do everything I can to savor your meat."

"Harder," she rasps. "Bite me harder, Kent."

Frustration buzzes to my jaws. Does she think I'm a pussy?

I bite down as hard as I can, and her skin finally gives way. A hint of a metallic liquid teases my tongue.

She cries, and I immediately lift from her. A tiny drop of blood pools on her skin, her thigh meat indented with my teeth. *Was that hard enough?* I want to howl. *Am I still a scared little boy to you?*

Then Mona's bottom lips quiver, and those irritations fade, replaced by the panic. I went too far, didn't I? This will be the act that pushes her over the edge, that forces her to leave me.

Then the shutter taps. I blink. She grins, encouraging me. *Go on*, her smile says. *Keep telling me your desires.*

If she's well enough to keep taking pictures, then she likes my piercing bite.

I'm back in my predatorial form again. There are so many fleshy parts of her body. Her breasts. Her stomach. Those mouth-watering thighs. I can barely keep track of what I want first.

"I'd make you watch me eat you," I say. "You'd become a part of me."

"Kent, *now*—" she says. "I need you."

She thrusts her pussy, practically bucking into my face. I growl, then push her hips until she's lying flat, ready to be sliced open. I lick her slit. Her liquid need drips down her crevices, filled with sweetness and salt, and I grab my dick through my pants. I bite her beady clit, her hood sliding from the pressure of my teeth, each movement tenderizing that bundle of nerves. Then I trace my finger down her cunt.

I pinch her folds. "I'd slice off these pretty little lips. I'd eat them first."

"Do it," she whines. "I need to come—"

The hunger rises inside of me. With two fingers massaging her meat sleeve, I swirl my tongue around her swollen clit, puffy from arousal or me—or both—and she tastes *so* good. Like a tender medallion sprinkled with freshly crushed peppercorns. Like a polpette drowning in garlic. Like a raw, meaty tongue dipped in stomach acid.

Her hips twitch, nearing that final peak, and I don't know if it's my skill or if she's already worked up from dinner. I keep forcing her into that abyss. My fingers jab inside of her, and my lips suction that meaty clit until she's convulsing around me and coming like a beast. Her legs wrap around my skull as if she's a praying mantis about to pop off my head and eat it.

As she comes down, I scoop out her juices and lick my fingers clean. I moan as I savor the subtly sour, *natural* taste of her.

She breathes heavily, still lying on the counter. I rest my head on her stomach and listen to her digest. Her belly gurgles and whines, a protest of the filet she's currently digesting. Even her internal organs know she doesn't need meat anymore.

I decide right then she's going to begin a new vegetarian diet. I'll stop spending my money at the butcher shop and start spending my paychecks on organic produce for her. I'll buy her the best fruits and vegetables.

We don't have to talk about her new vegetarian diet yet though.

She hops off of the countertop.

"Stand there," she says. I move where she wants, then check her camera. She probably doesn't want me to accidentally block the lens.

She fiddles with one of the kitchen drawers, and I suck the droplets of her drying juices from my hands and eat her arousal like she licked up the filet's blood at the restaurant.

My stomach growls. I'm still hungry.

Mona holds up a utensil. A steak knife.

My jaw drops open, and she sits on the counter and spreads her legs. Her pussy oozes more clear juices onto the countertop as she brings the blade to her thigh, right below my bite mark. The blade knicks her skin, and the blood beads along the seam of broken flesh.

My dick rages as panic flares inside of me.

That's blood. Real fucking blood. Blood that she needs to survive. Blood that I can't have. If I go overboard, I may ruin this relationship before it truly begins, and I can't let that happen.

But my stomach growls angrily. I want to taste her blood.

I want to taste *her*.

"Drink me." She points down between her feet. "Kneel before me, love, and drink my blood."

Conflict ripples inside of me and clogs my throat. This is some vampire queen shit, but we're not acting in a movie or television show.

This is real. Mona is bleeding. She cut herself.

For me.

She cut herself to feed me.

It's all for me.

And I'm so fucking hungry.

"T-this is wrong," I stutter. "This is real, Mona."

"Come on, love," she says. I take another step closer, and her voice taunts me. "It's only a little blood."

My breath catches in my throat. "I can't—"

"I want you to do it," she says, a hint of familiar anger appearing in her voice. "Are you going to deny me?"

When the sex workers made fun of me or when girlfriends told me I was messed up, I hated them, and I hated *myself* even more. I hated that I was a freak who liked something as disturbing as eating a woman, and I hated how those freakish desires left me alone. Does Mona feel like that too? Is she isolated? Does she think I'm mocking her?

The blood droplets pool on Mona's skin, and my dick grows painfully hard, my balls contracting against me. This isn't right; at the same time, I don't want to disappoint her. I've tasted her period blood, and now, I'm curious. So fucking curious that I need to know if her blood will taste different when it's fresh from the source.

I kneel down.

I lick the blood.

Warm liquid, like metal and pepper and nectar, swims over my tongue. I seal my lips around the wound and suckle more of her life source.

"Yes," Mona murmurs. "Go on. Eat more. Pull at the skin." She pushes her thigh, disrupting my suction. My nostrils flare. What the fuck is she doing now? "Chew it off," she commands. "Eat me—"

I didn't plan to chew anything off.

I just wanted a lick. A little taste.

But this isn't about me or what I want, is it?

It's about her power over me.

I don't want her to have power over me.

But I like how she tastes way too fucking much.

My chest compresses, and I adjust my pants. I swear I can't breathe around her right now.

"I need some air," I say, and I run out of the home.

CHAPTER 10

Outside, the winter wind whips past me. A lamp hangs from the mobile home, lighting the back of the property. I stare down into the shadowed offal pit, at the decaying meat covered by salt and flies. I should probably rotate the older leftovers out and mix a new batch of ground meat soon. Even if it's a risk to bring my ground meat to the processing plant, Jerry always likes it, says it gets him high because it's fermented or something. I don't know if he's right about the fermentation, but I admit, I enjoy sharing what I have. It's nice to give protein to others, especially knowing that back when I was a kid, I didn't have that option or anyone who did that for me. And I like my ground meat better than the supermarket variety. When I blend the animals together, it's easier to convince myself that the final product has a human flavor, even if it's only a subtle hint of it.

The flies swarm me for a few seconds. When they realize I'm as much of a part of the fields as they are, they grow disinterested and leave me alone.

I may have tasted Mona's blood, but I'm not a cannibal. I didn't hurt her; she hurt herself. On top of that, she did it *for* me. If I didn't consume her, it would have been rude. Wasteful.

A memory flashes; in it, I'm ten years old.

You shouldn't have pissed him off, my mother had said. *There's no such thing as leftovers in our family. You know that.*

Things were never good, but that night was especially awful. My mother couldn't leave me at home, so she took me camping with her boyfriend. They drank beers, and he even gave me a few, but when he fed me a third hot dog, I couldn't finish it right then. I wanted to eat it. My stomach was full though. I just needed a few minutes to digest.

You beg for food like a little bitch, and this is what you do when you get it? he asked. *Is my food not good enough for you?*

Then he punched me so hard, I fell to the ground and threw up.

Once I finally stopped vomiting from the impact of his fists, I crawled to the tent. My vision was blurry, and I could barely move, but that didn't stop my mother and her boyfriend from coming into the tent and fucking right in front of me. He barreled into her. Slapped her. Choked her. Bit her so hard, a blurry patch of red streamed down her breast. She panicked, writhing underneath him. He growled, and that primal noise made my mother moan as if she liked it. As if she wanted more. As if she needed it.

A cold hand snakes behind my back. I jolt and swing around.

Mona stands next to me. The flies rise to greet her. She gives me a funny look.

"What's that?" she asks as she motions to the dark hole in front of us. "It smells."

"An offal pit," I say.

"Huh. I didn't realize that was a thing here." She clears her throat. "You butcher animals at home too?"

I scratch the back of my neck. "Not exactly. It's another means of preserving meat."

"Oh. Cool."

I keep my eyes on the pit. In my periphery, I see Mona's bare toes sinking into the dirt, and I wonder if there's a chunk of animal flesh—a scrap I accidentally dropped—that's mixing with her feet. I'm too careful to drop meat, but there's something appealing about mixing her flesh with my collected meats, especially without her knowing. Like she could end up in the offal pit one day, and I'd eat her in a meatloaf.

When it comes to her, she'd never make it to the pit. And I wouldn't have any leftovers.

"I didn't mean to scare you," she says. "I guess I was trying to figure out why you don't go after what you want."

I grit my teeth. *Scare me?* I wasn't scared. I was just...resisting the urges. For fuck's sake, I was trying to protect her! I'm close to crossing a line I may not be able to come back from. I don't want to scare *her*.

I can't say that though.

"I'm the one who should be sorry," I say quietly. "I freaked out. You were just trying to indulge me."

"And get a good picture," she says with amusement. "I want to thank you for taking me and my project seriously. It's refreshing to meet someone who isn't so resistant, you know?"

Her words dance in my brain. Did she just thank me?

I left her in the kitchen, and yet, for some reason, she appreciates me.

She's right; I do take her seriously. So fucking seriously that I know there's real danger in our relationship. Mona is willing to cut herself for her art, for *me,* and if we keep doing this, I don't know where it will end.

I'm *not* a cannibal. I just have these ideas in my head, and Mona does too. We're both adults. We can make our own informed decisions.

And I can stop again like I did tonight. Even if she wants me to eat her, I don't have to go all the way.

I broaden my chest. "No, really. Thank *you* for including me."

She takes my hand in hers. Her small, dainty fingers envelop me in their coldness. It must be too chilly for her out here. That can't be good for her muscles. For her meat.

A shudder rolls through my body.

Mona tilts her head. "I want you to meet my friend and teach him how to be like us." Hopeful curiosity blooms across her face. "We'll show him how to create true art."

The mobile home lights gleam in her eyes, surrounded by the

dark makeup. Tension wraps around my gut, my head buzzing with cautious thoughts. Having another man with us ruins the intimacy of our roleplaying. He'll be a voyeur. A person casting judgment. A barrier to destroy.

And the idea of destroying her friend fills me with vibrating energy. Would Mona like seeing me prove to her friend I'm the alpha of our small trio?

"Will your friend be participating?" I ask.

"Not if there's no purpose for him." She squeezes my fingers. "We'll take it easy though. Just sex and roleplay. We'll teach him, and you can demonstrate how beautiful taking my flesh can be. Can you do that for me, Kent?"

Nerves braid their way into my thoughts. I don't want to share her; at the same time, I want to do this *for* her, like she cut herself for me. I want Mona to need me. To rely on me. To not have any choice but to be mine. My lover. My flesh. My meat.

My spine tingles. It's not a choice. I have to do this for her.

"Okay," I say.

"You're so good to me," she says.

And the rest of the night fades into a blur.

I get to see her again. She even invited me this time.

Mona wants me.

CHAPTER 11

MONA TEXTS ME HER ADDRESS, UNAWARE THAT I ALREADY HAVE IT, then sends me an exact time to show up at her place.

Two weeks. Two whole fucking weeks pass. The urge to know what she's doing crawls under my skin like slugs slithering along wet cement and exposed to stomping feet. I consider sneaking into her house again. I don't though. Respect is earned. I want her to trust me. Even more than that, I want her to need me like I need her, and you don't get something like that without developing a craving first.

Instead, I appease my own cravings by savoring the last tampon from her trash can. I cut it into quarter-inch pieces. I lick the dried red bits from my fingers, and I suck her menstrual blood a little more each day. I even heat one of the chunks in the microwave to pretend like the blood is from her thigh again, then I smooth out the warmed fibers on a cracker. It's decadently satisfying, like brie and blood pudding sausage.

My entire world is about her.

By the time the designated evening comes, I'm ravenous. I show up slightly early and park my cargo van on the curb. A car is in her driveway, an electric model this time. A bunch of crates crowd the back seat, each container full of putties and paints. It must be Mona's car too.

Under one of the boxes, two eyes seethe at me.

A replica of the classic Frankenstein's monster is smashed under a cardboard box. It's artistic, but it seems too predictable to be Mona's project. Who owns the car: Mona or her friend?

I dismiss those thoughts, then heft my duffel bag up higher on my shoulder. Mona can create whatever she wants as long as I get to eat her.

I knock on the front door. It swings open.

A shirtless man with sinewy arms stands in the entryway. Jagged veins rope around his neck. His chest is gaunt, and his long hair is tied back in a low ponytail.

I squint. How do I know this man?

He offers his hand. "You must be the infamous Kent."

His grip is shockingly strong, and his display of strength unsettles me. Then it clicks: the man from the art gallery. The one who tried to talk to me about Mona's art. The idiot who wouldn't stop trying to find meaning in a bunch of broken mirrors.

I force a smile, and I can feel it's come out awkward, like I've got food stuck in my teeth.

"And you are?" I ask.

"Artemis. My friends call me Arty."

I blink slowly, resisting the urge to roll my eyes. It sounds like a stage name used to impress a woman like Mona. He's annoying. A fucking peacock.

"Isn't that a girl's name?" I ask.

"I renamed myself after the Greek goddess of the wilderness and hunting because I wanted to tap into that power. Take the goddess's name and honor it." He chuckles. "It's fitting, isn't it? Especially for tonight."

A roiling heat churns my stomach. We aren't hunting Mona tonight, and she's not a wild animal.

He stretches his thin shoulders as if he's bigger than me, and in response, I expand my frame, caging him in. He's an ant compared to me, and I want him to know that.

He doesn't flinch.

"Come!" he says eagerly. "We were just getting into the spa."

I grit my teeth, then follow him through the house. He effortlessly weaves through the hallways, and that familiarity irritates me. He doesn't understand Mona's sexual needs, and somehow, he knows her house like this? I had to learn the layout of her house the hard way, without her help when she was out working. Why does he get more access to her than I do?

The glass doors to the backyard slide open.

A bonfire flickers, the flames licking the earthy night. Mona sits in the hot tub, her hair pulled back into a bun, tendrils streaming beside her face, similar to how she looked in the bathtub at the art gallery. She's in a stew again, cooking until she's tender for me. This time, her cheeks are red. She's probably hot, and judging by the bottles around her, she's probably a little drunk too. Her flesh is flavored with ale and wine, as if she's seasoned herself for me.

"You're here!" she squeals. She reaches for a champagne flute. "Here. I saved you some."

Before I can grab the glass, Artemis drops his shorts, his cock plopping between his legs like a scrawny turkey wattle. I forget about the drink. My cock is bigger and thicker, but his confidence is yet another thing that pisses me off. It's like he has nothing to hide.

A normal person doesn't have anything to hide. They aren't like *us*.

He takes the spa's steps gingerly, hooting as his body acclimates to the hot water. Then he scoots along the bench and sidles up right next to Mona.

The two of them stare at me.

My skin prickles with nerves. It's like they're waiting for a show, and I'm the rare, endangered animal brought out in a cage. A vision appears in my mind: my bloody hands splitting that cage apart, my fists bashing Artemis into a pulp, my jaws latching onto Mona's neck.

"There's a guest bedroom through the second set of sliding glass doors," Artemis says, like it's his house, and he has the right to tell Mona's guests where to go and what to do. "You can put your things in there and change your clothes."

Water swirls around them, the bubbles popping like a

simmering beef broth, and Artemis fucking ruins it. He's a chunk of metal found in a chicken nugget, a food you think is safe until your throat is slit in half.

I imagine gouging his eyes out. No—I'd chop off his fucking head.

"I didn't bring swim trunks," I say, my voice monotone.

Mona giggles. "You can wear your boxers."

I inspect her, my gaze hardening, and she leans into Artemis's shoulder, soaking in that shared bond. I'm back in that tent again, paralyzed as I watch my mother and her boyfriend fuck like rabbits.

Mona is mocking me, isn't she? Just like my mother did. She thinks I'm too insecure to be naked like her and Artemis. She thinks I'll bitch out.

This was supposed to be about us. *Not him.* This was supposed to be about us *teaching* him.

I refuse to back down now.

I throw my bag in the guest bedroom, then return completely naked, the cold stones under my feet as I walk to the hot tub. Mona's gaze lingers over every inch of my body, her purrs of approval drifting over the foaming water. Artemis nods appreciatively too.

"Artemis got us some wagyu," Mona says.

"It's on the table," Artemis adds.

I grab the tray of little red-and-white speckled slices of meat, then set it on the ground next to the spa.

Greed and irritation battle in me, my hands itching to hurt someone. Mona shouldn't be eating meat, but I can't tell her what to do yet. She has to choose it for herself.

At the same time, I'm not going to pass up a cut of meat like this.

I get into the hot tub, then grab a big portion of wagyu and let it slide over my tongue. It melts, and I groan, pretending the meat is a sliver of Mona's skin that she cut off for me.

Artemis says something I can't hear, and Mona laughs. A dull sensation surfaces in my stomach. I shove it down, blocking

Artemis out and pretending it's just the two of us. No one else. Mona and me.

Artemis whispers in her ear, then kisses her neck. Mona's cheeks redden even more, like he's telling her a dirty secret. A therapist once told me I didn't have a normal social upbringing, and I think about that a lot when I see couples like this. Neck kisses don't arouse me; I only do it because women like it. Dirty talk—unless it's about eating her—does absolutely nothing for me. I don't even like blow jobs, unless I'm watching a cannibalism montage, I guess. I'll never be like Artemis is with women.

Mona reacts to him. She's half normal, half like me.

Artemis nibbles her neck, and Mona's lips part, a moan escaping her. Artemis beckons for me to join him.

"Come. Help me," he says. I don't move—I don't want to help *him,* only her—but I do angle forward in an attempt to hear him more clearly. He turns to Mona and says in a husky voice, "You want me to bite you again?"

"Yes, baby," Mona whispers. He nibbles her again, a rabbit eating a carrot. She leans into him. "Fuck me. I want it so bad."

Artemis perks up, then makes eye contact with me. "Why don't we use her from both ends?"

A normal threesome. A normal person would suggest that.

I turn my neck to avoid their eyes. Acidic bile crowds my throat, then the water sloshes, and Mona snakes her arm around my back, her naked breasts smashed against me in the water.

"Come on, Kent," Mona whispers. Her fingers twist around my elbow. "You know how to make me feel alive. He doesn't."

She beams at me, her expression rich with lust and need. There's a hunger there, and I want that hunger inside of me.

"Teach him," she says. "Show him what we're like."

What we're like.

I don't know if it's the fact she included me or made this about *us,* but alluding to him as the idiot outsider is the encouragement I need. My head spins as I gesture for them to follow *me.*

Soon, the three of us are outside of the hot tub. Mona is on all fours, and both of us fuck her like a seesaw, Artemis in her mouth and me in her pussy. The classic spit roast position, Artemis's idea.

He must think this position is enough to indulge Mona's interests, and that annoys me for her.

The two of them grunt, and Mona's warm cunt grips me like a glove. In the distance, one of her sculptures catches my eye. It's vastly different from her other pieces; it's not abstract or broken pieces put together. It's a very realistic marble bird with one of its wings nailed to the ground. It doesn't belong with the rest of Mona's pieces.

I don't belong here either.

Especially not when Artemis is around.

What the fuck am I still doing here?

"You want us to go harder? Would you like that, baby?" Artemis asks. My scalp stings, and each knot of frustration ties tighter around my rib cage. Does he really have to ask every time they do something together? Where's the seduction in that?

"Yes," she croaks, as if she can hardly contain herself, as if she *likes* this haphazard attempt at dirty talk.

She turns over her shoulder and looks at me, her eyes glazed and dark, trying to tell me something without actually saying it.

Finally, I see it.

Mona is acting. Pretending she likes this constant negotiation. She's faking it like she admires the ridiculous amount of authority he's giving her.

I can't let him insult her anymore.

I pull out, then get to my feet.

"Where are you going?" Artemis asks. "We were just getting started, right, baby?"

I storm back to the guest room and rip a bundle of rope out of my duffel bag. I need more though. I wander through the other rooms swiftly as I search for inspiration, for anything to bring this night to where it's meant to be.

I skim over a room decorated with jarred rodent organs and bat skeletons. I stop on a piece of paper on the desk. Each line is scrawled in a different style, the strokes switching between black and red ink, and in the corner, there's a bright red doodle of a skeleton holding an umbrella, like Mona was brainstorming her next project or taking notes while she was on the phone with someone. I read the writing.

Desiree Duncan
Desire, the survivor
Desire, the non-victim?
Face her FEARS

Did she misspell the name, or did it switch from Desiree to Desire on purpose?

"Another fake name," I mutter. "Probably one of Artemis's idiotic friends."

With that thought, I exit and hastily plod over to the kitchen. A bowl of fruit lies on the counter. I snatch a red apple from the top.

In the backyard, I throw the bundle of rope at Artemis's feet. He raises a brow.

"Tie her wrists together. Hold her taut," I instruct.

Mona's eyes widen in glee. "Kent, I—"

I swiftly bend down and shove the apple in her mouth. "Meat doesn't speak," I say.

She stiffens, her nipples beading. I rub my dick and admire my stuffed pig, ready for a long, slow roast in the oven.

Artemis fiddles with the rope. My jaw ticks.

"What's taking so long?" I bark. "Don't tell me you've never tied up a woman before."

He lifts a loose knot. It's reminiscent of a soft pretzel. Annoyance and rage flame behind my ribs. He doesn't deserve Mona. He doesn't deserve the air he fucking breathes.

"Will this hold?" he asks.

I yank the rope from his hands and tie her myself, placing her into an actual hogtie. In porn, they like to tie the ankles and wrists behind the woman, but like this—lying on her side with her limbs tied to the front—she's more like a pig, ready to hang from the rotisserie.

I put a slice of wagyu on the curve of her ass and bite it off of her. She jumps, and I keep my mouth suctioned to her skin. The meat disintegrates on my tongue, and I stroke myself, enjoying every last flavor and texture as if it's a full body orgasm.

Once it dissolves, I pull back and marvel at my masterpiece. *My art.* I'm teaching Artemis about our art, like Mona wanted.

A bright light flashes, illuminating us like we've been caught by the authorities. It's probably a camera. I ignore it. All I want is her. Mona is alive, and it should be too cold for us to be naked right now, but with the bonfire and the blood rushing through my veins, I don't feel the cold, nor do I mind that she's not actually my meat. I squeeze the head of my cock, a groan bursting through me, and I imagine I'm a caveman, taking what's mine.

I stuff another handful of wagyu into my mouth, then I bite Mona's nipple so hard, tears pool in her eyes. Another flash of light. I bite Mona again. She's an offering, a delicious feast, and I'm her god. The pressure in my cock consumes me, a geyser bubbling with the need for release.

Artemis puts the camera on the table, then kneels down and removes the apple from Mona's mouth. Then he unties her wrists and ankles, before pulling her body on top of him and letting her take the reins.

Deep inside of my brain, I know there's some part of Mona that likes Artemis too. A weak little man. A person that lets her control everything. And right next to those thoughts, I know I'm jealous of him.

I'm not a caveman. I don't *have* to eat Mona. I can be like Artemis. I can be a good man who indulges. Who lets her do what she wants. She can have the best of both worlds with me.

Fuck that. I *am* the best man for her. I am better than my mother and my mother's boyfriend. I'm better than fucking Artemis. I am better than everyone who has ever doubted me.

And I choose her.

Mona tosses her head back in pleasure, but my dick stays limp. I close my eyes and focus on my own needs until I'm back in that prehistoric fantasy: Mona stretched out before me, her body flickering in the firelight.

My dick hardens again.

The visions push further: blood gushes from her cut labia as I gore her cunt with my dick. Then, when it seems like she can't take another thrust, I bring the fleshy slivers of her pussy lips to my mouth. Her ripe flesh disintegrates over my tongue.

And *that's* when I come.

CHAPTER 12

THE LAST PULSES OF PLEASURE COURSE THROUGH ME LIKE A TIDAL wave, cum splattering my palm and the cement.

I open my eyes and find Mona and Artemis staring at me like I'm the finale of their show.

"Was that good?" Mona asks.

Her mouth is open and wet. She enjoyed watching me come, then.

Artemis grins next to her, and my throat tightens. Is Mona being serious, or are they laughing at me?

I shrug. "It was fine."

Mona limps toward the house; she must be sore from either the fucking or the hogtie. My shoulders expand, knowing the effect I have on her body. She hobbles inside, probably to clean up.

I take that as my signal to leave. I get dressed in the guest room and bring my duffel bag to the backyard to gather the rope. A partially bitten apple lies by the fire, and a chunk of the fruit's flesh hangs by the red skin, the spot where Mona bit when she was my pig roast.

My head buzzes, the sensation fluttering down to my knuckles. I curl my fists. Wasting food is an insult, especially when it's food that's good for your health. Mona shouldn't be eating meat; she should be eating fruit.

I zip up the bag, then I stand by the fire and finish the apple.

Footsteps clop against the stone flooring, too weighty to be Mona.

It's fucking Artemis.

My skin crawls. If I leave now, he'll think I'm weak and bowing down to his authority.

And I'm not fucking weak.

"She's in bed now," Artemis says.

My jaw clenches. Did he tuck her into bed like a princess? Why is he babying her like she's some kind of fragile doll?

Does that irritate me because I'm jealous, or because I don't understand why he'd waste his time like that?

He's not into this like we are, and even if I try to teach him, he never will be. He's a coward, and a coward can't hunt a woman like a predator can.

A cigarette hangs from his mouth, the cherry burning like a single red eye.

"You're not into sexual cannibalism," I say.

"But I can appreciate it *for her,*" he says. "If Mona wants it, then I do it, you know? And it's kind of hot, right?"

I laugh, the frustration flickering inside of me. *Kind of hot. Go fuck yourself, Artemis.*

I narrow my eyes like he's disgusting scum clinging to the bottom of my boots. That loose leather jacket hangs on his frame now. He must think wearing animal skin makes him tough. I bet the leather is fake though, the fucking pussy.

I shudder. How can Mona like a wimp like him? Does she prefer men like him over me?

No. Of course not. She doesn't. She *can't* like men like him. That would give her too much power. Based on Mona's personal ad and her request to fuck her like she's my meat, I know she wants to be objectified. To be powerless. To be controlled.

And the idiot here asked her for her permission every single time.

"Why did you do that?" I ask.

A smirk dances on Artemis's lips. "Do what?"

"Ask for permission every time you did something."

"Did that bother you?"

"Of course it did. You sounded weak."

Both of us are silent, our eyes locked on each other. Two animals circling, waiting for the weaker one to back down. The pressure in the air thickens as a realization dawns on me.

I'm a hypocrite. I've been waiting and giving Mona a chance to decide what she wants. She even cut her leg and bled for me, and I was the coward who ran away. I'm more like Artemis than I want to admit.

With me, it's different though. Artemis is obedient to her every whim, and I'm only asking because I don't want to scare her away. I want her to see everything I have to offer before she reaches her final decision about me.

"You do understand that we're powerless, right?" Artemis says. "Mona knows exactly what she wants. She may enjoy being sexually submissive, but submissives are always in control. It doesn't matter when or how, but she can revoke her consent at any time. All women can."

My mind morphs, molding his words until they vibrate inside of my brain and take on new meaning.

She can revoke your power.

Your right over her body.

Your ownership.

You don't deserve her.

I shake my head and force myself back to the present. "No," I say.

"No?"

"She knows what I want too." I rub my nose. "What *we* want."

"Sure, but we—"

I stop listening. He's just like the sex workers, except he's worse because he's obviously using Mona for sex. He will never actually like sexual or romantic cannibalism like we do; he's only doing it so he can fuck her.

For a second, I tune into his ranting. His voice drags on. "Which is why we should always ask—"

"But *I* can overpower them," I interrupt.

Artemis's eyes widen to the size of summer sausages. Is he shocked?

Or maybe he's afraid.

A thrill creeps through my body and fills me with adrenaline. I *like* scaring him.

"Them?" he asks. "What do you mean? Are you talking about overpowering women in general or specific women?"

"Her," I correct myself. "Mona."

Ever since my mother died, I've stayed back. Kept quiet. Bounced around. I've avoided the government, but when it comes down to it, I've played by the rules. I've done the right thing. And at thirty years old, I've earned the right to control someone like her.

Artemis rattles on in disagreement. I block him out. He leans back, away from me. A stem of smoke rises from his cigarette, and *I* smirk this time. Mona doesn't smoke, and that means her lungs are still good. Her organs are fresh for me.

The memory of my mother lying on the kitchen table fills my mind. Her stomach wound was caked green, and her mouth was empty. A cave. A hole I could reach into to take what I needed.

The tongue is one of my favorite organs.

I wonder what Mona's tongue tastes like.

"All of us are driven by our primal instincts," I interrupt his unheard monologue. I look down at Artemis. "Food is the main drive for survival. And with my size, I'm capable of getting what I want out of prey, including Mona. That's part of why Mona is attracted to someone like me. I'm not afraid of society's expectations." I sneer. "I'll get it fucking done."

"In a way, you're right," Artemis says slowly. "This is role-playing though. It's simply a game to her." He lifts his shoulders. "Mona likes conquering the unexplored, and that's all this is. We're not actually going to eat her."

I laugh, but it hurts, like his words are stabbing me in the lungs.

He's right. Humans aren't supposed to eat other humans.

Maybe Mona does have power. Since the first time we met in

that art gallery's bathroom, warning bells have chimed, telling me to stay away from her. Those bells get quieter every day.

Maybe she's going to eat me alive, chew me up, and spit me back out like everyone else has.

Maybe I'm okay with that, as long as I get to eat her too.

"I should get going," Artemis says. "You should too."

I throw my bag strap over my shoulder. "What about the fire?"

"I'll put it out." He angles toward the front of the house. "I've got to fly out for work soon, and I'm sure you know how she gets. Take care of her while I'm gone, all right, kid?"

His hand slams onto my shoulder, his teeth clamped down in a smile, like a patronizing asshole. He can't be *that* much older than me, and yet he says his words like he has the supreme authority over her. Like he owns Mona.

I grind my teeth and nod anyway, then I head through the house to the front door.

I'll take care of her, all right, just not in the same way he would.

CHAPTER 13

Taking care of Mona is difficult when she makes me wait.

I'm working on our project. Patience, love. Wait for me, she texts.

Like a good soulmate, I do. It's kind of pathetic to let *her* lead the situation, but I'm not stupid enough to risk everything for a text message that gets on my nerves.

Instead, I go to her lectures each week and raise my hand when she asks questions. She never calls on me, probably because she thinks I'm auditing, but she keeps eye contact with me, as if she's lecturing solely for my benefit.

One day, her tongue flickers over her bottom lip, and it sends chills straight to my groin.

"And at the lowest point, when the soul seems to be eaten alive, *that's* when true art is born," she says.

In my mind, I pull pieces of her flesh from her skull and run my fingers over what's left of her tongue nub.

"Is that why you created the exhibition on sex worker trauma?" a student asks. "The recent one at Sway?"

"Sex work is art too," Mona says.

"They were being paid. It's about capitalism," the student next to me chimes in. "Money means capitalism."

"Capitalism *and* sex," another student says. "That's what sex work is. Duh."

Mona's eyes are hooked on mine as she speaks. "Every interaction we have is about the consumption of the other."

And just like that, I know she's teasing me. Begging me to be patient. To wait for her sweetest treat.

The next few weeks are like a loud, empty stomach, until she finally reaches out while I'm at the processing plant. My phone buzzes on the break room table. Her name fills the device's screen, and my stomach lodges in my throat.

I've got a surprise for you, Mona texts. *Can I come over?*

The urge to play hard to get surfaces. If she's going to make me wait, I want to make her wait too. Besides, my excuse isn't a lie.

I'm at work, I reply.

Call out, she sends.

No question. No request. No hesitation. It's a fucking demand. Mona is calling the shots again, and though some buried part of me is pleased that she finally wants to see me, a bigger voice demands to be heard too.

She can revoke your power, Artemis's voice booms in my mind. I've ruminated over his words so many times I can't remember what he actually said anymore. Every warning sounds like him now, his stupid words regurgitating society's expectations. *She's the one in control,* he says. *She rules over you.*

My stomach drops. I have to take back control.

Can't, I text.

She responds with an unhappy face.

I gaze at the big window, giving a view of the processing plant's main floor. I zone in on the furnace in the corner.

A hand slaps my shoulder.

"This bitch's pussy was unreal," Jerry says. "I ate her like a tuna sundae."

"Tuna sundae?" some new guy with a shaved head asks. "The fuck does that even mean?"

"Pussy is tuna, right?" Jerry explains. "But add ice cream cum and shit."

"You ate her cum and her *shit?*"

Jerry rolls his eyes. "Come on, man. You know what I mean. I didn't eat her shit. I just know she tasted good."

My dick pumps with blood, my erection growing to half-mast at his words. It's been too long since I tasted Mona's skin.

"How good?" I ask.

"Like a creamy little fish sandwich," Jerry says. "She came like a waterfall too. I showed that pussy who owns it!"

We both laugh, and he pulls out his phone, then scrolls through his gallery to show me a picture.

"What about you?" the new guy cuts in. "Have you ever shown a pussy who owns it?"

It takes me a second to realize he's talking to me. He's in the same white jumper as we are, but there are no safety glasses hanging out of his pocket or on his collar. The supervisor is a stickler with safety rules. How did this guy get away with that?

"What Kent and I say about chicks is our business," Jerry says. "The fuck kind of question is that anyway?"

"A question of complete domination," the new guy says. He nods at me. "Have you ever beat up a pussy before? Made it raw? Made the woman fight? Take away her agency?"

Agency? The word is off. Stiff. Like cardboard. A buzzword he's been hanging onto.

But why do I get the feeling he's attacking me?

"All girls like it a little rough," Jerry says. "Right, Kent?"

"A little, sure," the new guy says. "What about when they beg you to stop?"

Jerry forces a laugh, like he's trying to break the tension. "This chick wanted me to tie her up once," he says. A few other workers laugh too, and I bob my head. Jerry howls. "She was a real freak!"

"Sometimes I get the urge to tie them to a bed and force them to beg for mercy," the guy says as he examines me. "Don't you?"

He bares his teeth, and I swear, it's like he's insinuating I did something wrong, like I'm the guilty offender here when *he's* the one confessing these violent tendencies.

I straighten myself in my seat. "I don't know what you're talking about."

"I bet you do," he says. "I bet you know exactly what I'm talking about. I bet you like chaining them to the floor."

I snarl, my nostrils flaring. I may have chained a sex worker to the oven, but that doesn't count. I don't like being accused, and I certainly don't like the fact that he's trying to corner me.

I zero in on a woman in the corner of the room, sitting alone at a table with her smartphone camera lens aimed at us. Like she expects me to do something violent. Her next viral video.

She's wearing the standard uniform jumper too. Brown hair. Brown eyes. A completely unremarkable face, and yet there's something familiar about her. She's fixated on the phone's screen, her lips pulled back slightly, greedy for my next action.

She thinks she's smarter than me, doesn't she?

"Are you fucking recording me?" I ask. I stomp past the new guy and corner the recording bitch. "You think you can record me like I'm some kind of freak?"

Her face drops with fear, her skin pale.

"I-I'll delete. I swear," she stammers. "I'm sorry——"

I yank the phone from her hands and smash it into the ground. The screen shatters into a million pieces.

The room falls silent.

The woman gawks at me, her mouth hanging open, her wide eyes full of tears. Full of fear.

My groin surges awake. The agitation dissipates, replaced by adrenaline and desire.

She's afraid of me.

I storm out of the break room and through the main floor. I grab a chicken breast out of a bin, stuff it in my pocket, and find the quickest path to the storage area in the back. The need pulsates inside of me, and until I get rid of it, I won't be able to think straight. I unbutton my jumper uniform, pull out my dick, then wrap the lukewarm meat around my cock. I groan, the slick juices coating me, and pleasure shoots through my spine. It's like fucking a woman's gaping wound.

If the supervisor finds out about me breaking that girl's phone, I'll probably get written up, or maybe even fired, but the memory of the look in her eyes sends me soaring above the clouds, and I can't contemplate the future of my job.

I can only think of her fear.

The woman's fear was tangible, there on my tongue. Like she knew I could kill her. Like she knew, just from a single look, that I wanted to eat her and watch her die.

My chest tightens, my skin sensitive and itchy. It should be Mona I'm thinking about, not some forgettable brown-haired stranger. I scrunch my eyes and change the image until I see Mona cowering underneath me.

I hold the chicken meat to my lips. I lick the smooth flesh, my tongue writhing over the pebbled pink skin, the taste subtle and musky, and I imagine it's Mona's puckered nipple. I suck the blood and milk out of Mona's imaginary tit as the chicken's slimy pink liquid coats my tongue. Mona's tears roll down her face, fear crawling over her body like sweat. She gives me everything she has, whether she wants to or not, and when I'm done with her, I'll eat every last bite until she's only bones.

I come, my jizz squirting over the raw meat sleeve and covering my hands, down my wrists, and dropping onto my boots. It's more cum than I've had masturbating in a long time.

Usually, I try to think about the eternal love of cannibalism. This was different. This was like I was embracing the predatorial side of it: the total and complete control of a woman. And it's all thanks to the palpable fear of that woman who was recording me, because for a split second, she thought I was going to kill her.

She was filming me without my permission. The only person who has ever gotten permission to film me was—

Wait. Did Mona send that woman to record me?

The thought pops into my head, bursting any sort of leftover lust from seeing that woman panic. If Mona *did* send her, then we'll have to talk about it. I don't like being a part of her little art shows without my knowledge or agreement. It makes me feel off-balance.

I clean up, then check the dial on the side of the industrial furnace. The highest temperature is 2,200 degrees Fahrenheit. I picture Mona's decapitated head being tossed out of a basket and into the preheated oven.

I shake those images away. I'd never cut off Mona's head and put her in an oven or a furnace. I'm only thinking of that because the woman in the break room reminded me of the sex worker who freaked out when I chained her to the oven. Mona would appreciate the steak-and-knife play more than that sex worker. She'd probably enjoy it more than all the sex workers combined. We were made for each other.

And whatever surprise Mona has for me is probably even better than steak and knife play anyway.

Back in the break room, I slap Jerry on the shoulder. "Speaking of eating pussy, I'm starving," I say. I motion toward the supervisor's station. "I'll see you later."

"You're calling out to get laid?" Jerry says. "Yeah, bro. What a man. Make that pussy cream!"

I find the supervisor and give him an excuse about having an upset stomach, and though his face twists in disapproval, I don't hear his words.

I text Mona I'm home early. It'll probably take her a while to get to my place, and I want her to be there right after I arrive. I don't want to wait anymore.

But as I drive up and the mobile home comes into focus, I notice another car in the field.

Mona's SUV.

CHAPTER 14

FROM THE DRIVEWAY, IT LOOKS LIKE THE POWER IS OFF INSIDE. I dart through the mobile home anyway, scanning to see if she's there.

It's empty.

In the backyard, she stands over the offal pit in rain boots. Textured tights. A short black skirt. Her gloved hand clutches a grayed pig's heart, crawling with maggots.

"You didn't lock up," she says. She lifts the organ. A larva drops to the dirt. "Can I use this?" My upper lip curls. She giggles. "For my art, love. Just for my art."

I blink hard. "Right."

"Did you know they've used a pig heart for a transplant multiple times?" she murmurs. "This little thing could've helped someone, huh?"

The pig's heart *is* helping someone. She's using it to create art, and before that, I was planning to use it in my ground meat. How can she not see that it is helping?

Her empty, gloved hand, slightly damp from searching through the pit, touches my face. My temple twitches.

"Come on," she says. "I want to show you your surprise."

Mona wanders through my home like she owns the place, and my mind rolls with unease. I scratch the back of my neck. It's almost like she's been walking around my home while I'm gone, just like I've wandered her house when she's working. Except Mona would never stalk me like that.

Would she?

No. Stalking is a threat, and Mona isn't a danger to me.

"How long have you lived here?" she asks.

A question like that leads to even more penetrating questions, and it's like the interrogation in the break room again. A camera poised, ready to catch me in the act.

"Why do you care?" I snap.

"A farm is a beautiful place to live when you're into cannibalism," she says.

I adjust myself, my palm running over the pre-cum staining my pants.

"It's not a farm," I say, but my dick throbs in disagreement. "It's a field and a mobile home."

"Think of the potential though," Mona murmurs. "With this much land, you can have a human farm one day."

I sigh, and she squeezes my hand. It's been my dream to live on a farm and raise a woman for meat. A human farm is out of my grasp right now, though there's no telling where the future will lead, especially if I have Mona by my side.

I clear my throat. I still don't know if she sent the woman to record me. A thrill runs through me. I loved seeing that woman cower.

"Did you send someone to film me at work?" I ask.

Mona laughs, each cackle dripping from her mouth like torn rose petals falling to the ground.

"Why would I record you at work?" she asks.

I snarl. "I don't know."

"I have nothing to do with anything that happens at your work, I can assure you of that." She drags her finger through the dust covering the picture's glass. "Can I take this picture of your mother? I'll bring it back."

The woman in the picture isn't my mother. I don't even know who she is, but I guess we all probably come from the same original homo sapien couple.

I fixate on the wall, on the dustless circle where the picture frame once hung. My mind fills with my actual mother, lying on the dining table. Her legs spread. Parts of her stomach exposed. Chunks of her flesh carved from her skin like deep pockmarks.

"Do you think baby animals eat their mothers for survival too?" I ask in a daze. I don't know why I asked that. It doesn't sound like my own voice.

"Children always eat from their mothers," Mona says. "Think of how much stress the body goes through with breastfeeding."

Mona bends under the table, her belled breasts hanging down. They're small, yet meaty. If her breasts were full of milk too, would they taste moist? Would milk make them juicier? Would they be like soup dumplings, sweetness bursting with each bite?

On top of the teal dining room table, a camera is aimed toward us, a red light blinking on top. She's already recording.

The dining chair scuffs against the floor. Then Mona picks up a sealed black bucket and places it next to the camera. She removes the top. A giddy expression fills her face.

"Come. Look," she says.

Inside, the reflective surface is dark, almost black, with the faintest tint of red. Mona dips her hand into the bucket, and when it comes out, her gloved fingers are soaked in thick, red liquid.

She touches my cheek. I shiver. It's cold. Viscous. Possibly refrigerated before this.

Is it her blood?

No. It's too much. She'd die. She can't—

"Pig's blood," Mona purrs. "I got it from the butcher this morning."

The hairs on my skin rise. It's not her blood. That's good. She needs her blood to survive. Why am I disappointed though? She wants to play in animal blood. Should I be worried about that?

No, you fucking idiot, my brain argues. *This is roleplay. This is good. The blood would be wasted otherwise, and like this, you give it a purpose.*

That explanation feels forced though. I don't know if it's because it's not her blood, or if it's because it was her idea and not mine, but bathing in animal blood—even if the animals were already dead—is too close to real bloodshed, and I'm not sure how much I can handle when it comes to that. The temptations are too strong.

"Mona," I say, my voice straining.

"Don't be a scared little rabbit," she whispers. "Just follow my lead."

I grit my teeth. Did she call me a rabbit? Scared of what? *Her lead?*

She touches me again with bloody hands. Over my shirt. My pants. My neck. She removes my clothes one layer at a time. The jumper. The socks. The boxers. My body yields to her silent instructions, but my dick is hard and ready, and then I'm bare before her. Too naked. Too stunned to do anything. Too fucking vulnerable. She's not forcing me to do this, and yet, she is physically *making* me do it.

And, damn it, I want to do *more.*

She guides me until I'm lying flat on the floor. Finally, she undresses, and I'm glued to her body. Fingerprints dart against her pale skin in red blotches. Her stringy black hair drops over her collarbones like spider legs, and her dark eyes are tunnels driving deep into an empty soul. I'm not supposed to eat her, but I can still fantasize and pretend. If that means I'm reduced to role-playing with Mona, then so be it.

She glances at the top of the table, checking the camera.

It's just her art, I tell myself. *This is pretend. It's roleplaying. A game. Like that idiot, Artemis, said.*

I still want more.

She slides down on my cock and impales herself on me, her needy slit slick with arousal. Her cunt crushes me like a vise.

I want more than pig's blood, but I can control myself.

Control yourself. Control your—

"We could take off my toes," she says, her voice raspy with lust. "One by one."

I involuntarily thrust my hips, pummeling her meat hole. I know the answer; I just want to hear her say it. "Cut off your toes for what?"

"A toe here. A toe there. It's not much, but it's something. A little snack. An *hors d'oeuvres.* A mere, little morsel. Hah!" She grabs my hair like reins, then throws her head back. "What if you called me your 'little morsel'? That would be a cute pet name for me, wouldn't it, love?"

I grit my teeth, desperate to keep myself at that boundary, to protect *her* from the hunger raging inside of me. I can't give in. I can't do it. I'm not a cannibal…right?

Eating her toes wouldn't kill her though. We could do it safely. She may walk with a limp, but she'd be okay. She'd live. Knowing Mona, she would somehow do better without her toes.

It's wrong to eat people though. I know that. I swear I do.

"Mona," I try to say. I try so fucking hard to get the words out, to disagree, to do *anything* to show my resistance when I desperately want this, probably more than she does. "This is—"

"I need my fingers to create, but my toes?" A smirk spreads across her face, and she lifts her hips, then drops her weight on me. A harsh huff expels from my chest. It's like she's forcing me to submit, smothering me with her power. "Being off-balance will be difficult at first. I'm still young though. I can compensate. I can find a new way to walk."

She's reading my mind, and I love it. We are perfect for each other. The meat to my carnivore.

Is this love? Is this what I've always needed?

Control yourself, my brain screams. *Say something! Stop this, you pathetic piece of—*

"This is going too far!" I shout.

She freezes on top of me, her pussy contracting around my cock. My eyes roll to white, and I grind my teeth until the pleasure is numb, and I can't feel my cock anymore.

"We're taking this too far," I gasp. "It's dangerous. I can't eat your—"

"I thought you were better than Artemis," she snaps.

As she exhales, her entire expression changes. She cocks her head to the side and squints at me in disgust. Not because I'm a cannibal fetishist, but because I'm *not*.

My shoulders tense. I stay firm. I can be good. I may fantasize about cannibalism, but I'm not a cannibal. If I eat her, then she'll be gone. I won't have her anymore, and I won't let my stupid, fucked-up cravings get in the way of our potential future together.

"Don't be a scared little boy," she snarls. "This is me: my meat, *my* choice."

She grabs the bucket, then spills the pig's blood all over us, the liquid chilling me to my core. It spreads like oil. She slides back onto my dick again, and my body heats. Her harsh breath dances on my wet skin.

"Don't you dare tell me what I can or can't do," she says.

She pumps my dick with her cunt, forcing me closer to orgasm. The blood dashes across her naked, pale body and paints her red. It's not her blood, but it's so close, and I can't help it; I'm transfixed.

This is wrong. This is so fucking wrong. I can't let this go any further, but I want to—

"Stop thinking," she yells. "Stop thinking and fuck me."

My mind erases. I grab her hips, my nails digging into her flesh. Mona is everything I want, and this is what I've always dreamed of: a woman willing to give me things I can savor, a woman who knows what she wants too, a woman who will let me conquer her.

If I do this—if I go through with this relationship—I know what will happen. I won't be able to help myself. Pig's blood isn't enough, but if I try harder, if I do this right, I *can* control myself. I can keep Mona alive. I can show her I'm the cannibal she's always dreamed of, and neither of us has to give up who we are to find a mate. By some act of magic, we found each other. Cannibal and flesh. The conqueror and the conquered. The all-consuming god and the precious little morsel of meat.

But as my orgasm nears, a thought worms its way into my brain. I try to shove it out. I try to think of cavemen and decapitated women's heads, but my dick goes soft inside of her, and the thought grows until I can't think of anything else anymore.

Mona is the one who forced me to fuck her right now.

She's the one conquering me.

CHAPTER 15

ANOTHER WEEK PASSES. MONA TEXTS ME EVERY DAY. I DO MY BEST to ignore my phone. The irritation crests over my skin in goosebumps, the pressure building like a volcano each time my phone vibrates. Every text eats away at me like vultures consuming a flattened dog.

How am I supposed to ignore a woman like *her?*

Finally, I check the messages. *Come over,* the most recent text reads. *I need you to fuck me and eat me.*

I snarl at those half-assed words. "Eat me" is tacked on to the end, like she wants sex, but she knows I'll only be enticed if I can roleplay with cannibalism too.

Maybe that's true. Maybe I don't want to play by her rules anymore.

Busy, I text back.

You're always busy, she responds.

I shake my head, ready to toss my phone across the room, but the device vibrates again.

Come eat my blood, she sends. *My period is heavy today.*

My lips part. Tension curls around my groin, tingling over my veiny shaft and numbing me all the way to the inner tissue.

Period blood.

A period is monthly. If I eat her menstrual blood, I'm not causing any harm. I've done it before.

This time will be better though. Wet. Hot. Viscous. And straight from the source.

And like a pathetic little boy, I give in.

About an hour later, she opens the front door. A short pencil skirt clings to her hips, and her small breasts are pushed up in a lacy bra.

She dressed to seduce me.

I hate lingerie. It reminds me of the obnoxious sex workers, and the tricks they performed to finish our sad dates as quickly as possible. But, fuck me, knowing that Mona is *bleeding* under that skimpy fabric makes my stomach growl.

"I knew you'd come," she says with a smirk.

I grit my teeth, but she grabs my hand, and I follow her.

In the kitchen, Mona hoists herself up on the dark countertop. The skirt bunches around her hips like crumpled plastic wrapping. Her knees part, and the white tampon string lies on the marble surface. A faint reflection of the plug's tether echoes in the polished stone.

Her plump labia are stuck together like slices of deli meat in a sandwich, and the menstrual blood smeared on her inner thighs reminds me of tomato sauce decorating the bottom of a pasta bowl. My cock presses into my zipper.

"Pull the tampon out," she says.

For once, I don't hesitate at being told what to do. I tug at the string until the drenched cotton plops on the countertop. I move it to the side and take a mental note to save the tampon for later, all while I keep ogling her meat hole.

Her pussy muscles visibly tighten: a gloop of gummy liquid squishes out of her hole.

A blood clot.

My groin and face flush with heat. I rub my lips together. The blood clot is the size of a small sugar-coated candy. I bet it tastes like nectar too.

"Is that normal?" I ask. My tone is stunned, too captivated by her bloody cunt to form any emotion.

"Does it matter?" she says. She bares her sharp white teeth. "Think of it, love. By eating this part of me, you're not hurting anyone. Surely, you're capable of doing something as small as this."

A ball of shame tumbles around my stomach like sharp rocks. I can't decide if I'm turned on or if I'm pissed that she's questioning my abilities again.

She pinches the blood clot with her fingers, and it splits in half like a lump of gravy. Her fingers paint my lips, the rich irony scent of her blood wafting in my nostrils.

My head is on fire.

"It's okay," she says in a raspy voice. "Why throw this blood in the trash when you can eat this part of me?"

I blink rapidly and try my hardest to keep myself together. She's right. I can't waste something as precious as this.

I suddenly realize our relationship has been going on for way more than a month now. Why has she kept other periods from me?

I should've been tracking her cycle or digging in her trash this whole time. It's okay though. If I missed one or two periods, then fine. I've been good. I've been giving her space so that I can earn her trust, and that's how it's supposed to be. Day by day, Mona will be more comfortable with me, and eventually, she'll trust me with her whole body.

I need to ask though. "Is your cycle regular?"

She shakes her head. "That's why I had to wait until now."

For some reason, her word choices seem suspicious. Maybe I'm being paranoid though. I don't know how or why she would lie about a period.

I need to forget about those questions. I don't need those answers; I just need to taste her. The real her. I need more of her blood.

"Go on," she says. "Give it a taste."

I fall to my knees like a defeated man praying to his goddess, and I lap at her pussy lips. Her trimmed pubic hairs scrape along my tongue and send shivers down my spine. Then I suckle at the hole, dragging the edges of her pussy into my mouth, and a moan murmurs through her. Her musky scent, sour and acidic and metallic with blood, fills my nostrils. A drop of her blood swims into my mouth, and she tastes decadent—like a bite of fatty steak, covered in a red wine glaze—and that desire flames in my chest. My tongue swirls around her thick clit, and I resist the urge to bite it until it bleeds too. Her hips gyrate closer to the edge of the counter.

"That feels good," she says.

I unzip my pants and pull out my dick. My tongue penetrates her bloody gash. Her inner thighs cling to my head and stamp my cheeks with damp blood. I pump my dick and suck in as much of her life juice as I can and ruminate over the flavors.

Period blood is different from the fresh blood I got from her thigh. It's stale, like freezer-burned ice cream, but the undertones are sweet and metallic. It's still Mona, the literal shedding of her uterus, the shell of her motherhood. It's like I'm eating a baby that never was, and I hold on to that knowledge like it's the holy grail of cannibalism. Our perfectly crafted loophole.

This skirts the rules, because even normal people have period sex. This means I'm not a cannibal.

My eyes whirl to the back of my head as my tongue laps at her bloody seam. "I could eat you on toast," I murmur.

"Then do it."

My tongue stops. Is she serious?

Mona tilts her head toward a plastic bag of sandwich bread on the opposite counter.

"The toaster is over there," she says as she motions to the other side of the kitchen.

Each heartbeat in my ears is like a fucking drum, warning me that she's controlling me once again.

I keep going. I don't want to stop. Not when I can literally eat her like she's pâté. I take a slice of bread from the bag, then pop it into the toaster.

"Butter knives?" I ask.

She points at a drawer. "In there."

I pull the drawer out fully, then stare down at the contents. A serrated knife, a chef's knife, and a cleaver are thrust inside of a clear plastic block, and two narrow organizers contain butter knives and steak knives. A steak knife isn't the blade I need. All I need is a butter knife.

I grip the handle of a steak knife anyway.

A butter knife may not work for this, I tell myself. *Knowing Mona's current diet, the steak knives are likely used more, and therefore cleaner than the butter knives. And I can be gentle. I can treat her like a jar of jam. I've never broken a jar of food before.*

The toaster pops. I place the slice on the countertop next to her, then kneel between her legs. She moves her hips, positioning herself so that I can spoon inside of her. I carefully dip the knife into her cunt. She beams down at me, so pleased with herself, so pleased with *me*. She knows I'm using a knife on her.

But she must not realize it's a steak knife; otherwise, she wouldn't be so smug.

I angle the utensil to the side like I'm scooping peanut butter. She giggles.

"Is that okay?" I ask.

"It reminds me of a speculum at the gynecologist's office," she says. "This is way better though."

When I pull out the knife, a large clump of bloody lining clings to the edge of the blade, shining like a dark wine. I slather it on the toast.

I chomp into the treat. The first bite hits my lips and tongue; savory bread and her earthy flavors swim over my taste buds. My body throbs with pleasure.

"Fuck, Mona," I say. "You taste so fucking good."

She rubs the top of my head, her fingers combing my short hair. "Then be a good boy and eat me, love."

My jaw flexes. A good boy. Like I'm her toy. Her slave. Her little bitch.

No. I can't be mad. Not when she's letting me eat her period blood on toast. *I want this.* I want Mona. I even want the parts of her that fight me for control. I want everything she has to offer, and if that means I have to relinquish control for the chance to eat her period blood, then I'll be on my knees until her uterus is sucked dry.

I take another bite of the toast. This time though, the wheat dominates my palette. There's something incomplete about this, isn't there? I want Mona, but this isn't it. Menstrual blood is always going to come out of her. *I* have nothing to do with it.

I want to eat her. All of her.

But I also want her pain.

Before I can question myself, I stick the knife back into her pussy. She coos in approval, then I push the knife deeper, and she grimaces.

"Wait," she pants. "Hold on. What are you—"

The knife pierces the crust of her cervix, like cutting into a firm potato, and she screams, the cry raking through her and vibrating into me. I have no idea how deep I actually went, but liquid oozes out of her pussy, and I salivate.

It's blood. Red and fresh and vibrant against her pale thighs.

My dick is like a fucking baton right now, ready to knock someone unconscious, and the fucked-up part is that I *want* to hurt Mona like that. I want to choke her. I want to watch the will to live drain from her eyes.

I lick my lips, my mouth filling with spit. I want to taste her blood. Fresh blood. Straight from the tap.

She didn't cut herself this time. She didn't bleed on her monthly cycle. No. I cut her this time. Me, the predator.

My appetite grows. As my lips near her pussy, I clench my jaw shut.

I just hurt Mona. I'm not supposed to hurt her.

This is supposed to be safe. Pretend. What the fuck was I thinking?

"It's okay," Mona says in between hyperventilating breaths. "It's okay. Don't panic. It's only a little cut—"

She's right. It's only a little blood, but it's not enough. I still want to hurt her.

And I know I can't.

I drop the knife and race through the house. The front door swings open, and I'm in the van in less than a minute. Blood has dried on my cheek, and my hands are red. I must seem insane right now, but I have to stop this before it goes too far.

Mona chases after me. Her words are loud, but I can't hear a damn thing. I avoid looking at her directly. In my periphery, I see her shadow limping from the pain.

I can't think about what that means. I can't think about how much I *like* that she can't walk without being in pain.

I did that to her.

And I fucking love it.

She hobbles down the driveway, then bangs her fists on the driver's window. I suddenly remember the full tampon on the counter, but I can't go back now. I put the car in reverse, and she jumps back, avoiding the wheels.

I need to get out of here.

I drive faster than usual and swerve through a red light. Car horns blare after me. I can't stop though. I have to get away from her. I've eaten Mona's tampons on crackers before, and I just ate Mona's period blood on toast. The menstrual blood isn't what unnerves me.

It's the fact that I liked stabbing her pussy.

CHAPTER 16

FOUR BLACK GARBAGE BINS ENTER MY VISION. MY HEART POUNDS. The alley behind the butcher shop is just wide enough for a car, which means there's less traffic, and it makes my hunt for animal discards easy. Mona isn't meat, not yet anyway, but I didn't stab these animal discards, and they won't talk back or try to enforce their will on me. I'm the one who conquers *them*.

Then I see metal locks dangling from each bin, shiny and new, taunting me with their barricade.

"Fuck!" I shout.

I slam my fists into the top of one of the bins. It knocks over and smashes into my shin. I howl and heave until I'm back in a calmer state. It's been like this—clumsiness and agitation—ever since Mona spilled the pig's blood and let me eat her period. Everything is going to shit.

I can't let her control me.

"This is fucking bullshit," I groan as I hoist the garbage bin up. Is the butcher locking me out? I grit my teeth. Why would he lock me out?

There's a chance he's locking out wild animals. Bears. Coyotes. Raccoons. Sacramento is full of densely populated neighborhoods, but it's not unheard of to spot the occasional predator on the outskirts. And who knows what would happen if the zoo animals escaped?

I run a hand through my hair. This isn't about me. It can't be. Even if my favorite butcher shop blocks my access to their leftovers; even if my girlfriend—fuck buddy, professor, artistic meat hole, whatever the fuck she is to me—is the one leading our relationship; even if it seems hopeless, I can regain control.

The butcher can't control me anymore than Mona can. Make a copy of the butcher's key, and I'll be back in the premium discards. And when it comes to Mona—

Cold seeps into my bones, and every ounce of my control leaks onto the ground.

I don't know what to do about Mona.

But the butcher? I can figure him out.

I open the front door of the butcher shop. A small chime rings through the air. An old bitch takes her time at the counter. While I wait, I stare at the cold display cases, and my mind wanders: I imagine taking Mona to the grocery store. First, we'd find our favorite cashier, perhaps someone sweet and tender, someone who reminds us of an innocent lamb, and we'd tell the cashier that we just got back from our honeymoon.

The next year, Mona would come in without a leg. *It was the illness,* she'd say solemnly, explaining her missing limb, and once we were in the parking lot, Mona would wink at me.

The year after that, we'd return again, and this time, Mona would have a missing arm. *It was a terrible accident,* I'd say, and perhaps it would be. Maybe I'd try to argue with Mona about only taking her forearm, but she, the stubborn little morsel she is, would strongly insist on me taking her whole arm, and I'd have no choice but to fulfill my lover's desires.

And then I'd push her wheelchair. She'd only have an arm left, and yet, my precious little morsel would still have a smile on her face. The cashier would gawk at us, knowing there was something insidious behind our stories, our *lies,* and we would keep our secret close: there's no better connection than a love like ours, where you literally give yourself to the other, and the other consumes, never letting a single flake go to waste.

After that, I'd come to the grocery store without Mona. I'd tell the cashier my wife was in bed. I wouldn't mention the fact that she had to be spoon fed now, or that none of the food on the conveyor belt was for us but for me to cook *Mona with*. Naturally, I would ask the cashier to come visit my wife. *She misses you,* I'd say. *Please. Won't you come to our house and see her?* And because the cashier was sweet inside and out, she'd come to our home. By then, Mona's torso would be trussed like a turkey, seasoned with rosemary and garlic, a wreath of rainbow carrots surrounding her like a nest. Of course, the cashier would notice those were the ingredients I had recently purchased from the grocery store, and she'd be frightened. With the locks in place, the cashier would have nowhere to go. Nowhere to run. And then I'd—

The door chime jingles. I grimace and adjust my erection, a headache forming between my temples. This is why my relationship with Mona is a problem. Whether it starts with a toe or something even smaller than that, as the years pass and slices are taken from her body, I would have no choice *but* to continue eating her. Even if I supplemented with animals or other women, Mona would eventually become an inanimate object: a reliant torso, bed bound, and still serving me.

Whispers flutter past me. I turn over my shoulder and see the woman who was recording me in the break room, next to the same man with the shaved head who was goading me into talking about raping women.

The hairs on the back of my neck rise. Are they following me?

No. That would be crazy. This is a local butcher, the closest one to the processing plant in fact, and if they work there too, then they'd come here before or after work, like I do. This shop has the best organic meat in the city. It makes sense.

The woman stands on her toes and keeps her eyes on me as she whispers to the man. He bares his teeth at me.

I ball my fists. "The fuck are you looking at?"

The woman skitters closer to him like a bug hiding under the cracks of a tile. I sneer. The bitch would be better off as barbecue than a plant worker.

The butcher clears his throat. I blink rapidly. The old bitch is gone. I walk up to the counter, and the butcher glares at me. The fuck is his problem?

"I'd like a filet mignon," I say. I briefly scan the chalkboard for today's inventory. "And some pig's feet. Two pounds if you've got 'em."

"I think you've got enough to take home with you," the butcher snarls. "Your business is not welcome here anymore. Leave, or I'll call the police."

A painful pulse radiates between my temples. He must have seen me stealing the offal and rotten meat. So it was me then; I'm the reason he's got the garbage bins locked up. He must've added security cameras, and I must have completely missed them.

"So what?" I say. "It was in the garbage."

"I can't have perverts jerking off behind my store," he growls. "Now get the fuck out of here."

My vision reddens. A pervert? An outcast. A loser who will never be anything.

A cannibal monster.

"Fuck you, you wasteful piece of shit!" I shout as I storm out of the shop.

I sit in the van for ten minutes before I truly calm down. I remind myself that there are more butcher shops. Grocery stores have offal and meat scraps sometimes. Even if the stores have other waste clogging their bins, and it's harder to find the actual meat product, I can figure out another way to fill my pit. I can find a new plan.

I can deal with this.

I reverse out of my parking spot and head back to the mobile home. I switch on the radio, and the smog from the city winds through the streets like a fine mist. I take a deep breath in and force myself to relax.

Once my heart rate is even, I pretend like there's a neat package of white paper on the passenger seat, keeping me company. A slice of Mona wrapped like a present for me.

Everything is fine.

I glance over at the passenger seat. Black hair, pale skin, sunken eyes. Not a slice of Mona anymore, but the full ghost of her.

We don't have to pretend anymore, the imaginary Mona says. *I don't want to play games. I want you to eat me.*

I put my hand on her thigh, stroking her pliant skin and inching closer to her pussy.

"You want more?" I ask. "I don't want to hurt you."

Take me to the farm, she says. *Let me go free. We can run wild. We can do anything, Kent. Anything! You can eat me. I want you to eat me.*

"I'll take little nibbles off of you." My fingers worm closer to her meat pocket. "We could fuck like rabbits while I dine on your breasts."

How about a wolf and a rabbit? she says.

There's nothing in the passenger seat. Still, my imagination fills the emptiness: Mona smirks at me. Like she knows more than I do. Like she's better than me. This is just a fucked-up daydream, and somehow, she's still manipulating me.

A figure in a leather jacket leans over the center console.

Hate to break it to you, Artemis says, *but she's the wolf.*

The van bumps over an object. I swerve off of the two-lane highway and ram right into the fence. The metal crunches against my van, and I rail my fists into the steering wheel.

"Motherfucker!" I shout.

I stomp around the van. A few scratches scrape the front of the car; other than that, it's fine. The fence is bad—dented and ripped open. When the property owner finds it, he's going to be pissed.

No one pays attention to these lands though. I'm within walking distance of the mobile home, and the only people that come this way are the dump workers, and they stay in the human waste.

I suck in the dump's odor. The fecal stench of decay, rot, and humanity is strong here. I sigh deeply. The van looks like shit now, but there's no damage to the engine. After everything that's happened today, I have to take that as a win.

My phone buzzes. *Mona Milk* fills the bright screen, the *Accept Call* button taunting me.

I hit *Ignore*. I don't need to be manipulated right now.

I head around the van to the driver's seat, but in the grass, I see a flattened piece of fur. Two fluffy white ears poke up from the ground. I pick it up.

A dead rabbit.

A tendril of primal instinct creeps from my stomach and crawls around my groin. My chest inflates.

Maybe today isn't completely useless.

With the rabbit dangling by the ears from one hand, I drive the van the short distance over to the mobile home. Then I walk around the house, clutching those furry ears.

I jump down into the offal pit. The animal corpses deflate under my feet, and the flies rally against me.

The rabbit is still warm, and the fur reminds me of velvet. Red liquid drips down my hands. I think of Mona in the restaurant, the steak clutched in her palms, blood dripping down her wrists.

I pull out my pocketknife and rip a hole into the back of the rabbit, the only part that's still plump. I've fucked meat before, but I've never fucked it when it's fresh like this. My dick aches in my pants, and I wait for those contradicting thoughts, the ones that tell me that this is wrong.

My brain is silent.

I lick the blood from my knuckles. It's natural. Potent. Earthy. *Like Mona.*

My phone buzzes in my pocket, and I know it's her. I let the device vibrate against my thigh. My heavy balls clench for more friction, for the dead warmth, for the proof that this *thing* can't tell me what to do, because now, I own it.

I should own Mona by now too.

I bite into the flesh, and the fur wedges between my teeth. The skin is tough— too rigid for my teeth to pierce—but I move down the fur like it's an ice cream cone, and I take another bite. I pretend it's *her.* Two perfectly rounded crescents of meat, her breasts. Fuck it all—is there anything I wouldn't do to taste her breasts right now? To consume her like she consumes me?

Has Mona always been the wolf?

The juices run down my chin, skimming over my stubble. I unzip and pull down my pants. I stab my dick into the wound and rub the warm sleeve over my shaft. It's textured and bumpy like pussy walls, and it's sinewy too. It's got some give, enough to get me *there*. Enough to keep me satisfied for now.

I imagine Mona's corpse lying on the kitchen table. Her legs spread, her arms removed. Her blank eyes staring back at me as I fuck her pretty little hole.

When she's only a torso, will her pussy still be wet for me?

Fuck me after you kill me, she says. *Use me. Kill me. Eat me. Oh, Kent, eat me—*

I grip the rabbit tighter around my cock. In my mind, I pretend it's her scared little cunt crushing my shaft.

"You dirty, filthy bitch," I murmur.

And this time, it's different. I *am* the fucking wolf, ready to tear her corpse apart. Her art can be the medium she conquers, but with cannibalism—with *us*—she won't conquer or consume me.

I will consume her.

The jizz squirts into the rabbit's warmth, the pleasure drifting from my body.

Blood stains my pants and my shoes, and fur sticks to the damp splotches. Anger trembles through me. I didn't even kill the rabbit on purpose; I killed it by accident like a wimpy little bitch.

Even if she wants me to—even if *I* want to—I can't kill Mona. I'll go to jail, and in prison, if you eat another person, you will end up in solitary. I can't eat my own flesh. Male meat is too tough.

Eventually, you'll end up in jail, Mona's imaginary voice taunts me. *Or maybe you won't.* Her image reaches forward and puts her blood-soaked hand on mine. *But there's so much meat to hunt and eat before you get caught, right, love?*

I drop the rabbit's remains into the offal pit. Whatever this is with Mona, it's too much. She's gotten into my head and shown me that these games we're playing aren't enough.

I don't give a fuck if she's the wolf or the rabbit; I'm not going to prison for my sexual interests, and I'm definitely not going to prison for *her*.

There's more to us than our primal instincts. Animals don't think, but *we* are humans. We have brains that help us make complex decisions, and I know right from wrong. I can't control Mona, but I *can* do the right thing. If we keep doing this, I'll lose my mind and unintentionally hurt her, like the rabbit on the road.

And I refuse to accidentally kill her.

Chapter 17

A CAR HUMS, THE TIRES RUMBLING OVER THE DIRT. I CLIMB OUT OF the offal pit and check the driveway.

Mona's SUV.

My stomach sinks. I have to end this *now*, or something terrible will happen, and I refuse to let it happen to me.

Mona slinks out of the vehicle, then crosses her arms over her chest. "You haven't answered my texts or calls," she says.

I go around her to the front door. "Busy."

"Busy doing *what?*"

I spin around and stare at her. There's more than a foot of height difference between us, and yet her voice—her stupidly confident voice—echoes like she's a million times bigger than me. A monstrous giant.

I know better though. I know who I am and what she is. Even if she's taunting me, I have the power to do the right thing. I can end this.

"What happened to your pants?" she asks, her tone full of accusation. "Your hands?"

Rabbit fur and blood are caked on my palms, and my pants are drenched in red. This is going to start another argument, isn't it? Son of a fucking bitch.

I head to the bathroom; she trails after me. "Nothing," I say.

"Bullshit. That's blood!" she snarks. "You hurt someone else, didn't you?"

I snap around. "Are you jealous?" My laughter booms through the mobile home so loudly that Mona, the usually defiant little cunt, actually shrinks back. "You're jealous of a blood stain when you made me watch Artemis bite your neck like you were a corn on the cob?" She rolls her eyes, and I face the faucet and wash my hands. "Who the fuck knows what else you do in your free time."

She laughs.

Hollow tension rolls over my arms and neck. What's so fucking funny?

"You're right," she says. "There's nothing about love or respect between us, is there? You signed a contract; nothing more." She places a hand on her hip, then addresses me through the bathroom mirror. "Though you should keep in mind that our contract requires you to answer my phone calls and texts for the duration of your participation. We have an agreement, Kent. You can't just walk away from this."

A destructive fire simmers inside of me as I stare at her reflection in the mirror. Dust flecks the glass, the edges stained with brown rust.

Ever since I first responded to Mona's personal ad, she's been telling me what to do.

I'm sick of it.

"Fuck the contract," I say.

"I'll call a lawyer."

"Fine," I say. "Sue me because I won't eat you. I'm doing this for you." My voice is biting with frustration. "Cutting you off—"

She spreads her legs, widening her stance, and the image of blood dripping down her thigh fills my brain. The menstrual lining. The fresh blood. My cock is hard, and my drive to end our relationship leaves my body.

No. I *can* do the right thing.

I turn away from her. "This is for your own good!" I shout.

She puts a hand on my back. "I trust you. Isn't that enough?"

My head spins. She trusts me?

No. We're going too fast. Ending this is the right thing to do. It's not just about protecting myself from prison; I'm also protecting her. And if I want a future with her, then we have to take a break right now until I can better control my cravings.

I race into the master bedroom. "I stabbed your cervix——"

"The doctor said it was barely a scratch. I didn't even need stitches. Trust me, you didn't do anything. I've done worse with a dildo."

My muscles tense. A sex toy can do more damage than I can? Why does that bother me?

"Come on, Kent," she whines.

Fury undulates inside of me, the master of this fucking puppet show. I hate that I didn't actually damage her pussy, but *I can choose to keep her safe now.* I grab her head, her black hairs twisting through my fingers. Even as pain wriggles in my skull, I keep my expression blank. I don't want her to misunderstand anything I'm saying right now.

"You don't get it, do you? I want to eat you," I say slowly as I stare into her deep, black pupils. "I want to eat women. I can't do that to you or you *will* die. What part of that don't you understand?"

"Oh, fuck off," she says as she tears herself out of my hands. "You can't tell me what to do. I can make decisions for myself, and I trust you to keep me safe."

She bites her tongue, and tears fill her eyes, but there's an emptiness to her expression, like she's forcing herself to feel bad, to feel something, *anything at all,* for me. For us.

"Come on, love," she says, her words quivering. "We can do this. What we have is rare. I need you. I need you for my——"

The water in her eyes is like the bathwater at the art gallery. It's physically real; at the same time, it's a performance.

I don't want to hurt her. I swear I don't. Not emotionally nor physically.

But you do want to hurt her, my brain says. *You do. You want to watch what happens when she sees you rip her nipple from her breast and swallow it like an oyster.*

"I'm not a cannibal," I whisper. I'm not sure if I'm saying it to her or to myself, and I guess that's the point. Our whole situation is fucked. "You can find another muse. But this, Mona? Whatever this is"—I point between us—"this has got to stop. Someone's going to get hurt, and I'd be devastated if you—"

"What if I *want* to get hurt?" she says.

My dick palpitates, but my mind stays on track. "I don't have to do this," I say. I repeat it over and over again while she follows me to the kitchen. "I don't have to do this. I don't. I don't have to do this. Control yourself, Kent. Control yourself. You don't have to do this—"

My morals fight for the upper hand, but my brain screams until it's all I can hear: *Why stop now? Why stop here? Why can't you give her what she wants?*

What if it's her choice?

"You want to eat me, don't you?" Mona asks.

I freeze, my spine frosting with ice. I face her, meeting her dead on. There's pain in her black eyes, and I should feel sympathy for that, but my gaze wanders down. Past her pink lips. Down to her breasts. Her juicy breasts. There's so much potential in those small sacks of fat. And down further, there's her soft belly. She's got so much to give, but I know myself.

I want to eat her, but I refuse to do this to her.

"Mona," I plead. "Try to understand that I've held back with you, and you've been escalating at a pace I'm not ready for." I rub my temple and try to change my tone as if this is what I want. "This isn't right. Humans don't eat humans. We've got brains to tell us right from wrong. We're smarter than this. We know the consequences."

"Are you leaving me?"

A single tear runs down her cheek. My hand twitches by my side, desperate to wipe it from her face. To taste it. To savor the salty sweetness of her sorrow.

I don't. It's a piece of her rolling away, wasted into nothing, because I'm doing what's right.

"If anyone found out what we're doing," I start to say, "I'd probably be fired, and you'd be—"

AUDREY RUSH

"Nothing would happen to me," she snarls. "I'm an artist known for controversy."

"You're right. You're unique. But to the processing plant? Guys like me are easy to find," I say. "All you need is someone strong and willing to pretend to be a cannibal. You're gorgeous and smart. You can have *anyone*. Guys like Artemis who will do whatever you want. You just have to show them how to do it the right way."

He won't eat her toes though, my brain says. *He's too much of a pussy for that.*

Jealousy wages battle inside of me, while I force myself to act like I don't care. I check the fridge and pull out a plastic container. The green and pink ground meat assaults my nose, the stench rotten. It's vile, like hot roadkill mixed with sulfurous eggs, but you get used to it, and it's better than the alternative. You can't survive on nothing; you *can* survive on rotten meat.

And preparations like this—scavenging for discarded meats— aren't just about survival. Animal meat is the closest to what I truly want sexually, and if I have the meat with me, I can make the urge go away. At least for a while.

Going back to animal meat sleeves seems so depressing after Mona though.

"I don't want them," Mona cries. "Those men are fake. They're pretend. I want—"

"You don't want me," I say. "You want my hunger."

Mona's jaw drops. Our harsh breaths fill the kitchen. The fridge's generator hums, and her fingertips nervously scratch the countertop. She knows I'm right. It's not about *me;* it's about my obsession with eating women. It's about her art.

"I don't want to hurt you," I say again.

"This is who you are," she says. "Who *we* are. Humans are primal creatures, Kent. We may have brains that give us access to a deeper understanding of the world, but at our core, we're animals. That's all we are."

I used to tell myself that every day. If I eat someone I love, it's okay, because we're just animals, and we need to survive. No one can blame me for that.

116

It's wrong though. Mona is wrong. She's fucking *wrong*. We're not animals. We know better. We have thoughts. We make decisions. We can control ourselves beyond what a rabbit or a wolf is capable of.

My dick swells, and I lean on the cupboards in front of me to hide my growing erection. "Damn it, Mona," I whisper.

Her fingers graze my back. "This is what we—"

"No!" I grab her arms and lift her in the air. Her face flashes with a hint of fear, but then it's gone, and that proves it all: she's not scared of me, and she *should* be. My voice is rough with anger: "No, we're not animals. We're humans. We have power. Do you understand?"

I dig my nails into her arms, and she floods with tears again. This time, it's different though. This time, there's weight to those drops of salty water. They're real.

My cock rises, power filling my insides. I want those real tears so fucking bad.

But I can do the right thing.

"This is not who we are," I continue. "It's who *you* are. And this—" I shove her toward the door, and she falls to the ground. "This is for your own good."

She picks herself up, then waits for a few seconds. I stare at the ground meat on the counter. I don't want to fuck it anymore, but I'll force myself to fuck it if I have to. Anything to stop me from eating her.

She's the only person who has ever taken a real interest in me, and I need to protect her.

"Get the fuck out!" I scream.

She races to the door, abandoning me.

A familiar pain rises between my ribs and wraps its fingers around my heart. This isn't like before though. This is for Mona's own good. I can't tell her to stop her art project, but I can stop my participation in it.

Usually, I don't care about right or wrong. I didn't think about morals when it came to my mother. I didn't care if I was breaking the rules by destroying that bitch's phone at the processing plant.

And I sure as fuck didn't care if the butcher caught me between the garbage bins.

For once, I can do the right thing.

I have to do it for her.

CHAPTER 18

IT TAKES A LONG TIME TO COME DOWN FROM SOMETHING LIKE that.

I stare at the open front door of the mobile home for hours. I tell myself that Mona is gone for good.

Deep down, I hope that's not true.

Eventually, I go to the processing plant. I don't have a shift, and the supervisor says he can't pay me overtime. I dress in my jumper anyway and hang out in the break room. It's better than waiting for her at home when she'll never show up. She can't, because if she does, there's a chance I won't be able to stop myself from killing and eating her.

And I'm not a cannibal.

"Fuck," I mutter.

Jerry looks up from his phone. "What's up?"

"I can't stand women."

A grin spreads across his face. "That artistic slut again?"

I nod, and he slaps me on the shoulder.

"I know a chick. Real artsy, since that's your thing." He nudges me. "She's always listening to her earbuds. Wears these sexy fishnet stockings. I swear, one night with her, and you'll forget about your ex."

My ex? Is that what Mona is to me now?

Jerry flips through his phone and shows me a picture. The artsy chick is attractive: brown hair and nice, round tits. Tits like that would taste fantastic, and yet I know this stranger would ultimately taste worse, because *she isn't Mona.*

I shake my head. "Thanks, man. I'm taking a break from pussy." I shove my head in my hands. "The bitches are crazy around here."

The break room cackles into whoops and laughter. I get up and head to the large window facing the work floor. To one side, an industrial furnace stretches up and puffs smoke through the vents. The furnace's opening is big enough for the unnecessary shit we don't keep here, like the scraps we can't sell to the rendering plants that the higher ups like to call "toxic waste."

A random thought crosses my mind: Artemis could fit in the furnace.

I grimace. I don't even know why I'm thinking of him. I don't like wasting food, but the idea of eating him makes me sick. The pompous bastard probably tastes stringy and metallic like lean turkey meat. Flavorless, like his personality.

Not that I would kill him. I'm not a killer. And, for fuck's sake, killing Artemis won't bring Mona back. Though I would probably kill him if it meant keeping Mona safe.

If it meant keeping *me* safe.

I get bored of the mindless break room chatter and head back home. A mist hangs over the empty fields, and with the sun rising over the landfill's huge pile of waste, it's almost pretty. Hopeful. The kind of thing an artist paints to represent heaven. That idea soothes me as much as it hurts. Would Mona paint something like that?

No. It would be too simplistic for her.

My throat drops to my stomach. I keep driving. I didn't *want* to end things with Mona, but I did what was right for her. I can live with that.

As I drive closer to the mobile home, the fog clears, and an SUV comes into view.

Mona's car is parked in the driveway.

My mind stops. A thudding pulse clangs in my chest, my mind racing a marathon.

She's not in the front seat of the car. The SUV is empty.

I check the offal pit, where she was last time she came by unannounced. There's an empty bucket next to the hole, similar to the one she used for the pig's blood. It may even be the same one. I don't remember exactly.

The flies rise from the bloated rabbit corpse. There's no Mona.

Is she inside? Did I forget to lock up?

I push on the front door of the mobile home, and it creaks open. A trail of red drips across the laminate then becomes a red puddle.

Blood spreads in every direction.

In the kitchen, red stains every surface, clinging like it's half-coagulated, slick, and sticky. Red utensils. Red photographs. Red wood paneling. On each side of the dining area, two cameras, set up on tripods, are dotted with bloody fingerprints. She must have set them up when she was already halfway through her blood bath.

And in the middle of the floor, Mona sits cross-legged in a loose nightgown, so drenched in red that I can't tell what color the fabric is.

Her hands tremble. She holds a small knife in one hand; the other hand is lifted into the air, blood oozing from the tips of her fingers.

Did she cut herself? Is all of this her blood?

"What the fuck?" I whisper.

Mona offers me her cupped, bloody hand, showing me something in her palm. A small item.

"I did it," she says. "I did it for you."

I step carefully across the slippery surface. I don't see anything inside of her cupped hand. Once I'm standing within arm's reach of her, I finally see the pieces in her palm.

Three small slices, no bigger than pennies, lying in her hand. The flat ends of her fingers are turned up, blood dripping from the tips.

All of this blood—

It can't all be from her fingertips.

Can it?

Blood surges to my groin, filling me with hopeful desires. But then that dry itchiness wriggles in my throat and kills the wishful thinking in its tracks. Something is off. Where is this blood all from? This has to be a trap. A huge fucking game where I'm her pawn and she's playing with me.

But I can't stop myself from stepping closer to her. I want to see what happens next.

"It's not just pig's blood this time," I whisper. "Is it?"

She lifts her palm, and her body shakes uncontrollably, close to shock.

Three small pieces, like thinly sliced beef medallions, ready for a wet mouth. Meat like her fingertips won't melt on my tongue. Meat like that would be chewy. Savory. Gamey in a pleasant way.

My tongue thickens, my mouth salivating with desire, my throat finally wet again.

With fingertips like that, you'd have to savor it. Chew it. Let it break down on your tongue.

I can't throw it away.

"Eat it," Mona says. "It's like the menstrual blood, but I did this for you, my love. Just you. Now you have to do this for me."

Three small pieces of her body. Flesh she doesn't need.

Fingertips.

It dawns on me that she took pieces of her hands—hands she said she *needs* to create art—and yet she's destroyed herself so that I can eat her.

This is what I want. What I've dreamed of since my mother died. Men don't taste right, but women? Women are different. Tender, sweet, and pliable. I've waited so long for a woman who would be willing to do this for me, a woman who will give me a piece of her so that there's no distance between us.

She'll never be able to truly run away, because I'll have a piece of her in my body. She'll never be able to ask for her fingertips back, because they'll be inside of me.

If you do this, you won't be able to stop, my brain warns.

I know that. I know that. I fucking know that!

I inch closer. Into her trap.

"You know I can't eat that," I say, my voice hoarse.

"Stop thinking about me and my safety," Mona snaps. Then she begs in a soft, pleading tone. "Come on, Kent. Think about yourself for once. You keep putting everyone else before your own desires, including me. Do what *you* want for once."

She's pressuring me, treating me like a little boy again. I grit my teeth, but I'm focused on those red pieces of flesh.

Flesh she cut from herself.

For me.

"What I want," I repeat.

I kneel on the ground in her blood. It soaks my pants, the cold temperature creeping into my bones. Maybe it's not just her blood. Maybe it's pig's blood again. I don't know, and I can't ask. I can't do anything. I can only meet her on the same level.

Mona's dark caverns burn into me, ordering me to step into her darkness.

I should tell her to leave; it would be the right thing to do. After a refusal like this, after denying her bloody gift, maybe she'd finally give up on me and move on with her life. She can go back to art, and I can go back to sex workers and animal meat.

I don't want to hurt her. At the same time, I don't want her to leave. They *always* leave.

But not Mona. Mona understands me. And I understand her.

"Yes," Mona murmurs. "What *you* want."

I cup my hands under hers. The blood on her hands sticks to my skin. I bring her palms to my mouth, my heart beating against my rib cage. I'm a good person. I don't eat people. I just think about it. A fantasy never hurt anyone. It's a daydream. I can make the urges go away.

But wouldn't it be wrong to waste her meat, especially when it's a gift like this?

She angles her hands, and the morsels of meat tumble down her palm and skim my lips. I open my mouth and let them fall onto my tongue. Her meat is slightly bitter—perhaps from her carnivorous diet—and the skin is malleable, like a soft jerky. My mouth waters. Blood rushes to my groin, my dick full and weighty as I chew her fingertips.

Mona smiles at me, and that's when I realize that her meat reminds me of pork. It's sweet and mild like a pig, but there's something more complex about it. Something different. Something arousing. Something powerful.

That power is her. Mona.

And now, it's mine.

PART TWO

TONGUE

CHAPTER 19

YOU NEVER REALLY HEAR ABOUT THE AFTERMATH OF CANNIBALISM. Everyone is so obsessed with the actual eating that no one thinks about the practicality of it. And when your crazy girlfriend breaks into your home to surprise you with a devotional gift in which she literally removes a part of herself, no one thinks about the fact your house is now covered in blood, or it's going to take hours cleaning up the stains, or she probably won't stay to help you clean up.

No, you don't think about that.

You think about coming home from work.

You think about eating more of her.

You think about savoring every bite.

And that's where my head is at—exhausted and dazed—when I arrive at the processing plant. The supervisor stands outside of my locker, his head bowed.

"What?" I ask.

He pushes his glasses up his nose. "Look, Kent," he says quietly. "You're a good kid, but we caught you stealing on camera, and with your missed shifts lately, we just—"

I grit my teeth. We both know where this is going.

"You're firing me," I say.

The supervisor pats my shoulder. "I don't want to do this to you, but the other option is reporting you to law enforcement. I convinced the big boss that we should just fire you, and let that be it." His head bobs toward the locker. "You can clean up, then I'm afraid I have to walk you out. I told security I wanted to do it. You're a good kid, Kent. You deserve that much."

The way he calls me "a good kid" leaves a bad taste in my mouth. I'm thirty years old, and yet it's like the supervisor, Mona, Artemis, and everyone else in this world think they can look down on me.

I clear my locker, then we exit the building. The supervisor stays at the back entrance and watches me.

I pull out of the parking lot and take the van back to the fields. I don't have a job, but I don't care, because I have Mona now. For the first time, I've consumed human flesh consensually, and it's so fucking good. My mother, my boss, and everyone else rejected me, but Mona? She gave her fingertips to me.

Mona is everything.

In the mobile home, I clean the blood stains for hours. I become so physically drained that even the dried blood on the kitchen counter seems appetizing. I drag my tongue over it and relish the gamey taste. It tastes familiar, but there's something weird about it. It's not quite Mona. There's something missing from it. An emptiness.

I shrug my shoulders. It's probably pig's blood. She probably dumped the pig's blood inside, then left the bucket by the offal pit where I found it. She must've used it to supplement her actual blood. Besides, if it was all hers, she'd be completely drained. The pig's blood is another prop to include in her art performances.

Just like I'm another prop.

That's okay, I tell myself before the irritation gets under my skin. *It's better if she uses pig's blood. We don't want her to die just yet. Not until—*

The front door opens, and Mona's shadow fills the doorway. Afternoon light floods in behind her.

"You're back," I say.

She walks languidly, careful with each step, avoiding a slip in her own blood.

I scrunch my nose. The blood is almost completely cleaned up by now. There's no reason for her to walk like that.

She leans on the counter. "I went back home to get you something."

Her eyes twinkle mischievously. Black gloves cover her hands, and three of the fingertips bulge underneath the fabric; it must be from the bandages. That's good. She needs to heal so she can provide more for me.

"Bandages?" I ask, then tilt my head toward her thicker fingers.

She nods. "Now I can't be found guilty of a crime, right? And with my permission—my consent to your cannibalistic fantasies—you can't be found guilty either."

Her laughter cackles between us, and the hair stands on the back of my neck. Somehow, I've eaten her fingertips, and this is still a joke to her. I'm an object that she can mold for the sake of her art.

She thinks I'm stupid. Like I won't catch onto her game. Like she's the one hunting me.

I'm the one who ate her fingertips. I'm the one who is consuming her, and as much as I appreciate her, her smug attitude fucking irritates me.

"Mind if I take your picture?" she asks.

I grip the red-stained rag. "You want a picture of me cleaning?"

"No. I want pictures of you jerking off," she says dryly. "Yes! Of course I want pictures of you cleaning up the blood. I want to capture everything you do."

Before I can verbally respond, the shutter clicks. The camera's mechanics chant rhythmically like smacking lips. Each step of hers is weighted, sinking into the laminate, and it's like she's digging a deeper grave for me with her feet.

Tension crawls up my spine. She's following me and documenting what I'm doing, and it should feel good to know she cares about the menial stuff too, like cleaning. Instead, it pisses me off. It's like I'm another one of her many followers, cleaning up her messes.

Why doesn't she ask if she can help? It's not like I'd *make* her clean. I don't want her to clean, but for fuck's sake, I want her to pretend like she cares.

No—I wouldn't let her clean, even if she asked. I'd tell her to lie down before I tie her down and eat the rest of her fingers.

A normal person doesn't say things like that though.

I smear the rag over the counter absentmindedly. This is a part of Mona's art project too. If she wants pictures of me cleaning, then I can accept that, as long as I get another bite.

I turn over my shoulder. "You said you brought me something?"

She pulls a small object from her purse. The box is lined with blue velvet, the kind of container that holds a diamond ring or an expensive wristwatch.

"It's a present," she murmurs. "For you."

My nose wrinkles. "I like presents like your fingertips, babe, not watches or—"

She opens the box. A paper towel drenched in blood is folded inside of it, and on top lies a stubby toe. The cut end of the toe is frayed, the flesh mangled and raw, and the nail is painted bright red. It reminds me of the recording lights on her cameras.

Blood drains from my head and goes straight to my cock, an erection raging through me. I'd prefer to cut it off myself, but this is good. This is definitely a good start.

I look at Mona and realize she's keeping her weight to one side, favoring her right, giving herself time to heal. A limping woman is much easier to catch than a woman that can run.

My heart swells. She cut off her toe for me.

This is eternal fucking love.

A nagging sensation sews through my neck and worms its way into those pleasant thoughts. I swat it away like a mosquito, but it buzzes incessantly until I can't ignore it: I wanted to be the one to cut off a part of her, and she took that away from me.

No, my brain argues. *She did this for you. Be happy for once.*

I am happy. I swear I am.

"You cut off your toe," I gasp. I rub my dick through my pants. "Mona, you cut your toe—"

She winks. "You were so worried about doing the right thing that I knew you wouldn't—"

I smash my lips to hers and silence her words before she says something that ruins this act of love between us. I don't listen to the warnings that she thinks I'm not man enough to cut off her toes. I don't listen to the voices whispering that she's in control, that she's still manipulating me. I don't listen to any of that. I savor our kiss, my rock-hard dick smashed between us like a panini, because it's good—no, it's better than good. It's *euphoric* to call her mine. I've never exchanged I-love-yous with a woman before, but this? Her toe? A present for me? That's *more* than love.

Her mouth opens and lets me inside. The hint of toothpaste and the slightly sweet flavor of her tongue dances over my taste-buds. At the end of the kiss, bitterness leaks through, crowding my senses.

Meat-eater.

I pull back enough to speak, my words brushing her lips. "Don't eat meat anymore. I want to taste you. Not other animals. Just you."

"Is that a request or a command?" she asks quietly.

I don't answer that question; I simply expect her obedience, like she expects it from me. If she wants to argue about her rights to eat animal meat, then I can explain the health benefits to her later.

I hold the back of her head, my fingers tangled in her black hair. My fingers massage her ears as I kiss down the column of her neck. She presses her pussy closer to my dick.

Each kiss, each nibble, each thrust of our bodies drops me deeper into a fantasy: the two of us living on the farm together. My raised human meat. My little morsel. A woman like Mona needs luxury. She said it herself though: a farm is a cannibal's wet dream, and she can indulge me every once in a while. We can use the farm as our vacation home. We can even eat a person together. A second home like this could be a new way to jumpstart her creativity. Maybe I'll even give her a part of me too.

I unbutton her blouse and bite the tips of her nipples. A plea-sure-filled groan bursts through me.

"I still want those," she laughs. With more of her breast meat in my mouth, I bite again, deeper this time, enough to break skin.

She cries into me and stuffs her nose in my neck. "At least let me film it."

I suck the blood from her skin, savoring her metallic essence. It's not dull and empty like the dried blood from the countertop, but deep and rich, the sting of raw cinnamon peppering every drop. My eyes roll into the back of my skull. I suck out more. She taps the back of my head like she wants me to stop.

Reluctantly, I let go of her nipple. Only because I can eat her toe now.

"Too bad I can't milk you too," I say.

"You dirty boy," she says, and the filthy bitch flings her cunt up at me. I pull her leggings down and moan as I see the bandage wrapping around her ankle and winding obsessively around her missing toe, the second to last one. The childhood game with the toe piggies pops into my head, and my body warms as those words course through me: *this little piggy had none.* I'm not a little boy, and I don't have none anymore. I have so much when it comes to Mona. My little morsel.

I kiss down her calf, over her ankle, then hover above the bandage and swallow that gauzy, coppery scent.

"It hurts," she whines.

A guttural growl rips through me. "Good."

I let my pants hang around my hips, then I pick up her camera and snap a picture of her lying down, spread out before me like a mouthwatering feast. She yanks the camera from my hands and starts taking pictures of me. Behind the lens, her eyes are hungry, greedy, full of lust, and locked on me.

She did this for me.

I lay down between her thighs. "You're so good to me," I say. "You did all of this for me."

My tongue paints her pussy in saliva. Her meaty folds, even that beady clit, are salty, and I lick every crevice, tasting her cracks. I even lick her asshole and consider the possibility of eventually using her intestines as sausage casings.

Her breathing grows heavy. I fist my dick, and her pussy's

subtle bitterness and those sweet undertones envelop my tongue. She's warm, like meat straight out of the oven, and I swear, as I get back up on my knees, ready to fuck her, my brain fuzzes with heat. I get out that blue velvet box, and her lips part. The camera lens lowers; the red recording light glares at me.

I pull out the toe and lick the end. The fleshy fibers are wet and brittle, like a pinch of uncooked spaghetti noodles. I pop the whole thing in my mouth.

It's softer than you'd expect. Gamey and mild, without any crunch of bone.

With my mouth full, I ask, "The bone?"

"I wanted to use it for the project."

I grin. "Such an artistic little slut."

My dick slides inside of her as I chew her toe. Her pussy suffocates me, a boa constrictor murdering its prey, and I contemplate the possibilities. It seems infinite, but it's really not. How can I keep my meat alive for the longest amount of time? A sedentary pet, bound and helpless, reliant on me, will eventually die. It'll hurt to lose her—I know that—and I *still* want to go through with this.

"Kent," Mona moans. "I love watching you eat me. You're such a big, scary mon—"

Before she can finish, I choke her. The air squeezes from her lungs, her eyes bulging, and her delicious little cunt cinches me in a death grip. I get the feeling she almost called me a "big, scary monster" to mock me, but a vessel in her eye bursts, the blood spreading across her sclera like a drop of dye in water, and I'm satisfied.

She begins to thrash. Soon, she'll finally understand the real me. The parts I've been holding back. The secrets I've buried. The needs I must feed.

I swallow her toe, gulping it down like thoroughly chewed jerky.

"You're right, little morsel," I say. "I am a monster."

She passes out, her body limp and pliant, and I keep fucking her until I come. Once Mona learns what's best for her, she'll hand over that control. She'll give me her power like she gave me three fingertips and a toe. It's not my fault if this is what she wants. She *chose* this. And if the human body can survive this much, why wouldn't I push her further? Why would I stop now when I can enjoy all of her meat?

We only live once, and I'll make the most of her body.

It's what we both want.

CHAPTER 20

FOR THE NEXT WEEK, THAT'S OUR PATTERN. THREE FINGERTIPS—finger *slivers* really, not that I'm complaining—and two toes. It irks me that I don't get to see the actual carving, but when she comes to my home covered in bandages, I forget about the frustration. It's impossible for my dick to stay limp when she's vulnerable like that.

This isn't sustainable though. We'll have to make hard choices soon, decisions about what's next and where to go from here. I've always known a woman like her was a rare collector's item, and now that I've got her—now that I've confirmed that she's truly what I want—I'll never let her go. I'm not that stupid.

I pull the scratchy comforter up on the bed. It swallows us in heat. Mona rubs her naked ass against my crotch. My dick pokes the rim of her asshole, and though I'm not interested in anal sex, everything sounds amazing *if* I get to eat another piece of her.

I pull her into my arms and press my lips to her ear. "Let me cut one," I say in a low voice. "I want to watch your face as the flesh leaves your body and becomes a part of me."

"Kent," she murmurs. "It's hard to walk. I need time to heal."

I lick her ear, my dick growing at those words. She needs time to heal. Why do I like that so much?

Five pieces of her body in a few days is a lot of flesh.

But one more toe won't make that much of a difference.

"It won't be a toe you *need*," I argue. "Come on, Mona. I want to see your face." Warmth rushes over my body as I imagine her mouth contorting in love and agony. "I want to see the pain you have to endure for me."

She stiffens, her shoulders rigid. And with that small change, I know she's annoyed with me.

She curls away, moving her hips out of my crotch. "I have to teach soon," she says.

I sigh. Teaching. Right. She can't suddenly go to class in a wheelchair. That would cause gossip, and gossip can lead to personal issues for her.

Mona loves controversy though, especially if it has to do with her art.

A part of me knows that her irritation doesn't have to do with teaching at the university; it has to do with the fact I keep asking for more.

You warned her that this would happen, my brain argues. *How can she expect you to stop now?*

There's a solution somewhere. We can make this work. If I find another way to be satisfied—to keep *us* satisfied—then Mona can keep most of her fingers and toes. We can live together for a long time. Maybe even into old age.

The thought is barely formed before the words come out. "What if we eat people together?" I ask.

She rolls over to face me with a deadpan expression. "I'm doing a project where *I'm* the one being eaten," she says dryly. "I'm not a cannibal."

Her words slice through me. It's like she's cutting off the space between us, even though we're mere inches from each other.

Is she looking down on me for eating her?

Shame tingles in my toes. No. She's right. Eating people and being eaten are two completely different things. Feeding Mona another human won't please her.

What am I supposed to say now?

"That's not what I meant," I say. "I know you're not a canni-bal. I just mean—I don't have to eat *all* of you." I scratch the back of my neck. "I'll make it work with other meats, you know? I'll only eat from you one morsel at a time."

Panic flutters in my chest. I should be offended that she thinks being a cannibal is an insult, but I can't even be mad at her right now. I just want to keep her with me.

I fucked up. I fucked up big time.

This is love. I can save this.

I have to.

"Right, little morsel?" I wheeze. "Just one small bite each time. Enough to whet my appetite. I'd never really hurt you like that."

Her eyes hold mine, and there's a lack of emotion there, as if she's keeping herself together just to get this conversation over with as quickly as possible. Just like the sex workers.

Still, the words are on the tip of my tongue, full of weight and emotion, and so desperate to come out, to be everything for her. *I love you, Mona,* I want to say, *and I'm so grateful for everything you're doing for me. I'm so grateful, in fact, that I don't want to mess this up. I want to keep you forever. I want to keep you like you're mine, so that it's up to me— only me—to keep you safe. I'll keep you locked away for my pleasure. And I'll be good to you, Mona. I'll worship you the only way I know how until there's nothing left between us. Until we're together, combined in one body. One soul. One flesh. Isn't that what love is?*

My lips move, but none of those words come out. Instead, my head fills with images of my mother dead on the dining room table, the hole in her stomach crawling with maggots. Her sawed-off tongue in my hands, stiff and spongy. A savory cake.

Then those images morph and become Mona's foot with two missing toes. Patches of skin picked from her calves, like cupped pepperoni slices plucked from a pizza.

"It's just a toe," I say quietly. "I don't have to eat the rest."

"You're being selfish," she snaps.

Our naked bodies are so close that our heat is an inferno; at the same time, those words send ice through my veins. There are bandages on her fingers. Wraps around each ankle and each missing toe. Gloves on top of her hands and socks on her feet. Everything to keep her safe and sealed. Barriers guarding her from me. And she could have *more* protection. We could be in different beds, different rooms, different universes, and the fact would remain the same.

Mona thinks I'm selfish.

My mother used to say things like that. She'd call me selfish when all I wanted was to not be hungry anymore. To be full and satisfied for once. To feel like I had something I could call my own.

My mother never gave me any of that.

I shouldn't be comparing Mona to my mother though. They're different people. Mona gave parts of herself to me. Even if she doesn't realize it, Mona *loves* me.

Control yourself, I think. *You'll get what you want.*

"I didn't mean it like that," I start to say, but a drop of anger taints my next words. "Mona, you know I'm trying—"

"Can't you be happy with what I give you?"

Water brims the edges of her eyes. Pleading. Begging me to understand. But the longer I stare at her, the less those tears seem real.

It's another performance, isn't it? Or am I that callus?

I should be groveling, but I'm hungry, and fuck, doesn't she see that I haven't done anything wrong? All I did was ask. For fuck's sake, it's not like I actually cut off her toe.

A choking noise breaks up her tears.

"I have to amputate my toes at my house *for my project*, and you have the audacity to want *more* of me?" She recoils, her nostrils flaring. "Let me break it down for you. If I do it here or if I let *you* do it, then that won't fulfill my vision. And if I don't get what I want, then none of this will matter. I won't matter. My art won't matter. And *you* definitely won't matter. Do you understand what I'm saying, or do I need to make it simpler for you?"

Weakness clamors through my body. We're lying down, but my head spins like I'm about to trip down the stairs. I understand what she's saying, but I don't want her words to be true.

She's calling me stupid, isn't she?

It hurts, but she's right though. I am stupid. I shouldn't have let my desires get out of hand.

"Okay," I mutter. "Can I at least go to your house and watch, then?"

She rubs her temples. "Will you ever stop?"

I scrape my hand over my face and numb those emotions.

I can be good. I can be better. I can control myself. But will I ever stop asking? If I'm being honest with myself, I don't know. Maybe. Maybe after she gives me what I want. The question seems bigger than that though, like she knows that my hunger for her will never actually be satiated.

For a split second, I see it from her view: I have a woman who is finally willing to cut off parts of her body for me, and for some stupid reason, I need more.

Maybe I *am* selfish.

And I find myself begging her.

"I can be good," I say. My voice cracks, and I hate, hate, *hate* how I'm the little boy cowering in the corner and waiting for his mother to look at him and approve for once. I can't help it though. This is who I am, and I need her to need me too. "I swear I'll be good."

A low breath whistles from her mouth, and she reaches for my hands. "Let's wait until my body heals first, then we'll talk, okay? Right now, I'm starving."

My heart pounds. I can fix that for her.

I prop myself up on my elbow. "Let me feed you," I say. She raises a brow, and I brush the black strands of hair out of her eyes. "Not like the restaurant this time. I'll pick something up. I want to take care of you."

She gives me a curious half-smile. "Okay. Sure."

"Stay in bed," I say. She nods in obedience. I rush to pull on my boxers and pants. "I'll be right back."

At the nearest grocery store, I buy a beet salad and orange juice with cash. Next door at the antique shop, the display window catches my eye: a gold chrome vintage wheelchair. It's gleaming and borderline gaudy. I'm cutting it close to Mona's lecture, but even if we're a little late, this gift will be worth it.

I pay for the wheelchair with cash, and it easily fits in the back of my cargo van. A short while later, I roll the wheelchair into the bedroom.

"I've got a surprise for *you* now," I say. "I don't want you to waste any time walking when you can be healing those pretty little feet."

Mona lights up, and that expression of amusement reassures me that I did the right thing.

"Is this about my comfort, or is it about speeding up the healing process?" she says as she slips gingerly into her shoes. "Either way, thank you, love. This is perfect."

We don't have time to eat, so we rush to the university. In the lecture hall, everyone gawks as I push Mona's wheelchair, then the students gossip to one another. Mona beams, her eyes sparkling as she soaks in the recognition and the rumors; it's the same smile she had when she entertained her fans at the art gallery. She's in a wheelchair with missing appendages, and yet, this small change gives her power.

"What do you think they're saying?" she whispers.

I open my mouth to tell her how she's hypnotizing everyone with her allure, just like she's captured me, but Mona starts lecturing, and my answer falls silent as if what I think doesn't actually mean anything to her. It almost hurts.

But like a good, supportive boyfriend, I shake those emotions off and take my place in the front row. Her lips move, and her words dance around the room. I don't hear her though. My attention is solely on the way her body moves. Her neck muscles twisting. Her tendrils of arm flesh shifting under each movement. The bandage scratching against the bottom of her pant legs, waiting for me to unravel the layers. No one knows that there are chunks missing from her body, pieces of flesh that are inside of me now. How could anyone even imagine that my body is digesting her, taking her nutrients and transforming them so that I'm a better, more complete person?

I'm in awe of my little morsel.

I'm so lucky to have found her.

CHAPTER 21

AFTER CLASS, THE WHEELCHAIR RATTLES OVER THE CEMENT LIKE chains, and the zoo lion roars, but Mona laughs, not noticing the racket. During the ride from the lecture hall to her office, Mona keeps a smug smirk on her lips. The college students side-eye her, and a few professors gawk. No one asks any questions though.

I can see Mona enjoys the rumors and the controversy. There's a sort of power in it.

We roll inside of the elevator, and luckily, the wheelchair hides my erection. We exit on the fourth floor. I give Mona a hand as she walks up the ramp to her desk chair, then I take my seat on the other side.

Since her desk is on a riser, I'm in a lower position than her; it doesn't bother me though, because I'm confident now. I have Mona right where I want her. And I can admit that I have canni-balistic tendencies, but the fact is that I haven't eaten a whole person yet, so I'm not *really* a cannibal. Besides, I haven't eaten from her body without her consent. She wants it too. A cannibal doesn't wait for the meat's permission to eat it; a cannibal simply takes.

"Give me another toe," I say, my fingers thrumming my thigh. My dick pokes a tent in my pants. I'm aware that I'm being overly persistent, but it's *so* close. I know she'll give it to me if I just ask her the right way. "I'll wait for it if I have to."

A grin crowds her pursed lips. "I know you will."

She gestures for me to come back around the desk. I walk up the ramp until our feet are on the same level, then I look down at her.

She pulls my shirt until I'm on my knees between her spread thighs. She murmurs, "Tell me, love. What would you do to me?"

I exhale slowly. There's no camera in her hands for once, but she has floor-to-ceiling windows, and there are cameras set up throughout her office. I should assume she's recording with those devices, as I should assume that she's still using me for her project.

Art is what brought her to me though, and I'm not going to stop reaching for what I want because we're on display. Being watched right now is the least of my worries, especially when I'm so close to capturing the woman of my dreams.

My chest swells, and my blood vessels open up for that sweet, fantastical ecstasy. I'm on my knees, bowing before Mona right now, but in this position, I don't feel small.

I've eaten parts of her, and that gives me strength. Over others. Over *her*.

And I can take charge of what I want.

I swipe the contents off of her desk. Papers, books, pens, and paints crash to the floor. Mona's mouth gapes, her lips wet, her eyelids heavy with lust. I cup her ass and carry her, then lie her down on the desk. She bites her bottom lip, and I push the straps of her blouse from her shoulders.

She's a sacrifice on my altar. The mother of a feast. My little morsel warming under the heat lamp.

"I'd chain you to a bed," I say. I kiss and bite and lick her collarbone, then move toward her meaty neck. Goosebumps crest her body, and my own muscles relax as that juicy warmth spreads over me. My lips hover over her neck, and *fuck me*, prepared the right way, her esophagus would taste like pork rinds. My body grows taller, stronger, wider, as I embrace that sensation: my control over her.

"These goosebumps," I murmur. "I'd shave you to keep your

textures nice and smooth. I'd fry your skin until it was nice and crispy. I'd cut off small parts of you everywhere, my little morsel, fucking everywhere"—I nibble on her ear, her cheek, her lip— "until I had to move on to your limbs. I'd cut those too, you know. And let me tell you something, little morsel: I'd fuck you every day and every night, but I would *never* let you move. We need to keep your flesh tender, don't we?"

A breath escapes her. "Is that why you insisted on a wheelchair?"

There's hesitation in her voice, a new tone dancing under her words, and that tone sounds like desire and fear and selfless *love* wrapped into one. She should be scared. Love is a scary fucking thing; it can ruin you. And we both know she needs this as much as I do.

I'm going to take such good care of her.

"There's no need to be scared, little morsel," I say, my heated words breathing over her skin. "I'll feed you fruits and vegetables. Everything will be organic. You'll want for nothing. I'll get you everything you deserve. Only the best for my meat." I crush the head of my dick, then lower my lips to her ear. "You'll be sweet inside and out."

I pull off her pants, and those bandaged toes make my cock so painfully hard that I can barely move.

A few more cuts. That's all I need. It's a few more cuts, and she won't be able to move anymore. She'll be completely at my mercy.

"Kent," she whispers. "Why don't we wait to have sex until we're at your home later?"

She's posing it as a question, and that means she's finally giving me the respect I deserve, letting me decide, realizing *I* know what's best for us. She's probably worried about the windows, but this high up, away from the edge of the room, there's a good chance the students can't see anything. And it's not like Mona is asking me to stop. Waiting and stopping are different. Even if she did ask me to stop, I'm not sure I would listen. It's not up to her anymore.

Fear clouds Mona's eyes, a storm washing over her dark

pupils, and it's like she's finally seeing my true self for the first time. Me, the real me. The one that's always been here, waiting for her to open her eyes.

Her breath lodges in her throat like a lump of unchewed food. I shove my dick inside of her, and her cunt clenches around me like a cocoon. I concentrate on that frightened expression; it fills me with hunger for more.

If I got to cut her—if I carved her meat with my own hands—she would squeeze me harder. Deeper. Tighter. Like a rabbit snatched in a wolf's jaws, struggling to get away.

Her pussy walls close in on me, so fucking tight, so full of *fear*, it's invigorating.

"Would you hunt me?" she whispers. Her eyes are wide, and she asks the question like it'll give her power again.

"Hunt you, baby?" I ask. "I already have you."

As my dick impales her, I imagine it's not my dick, but a bone and keratin horn, goring her like a fighting bull. It slices through her pussy, her uterus, her intestines. If the horn was big enough, it could impale her from her ass to her esophagus.

I twist her nipples, and she cries, her sweet moan filling my ears with love. With need. With hunger. Like the scent of barbecued flesh on the wind.

This is too much though. I can't kill her. *It's just dirty talk*, I tell myself. *It's a fantasy. It's nothing. It's nothing. It's nothing—*

But it's *not* nothing. It's not like the sex workers or my shy ex-girlfriends. Mona isn't like those stupid cunts. She knows what I'm capable of. With Mona, it's *something*, like I'm only another fingertip away from my dreams.

"I'll fuck you and kill you slowly, little morsel," I groan, my dick pulsing, so close to orgasm, the crown of my cock dribbles with pre-cum. "All you have to do is ask."

A knock bangs into the door. "Who is it?" she yelps.

An angry male voice shouts, his voice muffled by the door.

"Tell him to go away," I order in a low voice.

"Come in," she squeaks, her voice eerily weak. "Come in! Come in!"

I roll my eyes and ready myself for whatever comes next. She's not listening to me. I'll have to change that. I'll teach her a lesson in obedience if I have to. I know what's best for both of us, especially when it comes to her meat.

It's the only way we can make this work.

CHAPTER 22

THE OFFICE DOORS SWING OPEN, AND THAT PONY-TAILED IDIOT walks in, his eyes like saucers as he takes in our bodies in the midst of sex.

Artemis draws his head back sharply. "What the fuck are you doing?" Mona jumps off the desk, and Artemis lifts his arms, his eyes bulging from his head. "You're fucking her while she's at work? When she's in a wheelchair? When she's clearly hurt?"

"What we do is none of your business," I snarl.

"Mona, tell him to get out," he yells.

"Kent," Mona says. Her voice is pleading, right on the edge of begging me, and for once, it's not a performance. She keeps her eyes on the ground, deferring to Artemis.

Irritation simmers under my skin. He has ripped the control I had over Mona away from me, when I was so close to holding it in my hands. It's fucking bullshit. If she had dumped him after that threesome—if she had *listened* to me—we wouldn't be in this situation right now.

I hate how this feels.

A situation like this takes more time though. I can't be hasty with how I carve my meat. If I want Mona to be mine until the day she dies, I have to respect her words. And if she wants to listen to Artemis right now, then I have to too.

"You don't have your car," I say. "We drove my van, remember?"

"It's fine." She nods at Artemis. "Arty can take me home."

There's a blanched quality to her expression, almost like sadness, or fear, or maybe dread. Like she doesn't want me anymore, and she's afraid to say it.

A sour taste crowds my mouth, and my scalp tingles with pins and needles. I wait, staring at her turned cheek.

She finally looks at me. "I'll see you later, okay?"

"Call me," I order.

She nods, then the double doors close behind me. Their argument penetrates the walls and rumbles into the hallway.

"You're overreacting," Mona says. "I know what I'm doing. He's harmless."

"He's not fucking harmless. He stabbed you in the cervix!"

"The doctor compared it to a love bite. He's doing this because he worships me—"

"This isn't just about *him*," Artemis shouts. "I don't trust *you* with him! You're going to get hurt! Not just a fingertip. Not just a toe. Not just a cut on your cervix. You're going to take this too far, and neither of us will be able to fix it. I can't let that happen."

I shake my head and walk down the hallway. Artemis is right, in a way. Mona and I *are* dangerous together. We are hunger and self destruction in the carcass of love.

Harmless. Gentle. They're offensive words, especially coming from her.

I focus on the good though. She's sticking up for me.

The elevator fills with bodies, the stench of mustard filling my lungs. Too many men. They smell as bad as they taste.

Once I step outside, fresh air fills my nostrils. I head toward the parking lot with a bounce in my step, because my morsel is upstairs, defending our love.

A woman steps on the walkway and blocks my path. She's half my size. Scars circle each of her wrists like bracelets or handcuffs. Can handcuffs dig into a woman's skin and leave a permanent mark like that?

Her clothes are white, and her skirt is impossibly short, her tits hanging out of her top. Floral perfume rings out from her skin. It's technically a naturally occurring scent, but fuck me, it's so strong, it's nauseating.

"You hurt me," the woman says.

She keeps her eyes on the ground, as if she's working up the courage to look me in the face.

A chill races over my shoulders. Who the fuck is she?

"I don't even know you," I say. I step to the side, and she steps in front of me again.

"You raped me!" she shouts.

Several smartphones light up in my periphery. I scan our surroundings and notice about ten to fifteen students using their recording devices like shields, capturing our interaction.

I grit my teeth like a predator, although inside, I feel small and attacked, like I'm pinned to the corner of the room with a knife in my hand. I'm desperate to defend myself.

Control yourself, Kent. Control, control, control—

"I don't know you," I say, raising my voice.

"You chained me to your bed. Kept me locked in a dog cage. You told me you were going to kill me and eat me. 'Meat doesn't talk.' That's what you kept saying, right? Every time I told you I didn't want to do it anymore, that's what you told me! I was meat to you, and I didn't get to speak."

My lips pull back in a grimace as the memory comes rushing back. It wasn't an oven, was it? She was scared of being tied to the oven, so I compromised and tied her to the cage next to my bed. Desire, the sex worker. Desire, whose real name was Desiree —the dumb bitch told me she switched her stage name to Desire, because she couldn't keep herself organized. The whore who wouldn't shut the fuck up. Who wouldn't stop crying when I gave her breast a superficial cut. Who sobbed like an infant when I untied her whiney little ass from the cage. Who limped away and rubbed her hands together, like she was so fucking destroyed, even as she carried double the cash of what I owed her.

I told her what I wanted. It's not my fault she didn't listen.

All I'd have to do is take a crowbar to the bitch's head, and she'd never be able to speak again, like real fucking meat. Then she'd finally listen to me.

She should be grateful that I didn't kill her back then.

The millions of recording lenses keep me restrained. Phones. People. Strangers. Online viewers. Everyone is watching me.

Her body trembles with rage. "You don't remember me, but I'll never forget you."

The urge to tear her throat out and stomp on her spinal cord lashes against my fingers, and I curl my knuckles in agitation. I'd eat her heart like a steak, straight from the bitch's body, raw in my fucking hands. Like Mona ate the filet in the restaurant.

I squeeze my fists at my side. I'm stronger than this. I have Mona now. I don't need a paid little cunt like this bitch in front of me.

And I'm not going to let her accusation fuck me over.

I peer up at the building to Mona's office window. Mona and Artemis look down at me, their expressions blank.

Mona knows me. She knows I would never hurt her like that, and that's enough for me right now.

"You got your fucking money," I snarl.

"I'm a person," Desire says, tears and snot dripping down her face like she's a fucking dog. I want to punch her in the fucking face like I should've done when I had her tied to my cage, and it seems like *that's what she wants.* To get a reaction out of me, like that shaved-headed man at work. To let these people catch me in the act of hurting a woman, like that frightened brunette recording me in the break room. To put me behind bars, when I'm so close to getting the only thing I've ever wanted for myself.

Of course you're not a rapist, Mona had said.

I'm not a rapist. I'm not. Desire knew what I wanted. She knew, and she cried, but fuck her. She got her money. It's not my fault she changed her mind. It was too late for that.

"You knew what was coming," I say.

I stomp toward the parking lot, muttering to myself. *Control yourself, and you'll get what you want.* I repeat the mantra, but I can't stop thinking about the sex worker.

I told her, didn't I? I told her *exactly* what I wanted.

She chose to stay.

CHAPTER 23

I TOLD MONA TO CALL ME, BUT MY PHONE DOESN'T RING.

I knew this would happen.

I tap my fingers on the table and check the grandfather clock. Do Mona's missing phone calls have anything to do with the accusations that bitch made outside of her office, or does it have to do with Artemis?

It has to be Artemis. He's a jealous parasite getting under her skin. Changing her decisions. Feeding on her.

Hatred bubbles in my veins as I realize that I'm that stupid, little boy again, waiting for his mother to wake up and feed him something. *Anything.* Waiting for her to love him again.

Except this time, it's not my mother.

It's Mona.

At Mona's next lecture, the front seats are taken, so I sit in the back row. Once class is over, she limps to the door, and I step in front of the exit and block her path.

"We haven't had dinner in a while," I say. "I'll cook for you."

She checks to make sure no one is watching us, then she grins at me. "I have a meeting later, but I can squeeze in a meal. How about that chain restaurant?"

I scrutinize her, reading past those words. Artemis must have told her to only meet me in a public setting. She doesn't trust me anymore.

Then I remember he said he didn't trust *her* with me either. As if we are two people destined to destroy each other.

It's more proof that we are made for each other.

No…It's not that. Mona is made *for* me.

"You're scared, aren't you?" I say. I corner her under my shadow. "You're scared, but you know me, little morsel. Let me cook for you. I'm harmless, right? You can trust me."

Her posture deflates, then she chuckles. "Okay," she says. "Your place."

By the time dinner arrives, she's dressed conservatively with a blazer over her blouse, a long skirt, and tights covering her legs. Every inch of her skin below her neck is covered like a fucking nun, as if I need to peel the bitch to get to the good stuff.

I don't say anything though. I tell myself those layers are simply extra butcher paper wrapping her meat.

I serve her a salad with fried tofu, and I serve myself a steak salad.

She gawks at the crispy chunks of white material, her jaw practically on the floor.

"You're giving me tofu?" she asks.

"You need to stop eating meat," I say.

"This is fucking rabbit food."

"And *you* are my fucking rabbit," I say through clenched, smiling teeth. "Are you criticizing the meal I cooked for you?"

She puts down her fork. I do the same. We scrutinize each other, our eyes hardened, our jaws strained, and the tension between us is thicker than a blood clot. An uneasiness pours out of her body, as if she knows that one wrong word can change everything for her. As if she finally understands who I am.

I link my fingers in front of me, waiting for her answer. Finally, she leans back in her chair.

"I'm not criticizing your meal," she says. "I'm grateful for what you've done for me. This is sweet."

I pick up my fork and stab another bite of juicy meat. "But?"

Mona pokes a chunk of tofu, then moves it on the side of her plate. "I just don't like the texture."

I keep chewing. "You'll get used to it."

Soon, a pile of golden tofu, speckled with drops of red wine vinegar, sits on the side of her plate, like dismembered toes pickled with red onions. The pressure builds in my groin and spreads to my chest. I should be insulted by her refusal to eat the meal I cooked for her, but my dick engorges as I dream of the possibilities for her appendages.

I can't stop myself.

"I want to cook your toes. Two of them," I say quickly. "You'll walk better if we cut off the same toe on each foot. That way it's even on both sides. It'll help you balance."

Mona's upper lip curls. "We're taking this too far, Kent. We can't—"

"It's just two toes, Mona. You cut off the first two. The second toe on each foot would be the same. You'd have three other toes on each side to give you balance. It's not that big of a deal."

"Not that big of a deal?" she says in a high-pitched voice. "And what happens after that? My foot? My leg?" She twists her neck, her nose lifted high in the air. "I've been limping since I cut off my first toe for you. I can't touch anything in my studio without getting sharp pains in my hand." Tears form in her eyes. "I did all of this for you, Kent. And now, you're telling me you need *more* of me?" She throws her hands up, the gloves on one hand still bulging with bandages. "I can't do that. I need to think about my art *and* my well being."

She continues lecturing me. The words fuzz into white noise, and I latch onto the one claim that kills the rest.

She did this for me?

How could she have done this for me? She wouldn't even let me cut off her toe. She knows how much cutting off her toe would mean to me, and she's the selfish bitch keeping that to herself.

"You didn't do it for me," I say. "You did it for your art. You even chopped it off by yourself, even though you *know* part of my fantasy is the actual dismemberment."

"For fuck's sake, Kent. Something is wrong with you." I clench my jaw, and she cowers, sinking into her seat. "I mean, something is wrong with *us*." She shakes her head. "Artemis is right. This isn't safe. We can't keep doing this, or I'll get seriously hurt, and I don't want to die yet. I don't think you want to kill me either."

My entire body goes rigid at his name. She has the nerve to bring him up now? *Him?* In my fucking home?

"I don't want to share you with him," I say.

A beat passes. Neither of us moves. We stare at each other, two predators circling. My jaw strains.

She rolls her eyes. "We never agreed to be exclusive, love. If you don't like it, you don't have to share me." She tosses her hair over her shoulder. "You can find someone else."

Her threat lingers in the air, like the stench of rotting meat from the offal pit, drawing the flies closer.

It took a long time to find her. She knows that. And she knows how easily she can cut me out.

I won't let that happen. I'll do anything to keep her.

"You're right," I say. "Artemis is right." I stab a cherry tomato. It pops between my molars, and I imagine her eyeball in the same position. Would it be as juicy as a tomato? "We'll stick to dirty talk."

"Thank the muses," she says. She forks a tomato too. "The brain is the biggest sexual organ anyway. We only need the dirty talk. Maybe a prop or two, sure, but nothing serious. It's just pretend anyway, right, love?"

Before I open my mouth to answer, her vision catches on the wall behind me, on the oval of bright wallpaper where the photograph used to hang, the one she asked if she could borrow.

"What happened to your mother anyway?" she asks.

"That woman wasn't my mother."

"I know, Kent," Mona says, her voice simmering with agitation. "That's why I'm asking. I know your mother was crazy, but what did she do that was so extreme that now you're a sexual cannibal?"

Every inch of my home takes on a red hue, like I'm seeing the world through tinted glass. Mona isn't the pale woman in the black clothes anymore. She's red, like raw beef on a cutting board.

I'm not a cannibal. I've only eaten what she's given me. I haven't taken anything from her, and I haven't eaten the rest of her body. But it's like she's accusing me of something. My jaw clenches, and I imagine I have the jaws of an alligator, able to snap her body in half and trap her in my mandibles.

Mona is different though. She's the only person who understands my inner struggle. I'm not going to hurt her like that.

I love Mona.

I swear I do.

And I can't waste any of my steak salad, just like I refuse to waste Mona.

"She was going to leave me, and she died," I say. I shove a forkful of lettuce into my mouth. "I don't know what else to tell you."

"Did you kill her?"

I drop my fork. Mona tenses, though to her credit, she keeps her expression vacant, like she wants to see what I say before she gives a full reaction. I cock my head to the side. My shoulders broaden, irritation taking hold of me. I stay neutral too.

Killing would imply that a ten-year-old kid has the gumption to be able to shove a knife into a dumb bitch, and I never did anything like that.

"No," I say. "What happened to her was an accident."

"What happened, then?"

I swallow a lump in my throat. "I don't want to talk about it."

"That's fine," she says in a high-pitched lilt. She reaches forward and holds my hand with her gloved, wounded fingers, a small attempt to connect with me. "You won't let an accident like that happen to me, will you, love?"

There's an expression on her face I don't quite understand. The tendons in her neck are sharper than usual, and her throat bobs, like she's gulping down an apple. I've never been good at reading people, but I've been around Mona enough to know that something is different tonight.

Is she afraid of me?

I shake my head. She's not afraid of me. She thinks I'm harmless, and I'm aware of how good I have it with her. She's a once in a lifetime opportunity, and I'm not going to fuck that up by accidentally stabbing her.

"No," I say. "Never."

"Good," she whispers. "Thank you."

The rest of the meal continues, and the silence is filled with the dings of our forks and plates. At the end of dinner, Mona leaves the chunks of tofu to the side of her plate. I clear the table, and in the kitchen, I eat the tofu with my hands, pretending it's her toes.

It's not the same though. Plants aren't meat.

I want her flesh.

"Thanks for the meal," she says, her voice drifting through the house. I wipe my hands and head to the door. She pulls her purse strap higher on her shoulder, her camera strap on the other. "I'll see you soon——"

"Wait," I say. "I got you a present."

Her posture straightens. "Oh?"

I run to the bedroom and pull out a film camera—the one-time-use kind, an item I found in the mobile home when I moved in—and I give it to her.

"Thank you," she says. "I love film. I'll use it for the exhibition."

She heads toward the door again, and panic forms in my rib cage. She can't go. I can't let her. If she leaves right now, she may never come back.

"Stay with me," I plead.

My forehead creases. I try to keep my eyes open and form tears, my own performance to manipulate *her* this time. It's so unusual to me though. I don't feel like other people. I didn't even cry when my mother died. Why would I cry when Mona leaves my home?

"It's the end of the semester. My next exhibition is almost here," she says. "I've got a lot of work to do."

She can do whatever she wants, even leave me, and she knows it.

I press down the anger and soak in the desperation, crossing my fingers that this display of emotion works.

"Please, Mona," I whisper. "Don't leave me."

Something about those words must unlock her sympathy, because she smirks and shakes her head. "You truly are persistent," she teases.

"What can I say?" I rise to my full size and tower over her. "You inspire me."

"Do I?" She trots over and grabs the olive oil off of the kitchen counter. "Let's use this."

Olive oil? To season her, we'd need more than that.

I force a smile. This isn't about seasonings. This is about Mona. I need to fulfill her fantasies first, and later, we can get to mine.

It's the only way to make my dreams come true.

CHAPTER 24

I LEAD MONA OUTSIDE. SHE PUTS HER PERSONAL CAMERA ON THE back porch step, and the glowing red light on the device reminds me of a lighthouse in the darkness. An ache grows in my chest and drips down to my cock.

She's here. So close to the pit. The flies buzz around us.

I could suffocate her under the flesh.

I would never do that though. Her meat is too good to be repurposed like that.

She slips out of her tights. Those bandage straps come into view, wrapping around her ankles and down over her missing toes, like carefully constructed lingerie leading the eye to the best parts of the body.

I've never liked lingerie; it always felt like it was created to hide something. And now, I tap my fingers together, struggling with the urge to yank those bandages off of her legs and see the healing flesh underneath. Mona needs time to heal though, and those bandages are the best way to make sure that her body can provide for me again.

"Rub it on me," she says. She shoves the olive oil bottle into my hands. "Pretend it's a marinade."

A marinade.

Pretend.

Another prop for her art.

When I don't take the bottle, she twists the cap and begins pouring the olive oil into my hands, then she moves me, making me do what she wants. There's a coldness in her movements, like she's a cardboard cutout at a puppet show, and this is a performance. Give her dirty talk and a bottle prop, and the artistic bitch has everything she wants out of me.

Maybe I'm just a prop too.

She moves my hands to her upper thighs, her skin slimy with the slick yellow oil.

My dick stays limp.

"Just like that," she says. "Pretend you're preparing me for the oven."

Pretend. There's that word again.

Heat funnels inside of me, filling my lungs with ash. Mona is the same as the sex worker in the black lingerie, the same as the stupid whore who accused me of raping her, the same as every shy cunt I've ever dated.

They all wanted to play pretend. They wanted me to hide who I really am. They never wanted me.

Mona is supposed to be different. Better than them.

She moves my hands closer to her pussy, and she giggles. "The oil tickles."

I growl. "Meat doesn't speak."

She avoids my eyes and subtly sighs. "I'm not meat. I'm obviously still livestock."

The anger rushes in, and every blood vessel and nerve ending in my body is scorching with rage. Her condescension is ripe. She wants me to pretend?

Then a marinade isn't where it stops.

"All right," I say.

I grab the hair at the bottom of her neck and drag her up the platform to the industrial meat grinder. She trips over the steps, and my fist tugs her hair harder, yanking at the strands.

"What the fuck are you doing?" she asks.

I force her head into the metal hopper. "Putting my livestock in the meat grinder," I say. "I've always heard livestock tastes best when the meat is ground while it's still alive. Let's test that theory."

I power on the machine, and it whirs, the metal screeching through the air. My fingers accidentally slip over the dial, and the metal grinding increases. A slosh of old meat drops to the bottom of the holding container, breaking up the metal orchestra, but it's Mona's protesting that brings it to another level. She thrashes, her small frame bucking against my erection, and my muscles are heavy with tension. It feels so fucking good to dangle prey right above its death.

Her oily body slips in my grasp. I reposition myself and use her extra clothing to get a better hold on her. It's enough to keep her still.

"Kent!" she screams. "Kent, don't you dare—"

This time, I purposefully twist the dial as I unzip my pants. It's only switching plates, but she doesn't know that. Mona's head isn't fully inside of the grinder, but she screams, and I pin my full weight against her body, keeping the front half of her stuck inside of the machine. My dick slips in the olive oil as I slide into her pussy. She's wet though. *No*—the dumb little bitch is fucking soaked, and *fuck*, my dick twitches with each of her greedy little protests.

"Let me go!"

She keeps screaming, but we're in the middle of nowhere. The nearest hint of civilization is the landfill, and even then, their machines are louder than mine. The workers can't hear a thing.

I squeeze her neck and her cunt retaliates, her cream squishing out around me. I always knew fear would make her wet, and that confirmation fills my head with a seductive mist, putting me in a trance. She pulls at my hands, but her oily fingers slip like mine did.

"You're mocking me," I say loudly into her ear. I thrust against her and her cunt constricts around me so nicely, it's like she thinks she can grind *my* meat with her pussy. "With your head in the meat grinder, it's a little hard to fuck with me, isn't it?"

I tighten my grip on her neck, and she struggles, her exposed skin bulging red with blood. Her pussy tries strangling me to death, but I'm the one with my hands around her throat right now.

I press my lips to her ear. "You know what I'd do after I cut off your arm? I'd cut a hole in the bicep and fuck the wound. Then you wouldn't mock me, would you? You wouldn't think I was a stupid, little boy then."

Her eyes roll white, her lungs stop, and that delicious unconsciousness pushes me over the edge. I come inside of the bitch, filling up her meaty cunt with my fluids. Pleasure tingles over my body, and the night air cools me down. I pull out of her pussy and power off the meat grinder.

Mona's body stays limp in the metal hopper, her pussy exposed, my off-white semen glooping out of her oily hole. My stomach grumbles at the sight, and I'm compelled; I drop to my knees and lick her pussy, tasting her fear, the olive oil, and my semen. I imagine it's like a Balut egg, half-formed babies seasoned with oil and salt rolling over my tongue.

She stirs, her pussy writhing against my face. I bring her hips closer and keep eating the juices.

"The fuck, Kent?" she murmurs. She kicks me in the shoulder, and I pull away. Her face twists into knots. "Are you seriously eating my pussy right now?"

I wipe the back of my mouth with my hand. "You liked it before—"

"That was different. This time, you—" Her lips quiver. Nothing comes out. Finally, she points a finger at me. "You raped me."

"Raped you?" I ask. "You're the one who wanted to be treated like livestock."

"I told you to let me go, and you didn't."

"I thought it was a rape fantasy," I say in a low voice, my tone snarling with mockery. "You said you had rape fantasies, remember?"

She bares her teeth, but she doesn't contradict me. She knows I'm right. She's the one who talked about her rape fantasies at our first dinner date. She should've anticipated I would do this. It's what she wanted, isn't it? For me to eat her. For me to treat her like my food. My livestock. My raised human meat.

"You're unbelievable, you fucking predator," she says as she backs away from me and bumps into the meat grinder. "One day, you're going to pay for it."

A grin spreads over my face. "A predator?"

All of this time, I've felt like Mona was the one luring me into her trap, and now, the rush of power in her accusation swims over me. Pride builds in my stomach, in my chest, in my shoulders. Puffing my insides. Making me taller. Bigger. Stronger than her. Me, on top of the food chain. Me, inspecting my meat. Me, the predator.

"You don't like it when you're not on top," I say, amusement in my tone. "You don't like it when *you're* the one who's captured, huh, little morsel?"

She shoves past me, then grabs her things off of the back porch and stomps to her SUV.

"Go fuck yourself," she shouts.

Her car door slams. I stand on the platform as she drives away. It's then that I notice the film camera—my gift—is still on the porch steps.

I pick it up and sigh. All of my life, every woman has ended up being the same condescending little cunt who thinks she's better than me. Who thinks she can walk all over me. Who thinks she can trap me in her spiderweb and suck me dry.

None of them realize that I'm the one who holds the true power.

I stare at the dark road. After I clear my head, I should go to Mona's next lecture and apologize. *I don't know what came over me,* I'll say. *I guess I was angry.* It'll be partially true; I am angry— fucking enraged—but I know what inspired it: her need to *pretend.*

Putting that aside, I don't want to end things like this. Maybe I'll tell her I was feeling insecure and return the gifted camera.

I should want her forgiveness too.

But there's an appeal in confronting her and realizing that

she's not going to forgive me, because she *wants* me to leave. Because she wants me to stay far, far away. Because she knows I'm the predator and she's my prey, about to die in my teeth.

And I like the way that feels.

CHAPTER 25

Armed with the one-time-use camera, I settle into the back row of the lecture hall. The class's start time passes, and as the minutes go by, the students' chattering gets louder. Mona isn't usually late.

Maybe she's late to class because of me.

Saliva pools in my mouth, like I'm waiting for the first taste of a giant feast. I like the idea of it: the bitch is so scared, she can't even come to class.

After the other night, I have to apologize. There's a chance she may never want to see me again, and I have to make it up to her.

I can't let her go like this.

A dark gray ponytail bounces down the aisle. A leather jacket swings on a man's shoulders. He spins around, his proud weathered smile gleaming at the students.

Artemis leans on the podium. "Professor Milk is hard at work on her new exhibition for Sway Gallery. I offered to cover for her today; I hope you all don't mind."

My chest compresses. Is her new exhibition actually that close, or is it an excuse because she knew I'd be here?

She's avoiding me, isn't she?

"I'm Artemis, but you can call me Arty," he says.

A student shouts: "Wait. Are you Arty Milk? Like the practical special effects artist who worked on *Hunting Sasquatch?* That Arty?"

He waves a hand in the air, dismissing the question with feigned sheepishness. "No one has forgotten about that shit show, have they?"

The classroom erupts into conversation, an energetic buzz floating in the air.

Artemis Milk, huh? Like they're fucking married.

I roll my eyes. His name sounded fake before, and now it sounds even *more* made up. Mona would never marry a lowlife like him. He must've stolen the name from her. And *Hunting Sasquatch?* So fucking what if it's a cult classic now? That movie bombed at the box office. They *lost* money on that piece of shit.

A few students raise their hands and ask Arty questions about the monsters and gore he's created over the years. I slouch in my chair and grind my teeth. Artemis substituting for Mona's lecture is a blow. She knew I'd be here, and this is like rubbing our non-exclusivity in my face. Just like my mother.

When my mother was going to run off with her boyfriend without me, she showed me how little she truly thought of me. Her only child.

If you could control your needy little tantrums, you'd get what you want. But you can't do that, can you? You're selfish, my mother said. *A spoiled rotten little boy who never stops whining about what he wants when he has more than enough. How much of a stupid, little boy can you be? Look at yourself!* She pointed to the knife in my hand. *You're making a sandwich out of ingredients that Daddy bought for you, and you want to complain about me leaving to go find him?*

I remember staring at the knife, then back at her. The bread was molding; I had to cut around the fuzzy blue spots. The cheese was as hard as plastic, and the meat smelled sour, but I knew if I wanted the stomach pains to go away, then I had to eat it. And deep down, I also knew she wasn't leaving to find him; she was leaving for good this time, and she would never come back. The home was empty without her boyfriend.

I wasn't good enough for her.

No wonder he left us, she hissed. *He takes care of us, feeds us, and does everything for us, and all you want to do is break us apart. Why can't you control yourself, Kent? Why can't you just be happy with what we've done for you? Why can't you be grateful for once? No, you have to ruin everything by being such a pathetic little freak.*

Thoughts rushed through my head; none of them were fully formed. They were more like bubbles floating in the air, each one of them popping as soon as they skimmed my fingertips. The only thoughts that stayed—that didn't evaporate as soon as I had them—were the memories of when her boyfriend, or Daddy as she so affectionately called him, *hurt* me.

Daddy kicking my ribs because I breathed too hard, while she pretended to be asleep.

Daddy forcing me to pretend to be happy at my tenth birthday as bruises healed on my neck.

Daddy knocking me out when I didn't eat the extra hot dog.

Did I have to be grateful for that too?

Anger simmered inside of me, threatening to boil over the edge.

He takes care of you, I said to her, putting extra emphasis on that last word. I tightened my hold on the knife's handle. *He told me he would be happier if I was dead.*

Maybe you should be dead, she said flatly. *You don't like living with us anyway.*

Those words were sharper than a knife, and I swear in that moment, I could've gutted myself and spilled my intestines on the floor, and my mother would've laughed.

My mother picked up her duffel bag, hiking it higher up on her shoulder. She angled toward the front door.

Panic rose inside of me, fighting with my inner rage. She couldn't really leave, could she? A mother is supposed to love you unconditionally. She gave me life. We were supposed to be connected beyond the umbilical cord. Why was she leaving me?

Please don't go, I said.

Control yourself, Kent, she muttered. *You really are pathetic sometimes.*

I tried to remind myself she liked her boyfriend because he was unafraid. Because he was strong. Because he had control.

Because he wasn't afraid to put us in our places. I tried to tell myself I could be like that too.

But it scared the shit out of me to be alone. I didn't know what to do.

Please, I begged. *I can't live without you.*

She spun around and faced me with the gleam of hatred in her eyes. She stepped forward.

You're going to die alone, baby boy, she mocked. *Sad and alone.*

She leaned down to my level to humiliate me more, so I thrust my fists forward to stop her. Her mouth dropped open, her eyes wide in shock. And that's when I realized I had stabbed her. So I did it again in the same spot. Then again. The first strike was an accident, but it didn't feel like I was doing anything wrong, so I kept doing it. It was like playing a video game, something I had seen her boyfriend play on the TV when I was supposed to be asleep, a game where your character can stab a civilian, and you don't feel any remorse, because it's not real. Nothing is.

My mother slumped to the ground, and my body buzzed with electricity. I stared down at her lifeless corpse. The vacant, dark blue eyes were the same in death as they were in life. Her gapped teeth. Her lipstick on, always on, always her crutch to get her boyfriend's attention, because he was more important than buying food for her own child.

The knife stood like a territorial flag in her stomach, the blood oozing onto the floor like a river.

I moved her onto the table. I don't know how I did that at ten years old. It might be that my memories are jumbled from everything that happened, but that's what I remember. The kitchen table. Her lifeless body. Her blank eyes. The knife in her stomach like a marker showing where the umbilical cord was cut, showing where she didn't feel anything for me, and where I no longer felt anything for her.

I didn't call the police. There was no reason to. She wasn't dead; it was pretend. She was used to playing pretend, wasn't she? She pretended to be my mother, and she pretended that she loved me. Why wouldn't she pretend to be dead too?

After that, I went back to the kitchen and made the rest of my sandwich. I told myself that stabbing her was an accident. I didn't mean to hurt her. I was just a boy, after all. It's not my fault that I was holding a knife when she came toward me. I was just trying to cut a slice of cheese for my sandwich. I was just hungry.

A few days passed in that hot house. Her boyfriend never liked having the air conditioning on unless *he* was home, which transformed the whole place into a living slow cooker. And the kitchen clock kept ticking. I guess I wasn't sad or angry or anything. My mother was home. She would wake up soon. Her boyfriend would be back too, and then I'd have to worry about what he would do to me when he saw her body. I couldn't even make myself care about that though.

Then her wound started rolling with maggots, the skin around the knife blooming into a sour green, and a gamey scent floated in the air, mixed with the feces expelled from her relaxed sphincter. And I was hungry. The deli meat was gone. The cheese and eggs too. There was some moldy bread left, and I could eat around it, but there was so much of her blue-tinted skin that didn't seem that bad. No, it even seemed *better* than the bread.

Her skin was blue and purple, and even green in some areas. I pulled the knife from her stomach, then stuck my fingers into the wound. Inside was slightly warm and sticky, and it wiggled. It was probably a maggot feeding on her. I had seen them eating rotten meat before. And if they could feed on her, why couldn't I?

While avoiding the living insects, I pinched what I could inside of that hole, and I pulled out red flesh. Damp. Metallic. I told myself that rotten meat is still nourishment. Maybe that's all I deserved anyway.

My stomach growled, and my muscles cramped so hard that it hurt to breathe.

I didn't see my mother after that.

I saw meat.

I put the flesh in my mouth. My stomach churned as the tangy flavor coated my tongue. I closed my eyes and swallowed it down. It was wrong, and I knew that, but I needed it more than she did.

And when I opened my eyes, I focused on her face. Her mouth was open, and inside, I saw that hunk of flesh. Her tongue.

I took the knife from her stomach and pinched the muscle, then cut off as much as I could. Then, without thinking much about it, I shoved her tongue in my mouth.

She couldn't talk now.

She couldn't tell me how pathetic I was.

And she would never leave me again.

Eventually, the police showed up, and when I heard the sirens, I grabbed some of her severed flesh and ran to the closet. Their footsteps got closer, and I knew I couldn't hold her meat anymore. They'd take her away from me. This was my last chance. I finally had her where I wanted, where she could take care of me, giving me unconditional love in the way a mother does best. Rotting meat probably wasn't a good idea for a growing boy, and to be honest, it made my stomach hurt, but it's not like she stocked the pantry when she left, and it would be wasting food if I threw her away.

Kent Baker? We just want to make sure you're safe, a female police officer said.

They were getting closer.

I stuffed the red flesh in my mouth, that metallic taste filling my cheeks. The meat was raw and rubbery.

But they couldn't take my mother away from me. She was already inside of me.

The officer opened the closet door. Her eyes widened. Blood coated my hands, my lips, and there were tiny pieces of flesh coating my naked body. She pulled back.

Jesus, she whispered. Sadness pooled in her eyes. *Are you alright?*

I salivated as I looked up at the police officer, wondering what she would taste like if I just cut off a piece of her stomach. If she was alive, if she was fresh, would she taste better than my mother?

Everything happened fast after that. I don't remember the rest of the police officers, the therapists, the judge, or the foster care system, but I do remember successfully avoiding them after a while.

"That's it for now," Artemis says. I shake myself out of the memories as he clears his throat. "Are there any questions?"

Mona had asked me if I killed my mother, and it was obvious

she had a hunch about the answer. But it's hard to explain that when you're ten years old, the judicial system doesn't see the full scope of your potential: they only see a child. So did I kill her? Maybe I did. Maybe it was my intention. Or maybe it was an accident. I can't go back and change what happened twenty years ago, but I can admit that now, when I think about it, I wish I hadn't just stabbed my mother. I wish I had kept her alive for a long time, slowly eating her alive as her body shut down.

I wish I had hurt her more.

The students rise from their seats and head toward the doors, while a few stragglers head to the front of the classroom to gawk at the supposedly famous Arty Milk. I stand behind them and wait for Artemis to meet my gaze. He avoids me so wholeheartedly it's obvious he knows I'm here for him. I just have to wait for my turn.

Then the last student comes closer to him, and he gestures toward the door. The two of them walk out together.

I hold the one-time-use camera up and take a picture. The cheap shutter clicks, and finally, Artemis scowls at me.

With bared teeth, I wave, then exit too. For now, Artemis is safe. I'm not interested in eating men. I'll kill a man if I want to, but I won't *eat* him. I'd rather use his meat to fuel a fire. There's no satisfaction in consuming tough meat like that.

With women though—with Mona—there's something unworldly about their soft flesh. Their lips. Their pliable stomachs. Their fatty breasts. I can cut off any piece of a woman and show her that she may not need me, and that's okay.

But I can still fucking eat her.

CHAPTER 26

IN THE EVENING, I PARK DOWN THE STREET AND WALK THROUGH the neighborhood to Mona's house. I think about hiding in her backyard again, but that seems stupid. I don't want to scare her. I'm not a stalker, and I'm definitely not a threat—not like she probably thinks—but I do want to apologize and give her the one-time-use camera. It was a gift, after all. It'd be wasted on me.

As I near the house, I run a hand over my face. Maybe I lied. Maybe I do want *more* than to apologize; maybe I also want to confront her for treating me like shit the other night and for calling me a rapist.

I also want to make things right. It's what I'm supposed to do.

When I finally get to her house, there are two cars in the driveway: Artemis's electric vehicle and another similar car.

My shoulders stiffen; if there are people here, then there's only so much I can say. I don't let it stop me though; I keep going up the driveway. This doesn't have to be more than a conversation. We can have make-up sex later.

I knock.

She doesn't answer.

I knock again, this time harder, and I don't stop banging until the door swings open.

Artemis stands in front of me. A loose shirt hangs on his body, but his usual jacket is missing. He shifts his weight to the side. There's a comfort to his stance, like he belongs here. Like this is his house.

Are they actually married, then? How could I have missed that? How could I have been so stupid this entire time?

No, no, no. I'm not stupid.

She fucking tricked me…for her art.

"What do you want?" Artemis asks.

He's not a threat, I remind myself. *And he's not her husband. He's probably just fucking Mona, and they have some sort of artistic pact to use the same last name together. Milk is a stage surname. A brand they've created for their mutual benefit.*

And he's not *a fucking threat.*

I scratch the back of my neck, doing my best to appear casual.

"Hey, Artemis," I say. I lift the camera. "I was just stopping by. Mona forgot this, and I need to talk to her—"

"She's not home right now."

Laughter echoes through the house. I lean to the side, looking around Artemis. Two people—a man with a shaved head and a woman with brown hair—sit close to one another, facing someone on the opposite side of a coffee table.

Someone. A person I can't see.

I know it's her.

Mona *is* here.

I pinch my lips together. Artemis is more likely to give me what I want if he thinks I'm harmless. I force the tension out of my posture and slump my shoulders.

"When will she be back?" I ask quietly.

"I'm not sure."

"Are you house sitting for her or something?" I ask, frustration leaking into my tone. I release a breath forcefully. "Are you having a threesome in *her* bed?"

"It's none of your business, is it?" Artemis says, his mouth tight. He presses forward into my space. "She doesn't want to see you."

"I need to fucking talk to her, all right?" I snap. I grip the camera. My guts are so twisted, I want to smash the fucking thing into his skull to see what the pretty boy does. "After what we've been through, I think I deserve a conversation with her."

Artemis runs a hand over his face. "First, you broke Lexi's phone, and now you're acting like you're going to break Mona's camera too."

I squint my eyes. Lexi? Is that the girl who was recording me at the processing plant?

"I knew this wasn't a good idea," Artemis says. "I told Mona it was dangerous working with someone like you. I even told Desire to find justice another way, but Mona kept pushing her, and *you* are obsessed." His shoulders twitch with discomfort. "You and Mona are done. You got that? You were only an art project to her. My wife wants nothing to do with you anymore."

Wife? So it's true then. The rejection is a fire burning through every cell in my body.

She sucked my dick in the theater like she was hungry for it.

She invited me over for a threesome.

She even gave me her fingertips and toes like she was desperate for me to have her.

She acted like she needed me to understand her.

She didn't tell me she's married.

How can she be married to someone like him?

How can she ignore me when I've done so much for her?

The couple from the processing plant glance toward the front door, and Artemis steps in front of me so I can't see inside the house anymore. I can feel it in my bones though: Mona is in the house, chatting with her house guests, pretending like I'm a *thing* from her past. Like I don't actually exist. The bitch ran away from me to be with her wimpy husband, and now I'm the whiny little boy she can't seem to get rid of.

I'm being ignored. Neglected. *Abandoned.* I'd rather she stab my chest than refuse to talk to me.

The rejection *hurts.*

"Have a good night, Kent," Artemis says. "Be careful out there."

I open my mouth to retort, but the door slams shut, and the porch light goes out, leaving me alone in the darkness. I stand there for a while, waiting for Mona to appear. To check and see if I'm still there. To explain that Artemis was joking. To take it all back.

None of that happens.

Eventually, I walk back to my van. Instead of going straight home, I drive past the processing plant to see who is working.

Jerry's car is parked outside.

If the supervisor is off duty, Jerry will let me in. With a man of Artemis's size, I can easily fit him into one of the furnaces, and then his meat won't be wasted. It will be fuel for the fire. I can live with that.

I'm not a killer though. Incinerating Artemis's body is only a fantasy. I think about things a lot, but I'd never do something like that on purpose. With my mother, it was an accident.

And I really hope another accident like that doesn't happen again.

CHAPTER 27

DAYS PASS, AND THEN WITH A QUICK INTERNET SEARCH, I KNOW
it's the opening day of Mona's exhibit. I have to see her, and that
comes with seeing her art.

The event listing on my phone states that the exhibition is
simply titled *Cannibalism*. There's no fluff around it, and that's
something I can appreciate.

My heart pumps at a steady pace while I stand on the opposite
side of the street, just like the last time, when Mona and I first
met. Guests walk in and out of the entrance to Sway Gallery.
Each person has their jaws open and their lips curved, like they're
haunted but intrigued too. The giant windows facing the street
glow like an aquarium. I scan the glass for Mona.

Champagne flutes on trays. Gourmet snacks in cupped hands.
Gaping mouths and sharp fingers. Mixed ages. No woman with
black hair, pale skin, and black clothes.

Mona isn't visible from here.

Last time, she was waiting in the bathtub for me. This time, I
doubt she'll be in the bathtub, and yet a part of me hopes she is.
Maybe we can start over. This time, I'll do it right. Just me and
her. Me, her, and the bathwater boiling the two of us alive.

Her husband claims that she doesn't want to see me. What if

he's lying in some misguided attempt to protect her? What if he's jealous of what we have?

And after all we've done together, what kind of person would I be if I didn't see her art for myself?

I'd be a stupid little boy. A pathetic child.

And I'm not stupid or pathetic.

Inside the gallery, I head toward the bathroom. Before I get there, I immediately stop in my tracks. My jaw drops, my pulse narrowing around my windpipe.

A pig's heart floats inside of a jar, suspended in liquid, and a light emanates from the bottom of the container. The backside of the jar is decorated with the picture of the old woman, the one Mona took from my wall, and that picture is surrounded by tiny photographs of me. My eyes scratched out with black ink. Blood on my face. My teeth bared and open, chewing on what I know are her toes.

The cannibal eats the mother, the caption reads.

The news articles didn't use my real name in order to protect me—a young boy at the time—from the public. How does she know what I did to my mother?

She doesn't know though. She *can't.* Mona is making assumptions about me.

I take in everything around me. There are photographs of us *everywhere* with our faces obscured. But in most of them, there's no Mona. It's just me.

I'm her main inspiration.

My gut spirals into knots. Why does that make me so uneasy now?

On the far wall, the film collage from our private screening plays, but now, the footage is spliced with video clips of me fucking her as I chew her toes.

As I draw closer to the main wall, the focal point of the entire gallery, my back crawls with invisible insects. In the giant black-and-white photograph, my eyes are scribbled over again. Red paint, what I assume is meant to represent blood, is fingerpainted over my hands, my skin, and my lips. A chill runs over me, clammy against my skin, as I read the photograph's caption: *You'd become a part of me.*

Next to the main wall, a silver platter holds tiny, flat sculptures painted a dull pink. I squint my eyes and realize it's fingertips. The platter has been arranged like a charcuterie board serving slices of hand.

A stranger reaches over me and takes a fingertip from the platter.

"Oh! She must've used tofu," the person says. She pops it in her mouth. "Hmm. It tastes good! Extra firm, maybe?"

Another man takes a slice from the platter and chews on it methodically. "No, dear. This is definitely pork."

I gawk at them, my stomach churning as everything spins around me. I scrutinize the charcuterie board. The silvery edge is decorated with red, delicate cursive: *You want your meat to melt in my mouth, don't you?*

I said that, didn't I?

Sweat beads over my skin.

What if she never actually fed me her fingertips?

No. That can't be. It can't—

Nausea wages a war inside of me, my stomach threatening to expel everything it contains. Instantly I'm small, so fucking small, as I stand there in the middle of the gallery, in a place where I don't belong. Strangers gawk at the pictures, at the sculptures, at the pig's heart in the glass, at the video clips of me, and it's like they're laughing at me. Me, the cannibal who thought he finally found the one. Me, the cannibal who was willing to do anything for her. Me, the pathetic little boy who risked it all for someone he thought loved him.

My mother's voice echoes in my head: *How much of a stupid little boy can you be?*

I'm not stupid.

There's an explanation for this. There has to be.

Another small display on top of a pedestal draws me in. The column is decorated with pictures of me, each frame slightly different, all of them with me covered in pig's blood from the night I told Mona that we were going too far, the night I tried to stop us. On top of the pedestal, a blue velvet box holds two bloody toes and red paper towels, an exact replica of the ones she gave me. Underneath it, the red caption reads: *And without your leg, you won't be able to run away from me.*

Then I notice the small table next to the pedestal. A platter, similar to the one with the charcuterie slivers, holds a horde of matching toes, each of them with painted red toenails.

A young man takes one, flinging it in his mouth like finger food. She made *hors d'oeuvres?* Is that all this is? Themed snacks?

Or is she making fun of me?

My chest clenches. I can't stop staring at the art. Another pedestal displays small squares of toast with dark red jelly. It's difficult to focus on the inscription, but I scrutinize the words until I can read it: *I could eat you on toast.*

Then I study a picture of us outside of her pool: Mona is naked with the apple in her mouth, and her stomach obscures the view of my genitals, but it's clear that my head is tilted back in orgasm. The caption reads: *What if we eat people together?*

I said that to her in private. I could have told her I love her like a normal person, but eating people together means more to me than love. It was my best attempt at a commitment.

I feel so fucking used.

As I reach the back corner of the room, I find a picture on the wall of Mona standing next to the woman who accused me of rape that one day on the university campus. The caption reads: *A special thanks to my inspiration, Desire, who goes by that alias for anonymity. I deeply appreciate her for sharing her story with me for this project.*

I wrinkle my brow. What the fuck does Desire have to do with this?

Underneath that picture, there's a black plaque with white text. Her artist statement. I read it.

Cannibalism, or the dehumanization of us.

What's left after a cannibal has consumed what he wants of her meat? Unfavorable scraps. Rotting flesh. Bones. Feces.

Eating human flesh isn't the only time we transform each other into consumable objects. Labor. Family. Sex. Rape. Romance. Even friendship.

Every human interaction has a power dynamic where the subject consumes and the object is consumed. The truth is that all humans are capable of canni-balism. We consume each other each and every day.

Once we honestly accept that and make changes to respect one another, we can begin to live fuller lives with our fellow humans.

And if we don't accept this, we face the consequences of consuming humanity and being devoured ourselves.

Laughter erupts, breaking into my consciousness. My scalp tingles as if knives are pricking holes into my skull. I can sense her there before I even see her.

We instantly lock eyes.

Mona smirks, then tucks hair behind her ears. Her hands are completely exposed. Her fingers pale and unscarred. Her red toenails peek out of her open-toe stilettos.

All ten fingertips and all ten toes are intact.

She dismisses her entourage. My chest pounds, drumming in my ears. I ball my fists and imagine her neck in my hands, where I squeeze so hard, her brain bursts like a water balloon, the flesh and blood splattering her shitty art and ruining everything around her. Even me.

"I was hoping you'd make it," she says.

She looks up into my eyes, challenging me. Even though I'm twice her size. Even though she knows I can kill her. Her lips curl at the ends, her permanent smugness digging a deep pit inside of my stomach.

If I reached out, I could touch her tits. I could rip her fucking nipples off and show her adoring fans what it's like to eat a bitch raw.

I grit my teeth, willing myself to be so angry that I kill her on the spot.

But the truth is I can't do that. My body is weak. Heavy. Useless.

"You didn't actually cut off your toes," I choke out. "Did you?"

"Come on, Kent." She tosses her head back in laughter. "Artemis's skills were a big help with all of this, but it was only an artistic experiment. You knew that."

Rage boils inside of me, and blood rushes in my ears. I see the eyes: guests, onlookers, art collectors, servers. Everyone watching us as they eat their fake fingertips and toes.

No, I didn't know it was a fucking experiment.

"You lied," I say. "You used me!"

She rolls her eyes. "You signed a contract."

That contract mentioned her art project. It went into detail. It said something about not giving me money out of the final profits. I kept getting stuck on the fact that it was about cannibalism though.

Did I miss that it was an experiment? That her husband was going to create fake, edible body parts for me to consume? Did I miss all of that because I was too fucking horny to read every detail?

Is this *my* fault?

I don't care who is watching or listening to us anymore. I raise my arms. "I didn't know what I was signing!"

"And you could've taken the time to read it. You even took the contract home with you, remember? But you didn't read it carefully." She lifts her nose. "I was completely up front in that contract. I even asked if you wanted a copy. Maybe next time, you'll be more careful before you agree to something where you don't understand the consequences."

Everything blurs around me. I'm hyperfixated on Mona. She's the center of a volcano, a natural, deadly force pulling me into its molten core.

Then an image flickers inside of my head: that woman from the university. The one that accused me of raping her. She was tied to the cage. Her tit was bleeding. Steak juices dripped down my face.

Is Mona talking about Desire?

Is she trying to say Desire didn't know the consequences of sleeping with me?

Mona cracks her neck, her eyelids languid like this is a bore to her. I imagine her head on a cutting board, my dick fucking the backside of her esophagus until my shaft tears through her throat and slides over her tastebuds.

I've always dreamed of being the hunter. The one who

provides, the one who feeds, the one who kills, the one who enjoys flesh. And with Mona, I thought I had that. I thought we could be together. Hunter and prey. The perfect match.

But instead, she hunted me.

I dig my nails into the palms of my hands, the pain scorching my flesh. "And the processing plant with the woman recording me?"

"That was all Artemis." She winks over her shoulder. That couple—the shaved-headed man and the plain, brown-haired woman—stand next to Artemis. "I didn't see the point in aggravating you in a place where you couldn't explore your sexual needs, but he insisted we record the whole thing. It was supposed to be evidence for the police or something. I guess he wanted to prove to me that you're dangerous."

Artemis wanted me to blow up like a cannon to put me in jail, but Mona knew I would need to let off steam after an event like that, didn't she? She used that opportunity to sneak into my home and tease me with the pig's blood, assuming I would be in an agitated state.

And I had felt guilty for fantasizing about killing the brown-haired bitch—a complete no one—instead of Mona, the woman of my dreams.

"Anyway, that's why I told Desire to confront you herself. It was part of her full arc, you know? Victim becomes survivor. You can't just *consume* a sex worker and flush away the trauma you caused her. You know that, right?"

A million images run through my mind, but I can't shake the memories of cutting Desire's breast as she bled and cried for me to stop.

Maybe I did rape her. I didn't kill her though. I wanted to, but I didn't.

I didn't kill her.

I didn't.

I didn't—

"You lying, scheming bitch," I mutter, spit foaming at the corners of my mouth.

"I never lied to you," Mona says emphatically. "I did what I had to do in order to prove a point. You were willing to literally eat me, Kent." She lowers her chin, and even though I'm towering over her, it's like she's looking down on me somehow. "Honestly, you should be locked up. Who knows what else you're capable of."

Artemis steps forward. He shows me his phone: *9-1-1* illuminated in bright numbers on the screen. His finger is lifted, ready to call for help.

How am I the fucking threat when I never actually ate her meat? When I never actually hurt her? How am I the fucking threat when I was the one who was lied to and manipulated?

And why does it feel like she's pulling out *my* intestines right now? She's basically gored me like an animal, and now I'm stuck on my hands and knees, picking up the last pieces of my soul.

"Did you even want to be eaten?" I whisper.

"Oh, Kent." She chuckles, and my spine tightens. Her tongue slithers over her teeth. "When Desire first told me about what you wanted to do to her, I was fascinated. Honestly, I was. I watched every video and read every article I could find. But did it *arouse* me? Intellectually, yes. Sexually, no." She clicks her tongue, then her lips peel back in a sneer. "I simply wanted to prove how a sexual predator is willing to dehumanize his prey for his own selfish gain."

The lights inside of my mind go dark, and it's hard to see anything besides Mona. On the surface, it sounds like she's using her art to do something good for society, but there's this raw, nagging sensation at the back of my throat, and I can't let it go.

She used Desire, that shaved-headed man, and that brown-haired woman. She even used Artemis, and fuck, she used me. For fuck's sake, Mona used *all* of us as stepping stones to gain notoriety in the art world. She's stepping on *me* to lift herself up, and not once has she mentioned anywhere in this exhibit how much I did for her. That I watched her film collage. That I participated in her threesome. That I ate her fake flesh. That I got her a wheelchair.

Not once has she mentioned that I fucking worshipped her.

"So cannibalism is supposed to represent dehumanization?" I

scream. I jab at the black plaque with her artist statement. "You used all of us! Everyone is dehumanized in your art!"

The gallery falls silent.

Artemis steps forward, his shoulders hunched and bracing for impact, like he can actually take me.

I growl at him, then face Mona again. "You don't care about sex workers," I say. "You don't care about Desire. You don't care about any of us."

"You're right," Mona says. "I don't care." She purses her lips, then dismisses me with a flick of her hand. "It was nice seeing you, Kent. Thanks for helping me with this little project."

Artemis heads toward me, and though I want to stand my ground and not move a damn inch, everyone in the gallery is watching me right now, studying the photographs of my obscured face and piecing it together. A man even puts his arm around his date's shoulder and pulls her closer to him, as if I'll break out of my human skin and attack her like a beast. I may have killed before, but I'm not a killer. I wouldn't do that to some stranger, and definitely not in a place like this.

And I still don't belong here.

Before Artemis can force me to leave, I head toward the exit. My heart pumps with rushing blood, and each muscle contraction is another step toward that abyss. Maybe the best revenge is to be a better person and *not* harm anyone, like everyone seems to think I will.

The night air swallows me, and I suck in, and in, and in.

But I can barely breathe.

There's so much I can do to be a good person. None of it sits right with me though.

Maybe I'm not a good person after all.

CHAPTER 28

INSIDE OF THE MOBILE HOME, I STARE AT THE PREVIOUS occupant's items. Photographs. Dust. Old furniture. The place is filled with another person's life. A widowed husband maybe or an outcast like me. No one abandons a good home like this in California, but I didn't kill him. He was practically dead already. I admit I got rid of the body, but he didn't move for days, and besides, he hardly even flinched when I chopped him up into smaller pieces. At least then, his carcass became fuel for the furnace at the processing plant.

I don't like telling anyone about him because I know what I did was against the law, but I didn't *hurt* anyone. He was already a corpse.

As I scan the area, *dehumanization* echoes in my brain. In the end, every person needs to live, fuck, and eat. Who can judge me if I make a home in an abandoned place? If I make sure there is nothing being wasted, whether it's a corpse or offal? If I search for sexual fulfillment with someone who knows about—and agrees with!—my particular fetish?

My neck itches, and though I scratch my skin, nothing satiates that burrowing ache.

I could find a nice slab of raw beef or dial the escort company. Both options would get me off, but after tasting what cannibalism *could* be, after being ridiculed and abandoned like a fucking rat, I know myself. I'd take out my frustrations on a sex worker, and if that happens, I won't be able to stop. Even if I ate her afterward, killing a stranger—or even two of them—won't satiate me right now.

Another option is to go to town and pick someone off the street. A flash of cash, and I can tell the bitch I want her to take a shower before we fuck. That's a normal request for something like that. And out here in the fields, I can isolate her. I can feed off of her until she dies.

But I don't want just anyone.

One day, there will be time to fill my appetite with beautiful women who fall for my good looks and awkward charm. Right now though, there's only one piece of meat I want, and I refuse to let her go. I need her, and even more importantly, I need *this*.

Mona Milk.

Maybe I am a cannibal. Maybe I'm not. After everything she's done to me, one thing is certain: I have to take back control. I can't leave it like this.

And I can't let her go.

Out the window, the grass sways with the breeze, like people drifting back and forth across the art gallery, whispering to each other as they mock me. I'm an animal in a cage, and Mona is the key to my confinement.

I tap my chin. The tall grass shifts, probably from a rabbit hiding behind the blades. Mona is high profile. People watch her. Wait on her. And then there's the problem of Artemis. He works on movies. How can I explain their disappearances?

I tense my muscles as hard as I can until my whole body vibrates, then I pace the house and wrack my mind for a plan.

Finally, I zero in on an old book, another remnant of the last occupant. He fit in the furnace at the processing plant. Why couldn't I fit Artemis inside of the furnace too?

I rip a weathered page out of the book. I grab the bucket from the fridge and dip my fork inside of the liquid. There's not a lot of pig's blood left, but there's enough to write. I use my opposite hand to distort my handwriting.

Artist Statement, I write. *Guilt due to my betrayal of—*

I hold the fork in the air. I could write my name, but then people will draw connections, and after I capture her, we'll need to disappear. I can't have them chasing after us, at least not until after I leave the state.

—the inspiration, I write, *has overwhelmed me. I should never have misled and used so many people for my art.*

The cold blood is thick and doesn't spread easily, and at the same time, the tines of the fork seem to dance across the pages, like the ink is sparkling with violence. No wonder she loved using pig's blood in her artistic experiment.

I write the final lines.

Thus, I need time to reflect on the next stages of my art.

Signed, Mona Milk.

I toss the fork in the sink and let the pages dry. Maybe Mona is right. Maybe I should have been more aware. Maybe it was my fault for not reading every line in that forty-page contract. Or maybe she gave me such a short time to read it because she knew I would never agree to it if I read it thoroughly. Either way, I let myself get too wrapped up in the hope of finally getting what I wanted. In my mind, I was her sole inspiration, and I let that flattery distort my vision.

That won't happen again.

In an hour, the blood is dry. I jump in my van and drive to her neighborhood. I park down the street, then walk to her house like I've done so many times before.

From behind the elephant ear plant, I can see through the sliding door to the kitchen. Mona is absent—probably at her exhibition, luring unsuspecting people with her sultry aura—but Artemis is singing as he stirs a pot on the stove.

I'll need to text Jerry. We'll hang out once or twice, and I'll be on his good side. I need access to the processing plant, and he's the best way to get in there.

It'll take time, but eventually, I'll get what I want.

I'll control myself.

I always do.

CHAPTER 29

ARTEMIS'S PATTERN IS SIMPLE. IT ONLY TAKES A WEEK TO FIGURE IT out. When he's not working on a movie, he ambles between the university, Mona's studio, and an old movie theater downtown. The idiot is fixated on his habits, and that makes it easier for me.

In the meantime, I gather my supplies, which includes a new cage: a bigger version of the one I used with the sex worker. This metal enclosure is large enough for Mona to comfortably crawl around in, as well as lie down in, but not tall enough for her to stand up. It's completely flexible too; it can open up on all sides. The infinite possibilities inspire me and keep me going, but before I can use it on my morsel, I have to take care of her husband.

Not many people—besides special effects artists reliving their glory years—come to this particular movie theater. So when the chosen day finally comes, the parking garage is nearly empty. A car here. A truck there. Empty spaces. Then an electric vehicle.

I park my van in the corner of the structure, a few spots away from Artemis's car. There's enough space between our cars he won't think twice about it.

I'm ready.

Artemis turns the corner; his footsteps tap across the cement. I pull the van out of the parking space, then change my angle until the headlights surround him.

He hits the key fob; his car beeps, and the lights flash. I drive. His eyes widen, a scared little deer in literal headlights, and his mouth opens in shock.

My ears are throbbing. I don't hear him scream.

His body thuds against the car. I jump out.

The puny sonofabitch lies on the ground, cradling his head and moaning like a heifer. The idiot can't move. I wasn't driving fast, but it was enough.

And the rest is so easy now.

I pull him into the van's cargo bay, then I find his phone, power it off, and stow it in my pocket. He's so distracted by the pain he doesn't even fight me.

I drive as fast as I can back to the fields. No one will see us there.

I turn onto the two-lane highway. The landfill's hill looms in the distance, and the back of the van rattles with yelps. I turn down the radio and listen carefully to his muffled words.

"What the fuck, Kent?" he screeches. The asshole must've found some sudden strength to be able to scream so loud. "You can't do this—"

My chest expands, my fingertips tingling under the gloves. I doubt he can hear me, but I say it anyway: "But I *am* doing this."

The asphalt becomes dirt, and the rooster continues to squawk like it can hurt me. It's just like Artemis to think that words hold any power.

Words can't save him. Words don't mean anything.

"That was always your problem," I say. The van rolls to a stop, and I go around to the locked doors at the rear of the vehicle. The pathetic idiot bangs on the doors. I hold the handles. I don't release the locks yet. "You think you can fight me with your big ideas, but do you think a monster will stop if you say 'please'?"

My laughter booms out, and for a second, Artemis's temper tantrum stops. I imagine him behind the metal doors, cowering in a fetal position while the fear courses through his nerves.

"You hear that, motherfucker?" I scream. I whack my fists into the van. "I control everything here."

I open the doors to the cargo bay. A fist immediately hits my face. It's weak though, like a toddler's attempt at fighting. Either the car crash is still working against him, or he's just as scrawny as he seems.

Another wimpy punch, and the idiot rolls onto the dirt like a tumbleweed. He scans his surroundings for an escape.

I pull out my knife.

He jets off, but his foot immediately catches on the outer edge of the offal pit, and he slams into the hard ground.

I stab the knife into the back of his calf and pin him in place like a housefly on a mounting board. Artemis howls, and I smirk at my own thoughts. He is a housefly, isn't he? A nuisance buzzing around where he doesn't belong. An insect like that belongs outside, where it can find a home in the offal pit.

Even the offal pit is too good for Artemis though.

His wailing agony vibrates through me, the heady rush of invincibility going straight to my dick. My shaft is half hard, not because I want to fuck him, but because of how good it feels to finally do this. I don't know why it took me so long. I've been dreaming of killing him since I first saw him at Mona's house, and now, the cock block can't stop what me and Mona have.

Had.

What we had.

Mona and I are different now. I'm adapting, and this is what I want.

Artemis rolls around, then reaches for his phone, but it's gone, and I grin. His eyes fill with panic as he realizes this is where he dies. I snatch the knife from his calf, then stab the other leg. Blood soaks through his pants and mixes with the dirt. It'll be hard for him to run now, and that makes me smile.

I grab his ankles and drag him to the industrial meat grinder. I slap handcuffs on his wrists, restraining his hands behind his back, then I grab his ponytail, and his whiny yelps fill the air.

We make it to the top of the platform, right by the hopper. My elbow flicks the power switch. The machine buzzes to life, the metal parts singing in their shrill cries. Artemis twists like a chicken right before you snap its neck on the factory line. I tighten my hold, and the stringy meat sack can't do anything now. I'm stronger. I always have been.

I fist his ponytail. "She's all mine now."

Then I shove his head into the hopper and keep him in place. His body convulses, fighting back, and he screams. Oh, fuck, he screams like it'll save him, and it's good, so fucking good, that my entire body buzzes with pleasure. I press him in farther, to the shoulders, then the chest, shoving him in deep enough that he actually hits the blades. The pressure mounts, and I press my entire weight against him—

The machine stops.

His bones or hair must've gotten caught in the plates.

I crack my neck. This is irritating.

Then I realize Artemis is quiet too, and those annoyances float away.

I pull on his torso, but it doesn't budge. His body is stuck in the machine. I wrap my arms around his stomach, then wrench the corpse with all of my might until we both tumble back, smacking down the steps to the ground. The wind is knocked from my lungs, and I wheeze, my body instantly sore everywhere.

Once I catch my breath, I sit up, and I see it.

Artemis's hair is disheveled, resembling a bird's nest, but the ponytail keeps his hair together. Blood drips down his face, and the top corner of Artemis's forehead is gone, the grayish-brown glossy surface of his brain exposed. His blank eyes stare straight ahead, no longer able to see anything.

I sway, dizzy with giddiness. After every time he tried to fuck with me, after every time he doubted me, after every time he tried to take what was mine, the world is right again.

Artemis is dead.

After stripping the corpse naked, I hastily cut off parts of his calf and thighs—the thickest parts of his body—and I even cut off his dick.

I also power down the grinder. It takes a few minutes to carefully clean the machine. Soon, it whirs with purpose again, and I add the chunks of his body into the hopper. Pride finds its way into my chest, puffing me up to my true size. Artemis doubted me, and now, he's where he belongs.

Mona probably still doubts me. That won't last much longer though.

I text Jerry a simple *Hey* before I go back to storing the ground meat in a container. I need to work quickly before Mona notices her husband is missing.

Two handfuls of meat later, my phone buzzes.

What's up, man? Jerry sends.

My gloved fingers slide over the screen, slippery with blood and mangled flesh. The words are visible through the thin, pink liquid. *I need a favor at the plant,* I type. *Is the supervisor there? Can you let me in?*

The asshole is on vacation, he sends. *Head this way.*

Another hour passes. I work fast. I dismember the rest of the body, store the ground meat, destroy the idiot's phone, bury the pieces, and collect the rest of the incriminating evidence. I even take a shower.

Finally, I head over to meet Jerry.

I park at the back entrance of the processing plant. Several black, heavy-duty garbage bags dangle from my fists. Smaller chunks make for easier disposal, and these garbage bags are top-notch. No leaks. No weaknesses. They're small in size, but they're heavier than you'd think. Human flesh is dense, I guess.

Jerry waves me inside, then wrinkles his nose at the bags. "What is it?"

"I bought extra offal from the butcher, and it went bad." I shrug my shoulders. "I gotta get rid of it."

"I thought it's better when it ferments? Those side effects, right?"

"Not this batch."

Jerry nods, then clears his throat. I clench my teeth. There's an uneasiness on his face as he studies me, like he suspects something is wrong.

"Are you okay, man?" he asks. "You look like you're high or something."

I can't help it; I beam at him. Even an unassuming person like

Jerry can see the adrenaline working magic in my veins, the power growing inside of me, spreading through me like a miracle food.

"Nah," I say. "I'm just finally getting the life I've always wanted."

Jerry nods again and watches me heave the bags into the furnace. His face is whiter by the second. He's seen me discard toxic waste before, but by the weight and size of the bags, it's obvious that he can tell that this—whatever is in my bags—is different. But the funny thing about someone like Jerry is that by the time he works up the courage to tell the supervisor about letting me in, there's a good chance that Artemis's body will be completely gone. There will be *nothing* left, not even ash.

Outside, we stop by my van. I grab the container from the front seat.

"I brought you the good stuff," I say. I hand him the ground meat. "Just wanted to say thanks, man."

Jerry flinches. He glosses over the van, then fixates on something. I wonder if he sees evidence of Artemis. If I missed something during clean-up.

It doesn't matter though. Jerry won't do shit.

He turns his head. "Don't mention it."

We shake hands. Once I'm alone in the van, I sigh with relief. I should've gotten rid of Artemis a hell of a lot sooner, but now I'm one step closer to getting what I truly want.

Artemis's head is still in the mobile home. I don't know if my mother or the mobile home's previous occupant count, but Artemis's death definitely deserves a prize. Depending on how you look at it, I figure his head is like a trophy of either my second or third kill.

And now, I can collect Mona.

CHAPTER 30

EVENING COMES. I DRIVE TO MONA'S HOUSE, AND THIS TIME, I park in her driveway. My whole body buzzes with adrenaline. I wait a few minutes to see if she'll check who's out here.

The cocky little bitch never comes.

I get out of the car and find my usual hiding spot in her backyard. She walks across the kitchen, her phone tucked between her shoulder and her ear. She laughs into the receiver. She's probably manipulating her newest inspiration right now.

I step out from behind the plant. I'm a looming shadow. A predator stalking her from a distance.

She doesn't notice me.

Irritation flares under my skin. She doesn't notice me, because in her mind, I'm insignificant. I'm nothing more than a stupid little boy she used for her art. She'll learn though. She'll have to, or this won't be pleasant for her. And it's almost funny. She's so absorbed in her own world that she doesn't know I'm watching, listening, and hunting her.

Imagine being that self-absorbed.

She clicks off her phone, then walks up the stairs. My dick hardens. The sliding glass door is quiet as I open it. It seems like a waste to be this silent, but I need to get her to the mobile home discreetly. There will be plenty of time to make her fight and struggle and cry. I've got so much more planned for us.

After dropping the fake Artist Statement on her kitchen counter, I pull the syringe from my pocket and tap the needle. Then I hide around the corner of the stairway and hold my breath.

She glides down the stairs, not at all worried that someone or something may be lurking in the shadows, and before she realizes I'm there, I plunge the needle into her neck.

Her eyes lock on mine, and in a second, I see it: the recognition, the hatred, the *terror*. Her wide pupils bare it all, and I know that finally, she understands she's the prey this time.

I've finally caught her.

She crumbles, and like a good human farmer, I catch my meat to prevent bruising. Her warm body hums with energy, and my dick wets my boxers, the pre-cum soaking through my pants. I suck in her musky scent, and my mind is at ease for the first time since Artemis caught us fucking in her office.

I set her down on the floor, then scout the rooms for her laptop. As I'm searching, it occurs to me that I don't see her vintage wheelchair anywhere; Artemis must have gotten rid of it. But then I find her laptop and calm myself with the knowledge that Mona won't need a wheelchair in a cage. With the computer, I book a vacation for her and her husband. I even pack two suitcases, including Mona's powered-off phone, and load them into the back of the van. Even if Jerry doesn't let me get rid of the suitcases in the furnace, I can get rid of them myself. The dump is close to the mobile home. The suitcases are the least of my worries.

Then, once everything is ready for her long-term absence, I cradle Mona in my arms as if she's a baby, and in a way, she is. She's my meaty baby. My pretty piggy. My little morsel. I place her in the cargo bay with the suitcases. Cable ties secure her wrists and ankles, and I briefly consider gagging her. The sedative should work until we get to the fields though, and by then, I *want* her to scream.

I shut the van's back doors, then whistle as I get into the

driver's seat. Mona will be on my kitchen table soon, in the same position as my mother, but for now, my little morsel is alive, waiting for me to feast on her. And though I can't stand the idea of someone like her teaching me anything, I can admit she's taught me a few things: You can't force a woman to agree to be your meat, just like you can't force a mother to love you.

But you can take what's yours and show the meat hole exactly who will be eating their flesh.

Whether they like it or not.

CHAPTER 31

AND JUST LIKE THAT, IN A SURPRISINGLY EASY FASHION, MONA LIES naked inside of the cage, right next to my bed. The cable ties are gone, her legs are spread, and the top of the structure is open. There's still sedative in her veins, but it'll run out eventually.

As I gaze down at those pretty pink pussy lips, my mouth salivates. I always knew I'd eat them first.

I step into an empty spot of the cage, then settle myself between her legs. I stretch her labia away from her, pulling the skin taut. The cravings are too strong for me to properly sew her up for extended harvesting, so I need to keep the piece small.

Besides, I only want a taste.

I zone in on the slice I want and cut; the knife melts through her skin like butter. Her body twitches, her nerves gradually becoming alert. It's no bigger than a strand of shredded cheese, and it's perfect. I hump the floor, my dick like an ax pounding into cement, and I shove that sliver of pussy in my mouth.

It's gamey and bitter, and *fuck*, it tastes good.

Soon, I'll cut off the rest of her labia. There will be no protection from me. Her pussy will be one giant clit and a hole. That is, if I don't eat her clit too.

The wound bleeds like a knuckle hacked by a cheese grater, and my tongue laps at it as if I'm a thirsty wolf. And then, I'm suckling it, a piglet at the teat, and the sensual pressure undulates in my groin. I suck up every drop of tin-flavored blood I can pull out of her, and my ears tunnel with overwhelming numbness.

I finally have her.

I want her to understand we could've lived a happy life together.

Now, I can't let her go. Not until I eat her.

And she made me this way.

Finally, she stirs, a painful groan gurgling up her throat. I take one last lick of her wounds before her hand swats down and cups her cunt. I get out of the cage and slam the top shut. The lock clicks into place.

She tries to sit up, but her head bangs into the metal bars.

"Fuck. That hurts like—" Her pupils round as she takes in her surroundings. Her cage. Her new home. "What the fuck is this?"

Power swells inside of me. For now, Mona's tone is forceful and accusatory. That won't last for much longer.

And besides, I've got a surprise for her.

I take another set of filled syringes from the nightstand and remove the first one.

"You see these?" I ask. She blinks rapidly, finally registering my presence just outside of the bars. I lift the syringe higher. "One is to help you grow. The other will help you produce milk. They're meant for cows, but you always wanted to be livestock, right?"

She gawks, her jaw quivering, and it's clear that she's not fully grasping her situation yet. She's refusing to accept her final form.

"How the fuck did you get hormones?" she asks.

I could tell her about how you can purchase anything online. I could also tell her how if you find the right local seller, they'll get you anything and take your cash offer. She doesn't need to know the details though. Meat doesn't have a need for information like that.

"That was always your problem," I say instead. "You always doubted my capabilities."

I tap the end of the needle. Droplets fling through the air. With this liquid, Mona will grow for me. And with some training, she'll crawl, moan, and cry for me too. But most of all, she'll feed me.

I reach through the wide bars toward her tit. She inches away as far as she can to the other side of the cage.

I smirk and square my shoulders. I don't mind her resistance. In fact, I *encourage* it. The harvesting is more satisfying when the meat puts up a fight. Without winning that struggle, how do you know you deserve the meal?

"Don't make this harder on yourself," I warn, but I swear, I *want* her to make it difficult for me. My shaft stiffens at the mere thought of her defiance.

Mona reluctantly comes back to the middle of the cage. I reach through the bars with the syringe and poke her small breast with the needle. The plunger goes down, and her eyes scrunch shut. I swap the needle for the next syringe, and that one goes down easily too.

I reach through the cage bars and massage her tit, imagining the milk in her mammary glands. I don't care for dairy, but the idea of eating milky tissue seems promising. The ultimate moist flesh. And there's something enticing about controlling a woman like this: forcing her body to grow, injecting her with animal hormones, treating her like actual livestock, preparing her for growth and slaughter.

Perhaps this is *my* experiment. Mona used me in her artistic experiment, and now I'm returning the favor. I can perfect my process until I discover what I truly want out of human meat.

"I-if you're going to do it, then do it the right way," Mona stutters. "Open the cage. Massage me. Knead me. Like *really* knead me. That's how you're supposed to stimulate breast milk, right?"

My lips stretch into a smile, and pleasure fills me. I can see through her latest trick, her first attempt at escape. Her odds are slim, but I've always wanted to hunt her.

I slide closer to the cage, and my dick presses against my pants. Her quick glance down shows she can see my erection. Her eyes fill with water, but she keeps the tears guarded behind her glare. Right now, she must be regretting her assumption that I'm harmless.

I play along with her game and use a teasing voice. "But if I open the cage, you'll try to escape."

"I won't," she says quickly. "I swear I won't. You can grow me and fuck me and eat parts of me. It'll just be better for the milk if you can properly massage my tissues."

My teeth are so ready for her flesh they chatter behind my closed lips. I can see what she's planning to do. I unlock the cage anyway, then click my tongue. As I sit back on my haunches, I gesture for her to come out.

Mona crawls forward like a dog. My chest expands, and even more blood rushes to my groin, the anticipation making my erection painfully stiff. The bitch stays on all fours, then peers up at me with those big black eyes, the dark makeup smudged around her like matted fur.

"Good girl," I say.

She stays still like a rabbit trying to blend in with its surroundings. She knows I'm blocking her exit.

I shuffle around the cage to the other side, giving her a way out. My dick pushes harder against my pants. I kneel again and grab her hanging tits. My thumb presses right on the pink needle punctures. Mona's spine becomes rigid. I knead the tissues, and I swear, it's as if her breast has already grown more supple for me. A groan forces its way through my body. There's no way she can avoid me now. She's mine; she just doesn't understand that yet, but she will soon.

I lean closer, and each breath in my lungs is another cup of blood filling my shaft. I press my lips against her ear.

"It's going to feel so good to finally kill you," I whisper.

The prey lunges forward, instantly on two feet, her stride wider than humanly possible. It's like the missing patch of her labia is painless now, all thanks to her fear-induced adrenaline.

The back door opens and closes. For a few seconds, I let her run. The landfill is too far away, and I've got the keys to the van in my pocket, and so the bitch's only choice is to hide in the grass and hope I don't see her.

I get my hunting knife and join her in the field.

Outside, the tall grass blades shimmy like they always do, and somewhere, my little morsel is hiding. My brain slithers inside of her, imagining her pure panic. Her heaving breaths. Her wide pupils. Her heartbeat thumping louder in her ears than an industrial meat grinder. And this is the best part about living out here where no one goes: I have so much land around me that I can chase her as far as I need to without any outside interference.

The grass flickers, dancing more than usual. Then I see my rabbit hiding in the brush, her black eyes peering through the blades, praying to the sky above that I won't find her.

But I'm the fucking wolf now.

I run faster than I ever have and howl at the top of my lungs. She gasps, and her feet run swiftly again, but it's too late. I crash into her, nailing us both to the ground. Her head smacks the dirt, and I shove down on the back of her skull, her face digging deeper into the soil, her ability to breathe cut off. She pushes herself up to get away, but with my body pinning her hips down, all it does is prop up her chest and ready it for carving. I slice the hunting knife against her breast. She wails a sorrowful noise I've never heard before, and it's like music swarming my ears. A symphony of her agony, the final cry of acceptance, the truth that she should have heeded the warnings that I'm a dangerous predator.

Blood gushes into the dirt, spreading over the grass like a red vinaigrette, and for a second, the little morsel lies limp, likely unconscious from the shock or loss of blood. I use those few seconds to unzip my pants and pull out my dick. I slap her breast blood over my cock, then I fuck her from behind.

Her pussy is loose, relaxed in her blacked-out state. I need her fight. With one aggressive thrust, the penetration jerks her awake. The pathetic little bitch coughs into the dirt, and I squeeze her dismembered tit. The blood drips out on her pale skin, and the fat coats my fingers, so utterly decadent, it should be illegal. And that's the funny part: it *is* illegal, and I don't care.

I shove the breast fat in my mouth, and my teeth snap, biting off a meaty chunk of her areola and ripping it from her skin. My tongue caresses her dismembered nipple, and it puckers for me, even now. Mona may never have wanted to be sexually eaten, but her body responds to me. Even now, her pussy is sloppy with blood and her natural lubrication. Fear is arousal, and pussy prey always gets wet.

I swallow the chewed-up nipple, skin, and fat, then I bring my slobbering mouth down to her neck.

"You know what comes next?" I say. "Your legs, baby. Once I roast those, you won't be able to run away anymore."

Her tears are loud and uncontrollable, snot stuffing her airways. My dick pounds into her sopping cunt, and I shove her face into the dirt again, propping her hips up for a proper fucking. Those noises begin to fade, muffled by the earth, until the bitch finally goes quiet.

I should sew her up, but I'm not done yet. I eat another bite of her tit flesh, and this time, I let it roll between my cheeks. I savor the flavor: notes of copper, pungent bitterness, and a gamey after-taste, like wild meat.

But the wild animal is finally caught. The bitch thought she was better than me, and that she could trick me again and get away. In reality, she can use tricks and lies until her very last breath. It won't change anything for her now.

No matter what she does, she'll always be mine.

CHAPTER 32

THE BLUNT END OF THE THREAD HANGS DOWN FROM MONA'S stitches. I cut off the excess, then marvel at my work.

Her left nipple is gone now, replaced by a blue-threaded line. This time, she doesn't ask where I got my suturing kit. The explanation about the hormones must have been enough for her to know it's better not to ask any questions.

"There," I say. "Good as new."

Once the orgasm subsided, I knew I had to get to work before she gave out on me. It turns out I didn't actually cut off that much of her tit, but to be honest, the bitch never had more than a handful anyway.

I slam the top of the cage shut, then slap the lock together and sit on the edge of my bed.

"Get on your hands and knees," I bark.

The meat hole flips around, more obedient *now* than she's ever been, and I rub my dick through my pants as I stare at her. Her tits are clean—I mean, her only whole tit is clean—but the rest of her body, including her face, is streaked with dirt, snot, and blood. I should wash her, though it seems like a lot of work right now, especially after the stitches.

A low hum drifts into the house, the mechanical noises rippling through the rooms.

Mona's body shifts.

My teeth snap together, and I know what she's thinking.

A car.

Cars rarely come down this way. Even the dump trucks drive in the other direction. If it was a car though, this could be her *only* chance.

It's not a car though. It's the echoes of the compactors restarting at the landfill. I know the sound well. Still, the hope erupts in her eyes, and her chin shudders in panic. My cock thickens in fascination.

"Help me!" she yells. "Please help—"

My upper lip curls into smugness. "Please" isn't a word I've ever heard from her mouth. It's not like Mona to ask for something, but I guess when you're stuck in a cage, your breast is hacked to shit, a sliver of your labia is chopped off, and a monster like me holds the key to your confinement, you don't have much room to be entitled or demanding anymore.

The machinery dribbles into white noise, and her lips keep shaking.

"That was the landfill," I murmur, cutting off her cries. "No one is coming to save you. After all, no one can hear you. You know that, right, my little morsel?"

Her pleading words transform into a blood-curdling scream. My cock bobs, yearning for more of that fear.

"You fight too much," I laugh. "You shouldn't waste your energy on that."

A tear rolls down her cheek. Her eyes stay on the floor. I like that.

Blood expands in my vessels, and my chest pounds. Fuck me, I *really* like that. I don't know if she's avoiding eye contact with me because she's scared or petulant, but my dick is harder than a boulder, and fuck, I'm feeling so powerful right now.

I unzip, then thrust my dick in one of the cage's openings. There are many reasons why I bought this cage in particular, and the most amusing reason is the fact that my big dick can actually fit through the openings. Technically, I can fuck her while she's inside of it.

Mona stays perched on all fours with her ass against the side of the cage. The crown of my cock dips inside of her warmth, and her heat sucks me in, but she remains lifeless, a rotting corpse.

I want more from her.

I move my hips forward in a sharp jerk. "Are you scared now?" I ask. "Tell me."

I smack my hips against the cage again, aching more for her tight heat, but my thrusting is a rhythmic drum without a song, and her pussy stays flaccid and bored. Like she's playing dead.

Irritation froths in my mouth, but I push it down. I'll get what I want out of her. I don't care what it takes.

"Answer me!" I shout.

Her shoulders harden. "You just told me to stop fighting, dumbass."

I freeze with my tip inserted inside of her. Mona stiffens. She has a good point though. I like the idea of keeping her caged like a wild animal, but our time is precious. I can't waste these last moments keeping her confined.

I want her to fight me.

I also want her to understand that she can't get away.

"You're right," I say in a low voice. My neck tingles, and those nerves pinch down my sides, reaching all the way to my balls. "A cage isn't a suitable place for my little morsel."

She cracks her head to the side. She's listening, but she knows not to fully trust me anymore.

"Keep your eyes on the ground," I say.

The submissive little animal does, and I leave her for a minute. In the kitchen, I grab the cleaver and tuck it inside my back pocket. Then I turn on the stove burner to its maximum heat setting and put a cast iron pan on it to get hot.

Back in the bedroom, the livestock continues to do as it's told. Eyes on the floor. Obedient. Submissive. Silent. My perfect meat.

"Come out, pretty girl," I say as I unlock the cage. "I'll bite, but it won't be that bad. I promise."

Her head subtly shakes. When she looks up, her bottom lip is swollen, snot is crusted around her nostrils, and dried blood is caked in a thin stream from her nose, down over her lips. The facial damage is probably from the tit harvesting in the field.

She notices me staring and hesitantly touches her lip, perhaps checking to see if it's still there, to see if maybe I cut it off and ate it too. *Not yet,* I think. *But soon.*

Fear clouds her bloodshot eyes, and my tongue fills with saliva. Fear is the best seasoning on a woman; I can already taste it.

"It would be nice to go pee," she says quietly.

"Then go pee," I say.

Her pupils jump back and forth as she studies me, searching for a clue. I keep my expression blank.

Bravery dips into her mind, and she inches forward. Her head pops out of the cage.

Impatience stabs my body. I don't want to do anything too soon though. I have to wait for the exact right moment. I step closer.

Another crawl forward. Her arms are out now.

I take another step.

She meets my eyes again. "Kent?" Her bottom lip quivers, adrenaline dancing frantically in her veins.

I lick my lips. "Yes, little one?"

"It would be wrong to force me to pee like an animal. You're going to let me use the bathroom, right?"

"Of course," I say. I tuck my hand behind my back and grip the cleaver's handle. The bitch can't see it. I bet she thinks she's finally going to escape.

But I'm ready too.

"You're not an animal. You're human," I add.

She's human.

She's only human.

Human meat.

My meat.

And I want to eat all of her.

She crawls the final inches out of the cage, and as soon as her bubbled ass is past the metal bars, I smash down the cleaver with every ounce of strength I have. The sharp blade hits the backside of her lower thigh, a few inches above the knee, slicing through the skin, the vessels, the nerves, the muscle, and into the bone.

Blood gushes like a fountain. The bitch falls onto her stomach; the sobs spew from her throat like a gurgling lava pit, and the cleaver is stuck in the bone. I howl with laughter. I didn't think I'd be able to cut through the bone in one whack, but with two more whacks in quick succession, it's completely cut off. I guess her meat has given me the strength I need. I step closer and she curls into herself, moaning in pain and trying to get away from me.

I need to work fast; if I hit one of the major arteries, I'll only have a few minutes.

But I desperately want a taste first.

I pick up her leg and lick right over the bone. The sourness invades my tastebuds, my blood vessels expanding to better consume her energy. And that's when I smell it: her rancid fear. It's nasty, like a mix of armpit sweat and sewage. My nostrils flare, soaking up as much as I can. My dick spasms against my legs.

The bitch inches to one side and pulls herself forward in a pathetic attempt at an army crawl. She looks like a worm. Her good leg shoves her body toward a nearby cupboard, and she pulls herself up. Her face twists, pain shooting through what's left of her body, but adrenaline is a funny thing. She's doing so much more than I thought someone could do with a freshly amputated leg.

"You can't run away," I say, my laughter roaring. "You can't do *anything*. What, little morsel? Are you going to crawl to safety?"

As she falls to the ground in her failed attempt to escape, I can't help but smile. Maybe that's one of the reasons I'm so attracted to Mona; I knew a stuck-up cunt like her would give me a good fight. She's too stubborn to give up. My little morsel has the mindset of a wolf; she's only just now finding out she's trapped in a rabbit's body.

With each of her movements, the adrenaline fades. Her will decreases, her limbs jerking. The little rabbit is finally in the wolf's teeth.

I can't have her dying on me yet.

I grab a fistful of her hair and drag her over to the kitchen.

The cast iron pan stinks of charred metal, and smoke fills the air. I'm high on my own actions as I take in the blood. So much fucking blood. On the walls. On the laminate. On her skin. Though this time, it has nothing to do with a pig. It's all Mona. Only Mona. She's going to need serious recovery time after this.

For now, I'll savor her life, and later, I'll relish in her death.

After I slap the veterinary tourniquet on her thigh, I move to the cast iron. The metal sizzles against her thigh, but it's so wet and fleshy it barely cauterizes anything. Her body goes completely limp, her mind and body unconscious. I push the pan to another area. The blood smokes, and the scent of seared meat wafts in the air. My mouth salivates. It smells fucking delicious, but no matter how difficult it is, I have to stay focused.

Heat the pan. Wait. Remove the pan. Press it to the flesh. Again and again until it's completely closed up with burned flesh.

Finally, I power off the stove and remove the tourniquet. The mobile home reeks of barbecue. I make a mental note to sear part of her severed leg in a similar way and enjoy the meal later. Right now, my body wants something else.

I use the strength meant for Mona's full body as I scoop her into my arms, but I almost toss her into the air. She's so light now, it's like she could fly out of my hands.

Less meat. Less muscle. Less strength.

More food. More meat. More control.

I kick open the back door. Outside, I bend her over the steps that lead up to the industrial meat grinder. She stirs and squints her eyes. Her face contorts. Her entire body must hurt, and fuck, it's got to be confusing to wake up outside like this.

"Kent?" she asks. "The fuck—"

I point up to the machine. "You see that?" I whisper. "I'm going to put you inside of it one day. Maybe your head," I murmur. "Maybe I should do that right now."

"Please!" she sobs. "Please, Kent. Don't—"

There's that word again. *Please.* You'd never know that an entitled bitch could be broken down into common courtesies. I guess all it takes is a missing tit and a leg to get her manners straightened out.

I've never wanted to grind a woman up—not yet anyway—but she doesn't know that. And if I want to keep her alive, I'll need to go to the store soon. With her here, I obviously have enough to eat, but she needs food. Greens. Organic vegetables. Fruits. Berries. Everything to keep her meat tender and sweet.

I prop her waist up, bending her at the best angle; she's too weak to fight me right now. Then I grab her hips and slide my dick inside of her wet pussy. Laughter rolls out of me. She claims she would never be into sexual cannibalism, but the fight-or-flight response activates, and suddenly the bitch is as wet as beef stew.

Her pussy walls clench me, contracting against my movements, and eventually, she's quiet.

As I fuck her, I think about what I'll do with her leg. I'll smoke and sear some of it. With the rest, I can buy a rotisserie. Or maybe I'll dig a fire pit and cook her flesh over the open flames.

A roast, maybe.

A roast sounds nice.

Chapter 33

After the first leg amputation, Mona slept for a day. She needed it. And during that time, between sharpening my knives, getting rid of her phone, removing the skin of her leg, roasting the flesh, and eating every single scrap from the bone, I decided that once she was up for it, my little morsel could move around the home as much as she wanted. I even got her a walker. I like the idea of giving her a false sense of autonomy. It seemed fair when she had given me fake meat.

And it's not like she can run away.

When she wakes up, she stays in bed for a while with her eyes closed, pretending to be asleep. It's obvious she's awake—you don't go from snoring with a slack mouth to "sleeping" with silent nostrils and pinched lips—but eventually, she accepts my gift and finds her wobbly balance with the walker.

I wait for her in the kitchen and clean the blender in the sink. The little morsel appears naked in the hallway, her mouth-watering flesh completely exposed for my viewing pleasure. She leans her weight forward, then shoves the walker a few inches ahead. Her balance is shit though, and she teeters like a bobble-headed toy.

As she ambles forward, she doesn't turn in my direction.

My jaw ticks. Seeing her struggle like this should arouse me, but this rude behavior gets on my nerves.

She can't even look at me?

I can understand where she's coming from though. It must be hard to be respectful to someone when they cut off your leg before you're ready.

"Good morning, little morsel," I say. I dry my soapy hands on a towel, then lift a full glass. "I made you some breakfast."

Her head swivels, then latches onto the green smoothie in the raised glass. Her upper lip twitches. Spinach, pineapple, coconut milk, strawberries, tofu, and a special ingredient just for her.

"I added your favorite protein," I say. "My semen."

A dry heave gurgles up her throat. Her lips clamp shut, keeping the potential vomiting at bay. Finally, she straightens herself, then gives me her best pleading, watery eyes.

"Kent," she whispers. "Can't you give me something else? You know I hate—"

My ears fizzle, and my vision reddens. Her lips move. I don't hear her anymore.

I'm giving her freedom. I purchased a mobility assistance tool, though she won't need it for much longer. I even prepared a meal for her. I give and give and give.

And she still thinks she can disrespect my courtesies?

I rip a wide silicone straw from the kitchen drawer, then slam it into the smoothie. I never had any use for a straw before; it was another purchase I made *for her.* With all the shit I've done, you'd think she'd be a little more appreciative.

I stomp forward. My lips widen into a grin. My gait is furious, each step pounding into the floor. Mona's knuckles blanch against the handles of her walker.

"Drink it," I say cheerily. Mona stares at me. Her refusal isn't verbal; it's there in her body language. The cunt thinks she has a say in her nutritional intake. Now, she's the stupid one.

This smoothie is better for her body. Better for the meat. And I'm doing it all for her.

"Drink it," I order. My voice is chipper, but the words are harsh. My chin drops, and as I try to smile again, I bare my teeth.

Mona bows her head, the tension finally getting to her. Then she bends forward and wraps her lips around the straw. The sides of the silicone pinch together under her suction, and my shoulders relax. The spinach will flush out her system, and the pineapple will help bring out the sweetness that's buried underneath the bitterness of her past carnivorous diet.

"That's it," I say. I salivate, my eyes glued to her sucking lips. "That's my good little meat hole."

She sneers at me over the straw, seething with visible rage. The straw inflates; she's not drinking anymore.

I scrunch my nose. "Come on, little morsel," I say, encouraging her. "Keep drink—"

She smacks the glass out of my hand. The glass shatters. The smoothie splashes down and paints the laminate in ugly green globs.

I gawk at the floor, my jaw hanging.

What does she think she'll get out of spilling the smoothie?

Why did she do it?

What's the purpose of being that defiant when she knows that I own her now?

Mona tightens her palms on her walker, and her spine straightens into the air.

"I am *not* your meat hole," she snarls.

My shoulders vibrate, and my teeth clamp shut. Everything around me spins like a carousel until I can't concentrate on anything but Mona's complete and utter disrespect.

I have to teach her a lesson.

I yank the cleaver from the knife block. Mona gasps and moves snail-like inches across the mobile home. Her escape is slow, too slow, and so fucking clumsy, and after I finish this next punishment, her abilities will continue to decrease. She will barely be able to fight me, and that loss will be her fault.

I don't care right now though. I'm too greedy. I need her fucking pain.

I ram the blade through the air. The cleaver smashes into her arm, a few inches down from her shoulder joint, cracking right through the bone.

It's the same hand she used to spill the drink.

On the ground, she wriggles like a cockroach stuck on its back. Desire floods my veins, my body vibrating with built-up lust. I've been holding back and waiting to let her heal. If we did as much as I wanted, she'd be on my dinner table right now. I've been giving her space to get used to our new pattern. I guess some sad part of me was still hopeful that we could build a long, happy life together, carnivore and meat, but I can't stop myself now.

I want to eat everything inside of her, even her fear.

"Not so fucking proud now, are you?" I growl.

I pick her up like a sack of potatoes and clutch her torso to my side, slinging her sideways. The bitch kicks and fights with the limbs she's got left. I grip her with so much pressure that she whines, her sniveling cries surging straight to my dick. I'm hard— so fucking hard, stars fleck my vision—and I won't be able to do anything the right way until I release this tension.

I throw her on the bed, and the blood soaks into the comforter, the sheets, and the mattress. I should've gotten a better mattress protector before I kidnapped her. Now, the bed is ruined. I don't care though.

Taking the severed arm, I cut a diagonal hole inside of the bicep, then I pull my dick out of my pants. The hot, fleshy insides swallow part of my shaft, but it's not deep enough for the full length. I lock eyes with Mona. Her energy fades, and my limbs buzz with need.

The arm flesh is lifeless. There's no struggle with it.

I want to *feel* her scream.

I cinch the tourniquet around the arm stump as fast as I can, then I mount the bed and shove my dick inside of her pussy. Her scared little cunt constricts around my cock, and it's like my head instantly severs from my body, my mind in the clouds as I look down on us. I see her, my little morsel. I see the savory fear and sweet desperation mixing on her face, and it gives me life. It gives me energy. It gives me so much strength that I don't know why I didn't accept this part of myself sooner.

I can give as much as I want to her, and she may reject it. But the fact is she has no choice; she must give me her meat now. I've got her right where I want her.

Her arm flails, her nails scraping at my chest. She kicks her leg, and the thigh stump twitches, the phantom limb fighting me too. She should be unconscious from the physical trauma, but no, my little morsel fights like a wounded beast. Her hips thrust forward in an attempt to throw me off of her, but it's no use. She doesn't even have two matching limbs to fight me anymore, and it's entertaining that her brain still thinks she can try. As much as I hate her, there's a part of me that's proud right now. Proud that I picked such a stubborn, feisty little cunt. Proud that I knew her potential, even early on.

I can admit it to myself now: she's exactly the kind of fighter I've always dreamed of.

My hands scoop against her fresh arm stump, gathering as much spilled blood as I can, and though there's a tourniquet stopping the flow, I'm still able to lift a few drops to my mouth. It stains my teeth, my lips, my neck, and it's so much better than menstrual blood—this is fuller, richer, spicier—and yet, there's something *off*. A missing secret ingredient, and I know what it is. I hadn't realized what it was until now. It's something I need more than her fresh blood.

Her eyes go dark, unconscious again, and we both know her future.

Drinking her blood from the veins will only quench my thirst for so long. Eating her roasted leg can feed me, but it doesn't completely satisfy me. Even this—taking her limbs, one at a time—even *this* isn't enough.

Eating her living body will taste only so good.

I have to eat her *and* kill her.

Until then, my hunger will never be satisfied.

CHAPTER 34

ANOTHER LEG.

I keep her bones in the fridge. Eventually, I'll use them to make a broth.

And then, there's only one limb left.

Mona can't do much these days, and so I keep her in my bed. I've given up on the growth hormones and the milk; there's no reason to waste the injections on her when she won't last much longer.

She stares up at the ceiling, her skin paler now, with a sickly hue. Sometimes, I prop her up so she can almost sit, but the meat likes to slide down. I guess it's more comfortable to lie flat and imagine you're already in your grave, than it is to face your butcher.

Now, she has one full arm and three rounded, inflamed red stumps with bubbled white ulcers. Her body reminds me of a fashion doll with its parts ripped off.

All that's left is her other arm and her head.

A lot can happen in a week.

A green smoothie—this time with blueberries instead of tofu —sits next to her attached arm, the cold glass leaning on her torso. An oversized straw is upright in the middle of the thick drink.

I stand in the doorway. I tear off a piece of her smoked labia and chew on the tender meat. The flavor is similar to brined salmon.

"Drink it," I say with my mouth full.

The meat keeps its eyes on the ceiling.

"Don't you want to be healthy for me?" I say with laughter. It's not like she has much of a choice.

Finally, she turns to me, shooting with more venom than she's had for the last few days. Her lips hang low, hopelessness settling into her muscles, but the strong-minded woman is still visible in her hate-filled eyes.

"If you gave me something besides fruits and veggies, maybe I would eat," she says.

"The only meat I have right now is yours," I say. "Do you want some?"

She hides her tears from me, another small way to defy me when she knows how much I love watching the pain flicker in her eyes.

I step forward. "Drink your fucking—"

The dumb bitch smacks the glass again, and the green liquid spills on the sheets.

I exhale fully, then lick my teeth. I thought she was smarter than this.

I guess I was wrong.

Instead of chopping off her other arm in punishment, I scoop the smoothie into the glass, saving what I can. Mona's eyes are still on the ceiling, and that refusal to acknowledge me burns every nerve ending in my body. How can a smart, well-known artist be so fucking stupid when it comes to a situation like this?

There will be no other meal. She knows that.

I grab a funnel from the kitchen. She's not going to waste what's left. As soon as I stomp through the bedroom, she squirms her head, her stumps and outstretched arm flailing. A normal person would feel guilty for overpowering her like this, but how can I feel bad for her when she's manipulated so many people in her life, including me? I refuse to feel bad for forcing her to drink a healthy meal.

I yank her chin toward me. She keeps her teeth clamped shut. I backhand her, and she finally opens her mouth. I shove the funnel between her teeth, then dump the green sludge into the plastic. Mona chokes, and the funnel flies out of her mouth. Apparently she wasn't ready for the liquid meal.

Once she can breathe, I do it again. I imagine babies are like this; you have to teach them everything. I guess that's what Mona is to me now: a baby I'm taking care of, an animal I'm raising on a farm, meat that will eventually be completely slaughtered for food.

After a while, she swallows the liquid, getting the hang of the forced feeding. She continues to drink, and I stroke her whole tit. Her perky little nipple pebbles for me.

"That's it," I say quietly. "Keep drinking like a good girl."

Mona's rage-filled eyes dart back to me. My dick pulses in response. I rub my shaft through the fabric, then tap the funnel with the other hand so that she gets every drop. More organic sludge pools in her mouth.

Once she's done with her meal, I put the funnel on the floor, then unzip my pants. I mount the bed, readying myself between her legs.

"He'll find you," Mona says.

Curiosity forms in my temples. I keep my dick in my hand. "Who?"

"Artemis. He knows everything."

I tilt my head to the side. "Does he?"

"He's the one who made the fingertips and toes. He's the one who told me not to actually hurt myself, but said we should trick you. He'll find you!" An ominous cackle bursts from her chest. Darkness and chaos flood her black eyes. "He'll find you, you stupid motherfucker. You can eat me, but he'll find you, and then you'll *never* be free."

I lick my lips and mull over those words. Artemis is dead; he hasn't been a problem for me for quite some time. But perhaps there is some truth to her claims. There is a chance *other* people could start searching for her, especially with her "vacation" coming to an end soon. It's almost time for me to move on from the fields.

With my pants hanging around my hips, I crawl to the ground and dig under the bed, picking through the last occupant's knick knacks for my first trophy. My back heats under Mona's heavy stare, and I'm glad for it. She's not backing down; she's still willing to challenge me. I like that. There's a thrill in her defiance, especially when she doesn't know the full scope of the situation.

She thinks I'd let him live? If I had, wouldn't he be here right now?

She's the stupid motherfucker.

I dangle what's left of the ponytail, and the decaying head swings back and forth, the exposed section of brain wriggling with maggots.

Her chin trembles. Her lips open.

She can't speak.

I put his head right next to hers, then I hold myself over her, resting on my forearms, my dick right at her entrance. Her mouth gapes at her dead husband's head, his lips opened in a silent wail. Her rounded stumps jerk to push me away, but she's so fucking helpless.

I lick her ear, and it's salty with her sweat. Maybe I'll make chips with her cartilage, or maybe I'll cook it down until it's soft and chewy.

I wrap my lips around her earlobe. "I killed him," I whisper. I shove my whole length inside of her. She whimpers, and I stick my tongue in her ear, lapping at her waxy flesh. "I killed him and ground up some of his meat. I even stuffed the rest of his body into the furnace at the processing plant. He won't bother us anymore."

Tears roll down her cheek. I lick from her ear down to her neck, tasting her natural sweat and oils. How hard do I need to bite to get a chunk of meat straight from a woman's skin? One day, I'll test it out.

A shrill cry explodes from her, stabbing my eardrum. I pull back.

"You're jealous," she says, her lips curled at the ends. "You're fucking jealous of my husband."

I realize then that the piercing noise was laughter. She's too scared and shocked to be able to laugh normally. Maybe forced amputations in quick succession fuck with your entire body, even your vocal cords. To be honest, I don't know why her laugh sounds so weird, but I know she's laughing at me.

"I didn't kill Artemis because I'm jealous," I snap. "I killed him because he would've tried to protect you. But you don't get it, do you? All I wanted was a true connection with someone who understands me, and you and that stupid motherfucker—"

"You don't want connection," she shouts, green spittle splattering my face. "You want to *control* me. You're like a rat, clinging to the first shelter you've found, and the fucked-up thing is you *know* you can do better. You even tried. You promised me a life where you'd only eat little parts of me, but you *chose* to be this person. You want to be a rapist. You want to be a monster. You want to be a fucking cannibal!"

I pull out and kneel on the bed, straddling her, my limp dick hanging between my legs. I don't see Mona anymore. I see my mother lying on the dining table. Her rotting stomach. Her missing tongue. Her teeth clacking, the dead bitch returning from the grave to mock me one last time.

"You're just a needy, stupid, *pathetic* little barnacle, latching onto the first person who gives you attention," Mona shouts. Her harsh laughter reverberates in the small room. "No wonder your mother left you."

She keeps yelling. Laughing. Making fun of me. Everything out of her mouth is about how pathetic I am.

I'm not the one who has one arm and no legs. I'm not the one who has no choice but to eat green smoothies for the rest of my short existence. I'm not the one with my dead husband's decapitated head next to me.

I'm not the one who has to watch a cannibal eat her body.

Ever since I left the art gallery, the idea of killing her has been cooking in the back of my mind. I told myself I'd capture her, keep her, and feed on her. I knew she couldn't live forever, and I told myself killing her wasn't the point. I told myself I wanted to savor her body until she understands me.

And then what?

It's not like I can let her go. If I drop her off at her house, the police will eventually arrest me. And if I throw her out into the field to survive in the wild, she'll die anyway. The wolves will find her, or her corpse will become fertilizer.

A barking laugh chortles from my chest. This time, Mona freezes, suddenly aware that now, I'm the one who's mocking her.

Maybe she is right. I've always been terrified of being abandoned again, and that's why I stopped dating and stuck to sex workers for so long. It's why Mona seemed like the first good thing to happen to me.

Maybe I am a clingy, needy, obsessed man who needs to feed on a woman to be complete. Maybe being that pathetic is worth it, because I get to see the struggle, the reluctance, the beautiful fear in her eyes as she bows down to my control.

I tried to suppress it. I tried to tell myself killing a woman wasn't a part of my fantasy, but now I know it's the divine part I've buried deep inside of myself so that no one knew the real me. I'm mad at myself for that. Why did I want so badly to be like everyone else?

Everyone has fantasies, and maybe some of us—the rare, exceptional few of us—dream of human meat. Even then, some of the fantasizers try to act like death doesn't actually exist in our sexual dreams. No, these sensual interests aren't that scary. After all, it's just a pornstar wriggling in a sleeping bag, pretending it's a giant carnivorous worm; it's just a computer-generated dinosaur eating a screaming, naked woman; or maybe it's just an erotic horror story about a man devouring a woman piece by piece. Maybe all of it is just a reflection of the way we dehumanize each other in our daily lives, just like Mona tried to explain in her tired art project. Maybe it doesn't mean anything. Maybe none of it is real. Maybe we only like the idea of it.

But I know I'm different from *them*, and I'm done acting like death isn't a part of the desire for me. I'm not going to pretend anymore. I'm done with roleplaying.

Fuck the fantasies.

I hate to think I had always planned to kill her and denied that need to my inner self, but I guess I have. I need to kill her as much as I need to eat her. Maybe even more.

And soon, I *will* kill her.

I bare my canines, and Mona creeps back into the bed as far as she can with her one arm. Her neck bends against the headboard. She blocks her face with her arm, protecting herself from me.

But the thing is that if you cut off someone's legs and arms, then they can never leave you. And when you eat parts of them, they literally feed your body and soul. Your system digests their flesh, and they become a part of you.

This is who I am. A cannibal. A man who kills and eats women. Mona isn't the first woman I've killed and eaten, and she won't be the last.

Finally, after all of this time, I can accept myself completely. I should thank her for that.

"I was going to keep you alive for a long, long time," I murmur as I bend down, close to her face. "I thought I loved you, but I guess I never did. You can't kill someone you love, can you?"

Her pupils dilate, her mouth dropping slightly, and I see it there, right where I want it: her desperate need for survival, even though she knows it's fucking hopeless, and that fear is savory, like crispy slices of skin sautéed in a garlic butter sauce.

I pin her arm to the side, then I lean on my elbows again. I lick her face, then her nostrils, her eyelids, and finally, her lips. The sweat and grime coats my tongue, and there's a sharp sourness to her mouth, like an expensive cheese, mixed with the mild sweetness of the green smoothie. I've been sponge-bathing her, but I guess I haven't paid much attention to her teeth.

Her rancid breath doesn't stop me.

I shove my tongue back into her throat, tasting everything: the sharp, sour flavor and that mild bitterness. I stretch my tongue, eager to tongue-fuck her esophagus. I'll never make it, but my dick is so fucking hard as I try and try and try until *I* can't breathe.

I pull off of her, swallow some air, then dive back down with my tongue. My fat muscle snakes between her teeth.

A sharp pain pricks me.

I rip myself off of her and clutch my mouth.

Blood drips over Mona's lips. As she chews, she smirks at me.

I touch my tongue. She didn't get much—not more than a pinch of muscle—but she succeeded.

She fucking bit me.

Maybe she *does* understand me.

I try to smile, but the rage overpowers it. I grab pliers and a knife from the dresser, then mount the cunt again. The sobs rake through her chest, and the meat panics, clamping her jaws and lips shut. So I punch her, my knuckles crashing into her eye sockets, and she relents. Then I yank that fucking organ out of her mouth, and her garbled cries are like screams from a drowning victim. I saw through the flesh. The muscle frays like the strings of a wet blanket. Her sloshy sobs become screams, and those chortled noises push me on.

Finally, the pressure releases. The tongue is severed from her body.

I toss it in my mouth. It's chewy. Metallic. A slight toughness to the tastebuds, more than I remember with my mother. I gnaw on it as I stare down at Mona, and my dick throbs, ready to impale her.

I lift her hips. She's light now, like a blow-up doll from the sex shop, and it's so fucking easy to fling her around. We can't stay here for long, but maybe for these last few days, I'll indulge as much as I can and fuck her like a sex toy.

Mona twists to the side and spits blood.

"Look at me," I say with my mouth full. I let our blood trickle down my lips. Pain stings my tongue. I scream it again anyway. "Look at me, you fucking bitch!"

She doesn't move, so I grab her chin and force her to face me. She scrunches her eyelids shut, but then I push my thumbs on her eyeballs for a few seconds, and she opens them.

Her pupils are dilated, and her sclera is streaked with blood. I tuck her tongue into my cheek.

"Good girl," I mock.

I slide my dick inside of her, forcing her to watch me as I eat her voice. The blood stains her pale skin so beautifully, and I'm grateful for this moment. Take away someone's tongue, and they can't even verbally refuse you anymore. There's no reason for me to feel anything right now, except for inner peace. She's mine. Mine to fuck. Mine to eat. Mine to kill. All fucking *mine*.

Her eyes are so glossy, they're almost like cups of water, and I love it when she looks at me like that.

"One day," I say, her tongue barely muffling my words now, chewed down to a smaller size. "As soon as you stop being worth my time, I'm going to kill you, and you can't do anything to stop me," I say. "And I'll enjoy watching you die as much as I enjoy eating you."

With that thought, the orgasm punches through my body and fills my head with overwhelming bliss.

And as I come, I swallow the mangled bits of her tongue.

CHAPTER 35

THEN SHE'S JUST A HEAD AND A TORSO.

Two days ago, after her final arm amputation, she stopped eating. Even when I used the funnel, she managed to vomit and heave until I grew tired of trying to feed her. At least with self-starvation, there's less shit and piss to deal with. I don't have to clean her as much anymore.

Now, her face is sunken, her eyes yellow, the last layers of black makeup finally washed away. The bits of her limbs, the red and white nubbins of bone and flesh, are bound in twine, trussed like a fine roast. She's decadent like this, her skin bulging between each length of string. A cannibal's favorite lingerie, the only kind I gladly approve of.

I rub olive oil over her naked body and massage her muscles just how she likes it.

She stares straight ahead, never bothering to look me in the face anymore. My little morsel is stubborn until her very last breath, and I wouldn't have it any other way.

I used to think that I would take my time with her, savoring each bite. Now I know that one bite isn't enough to satiate my hunger. I want to kill her. I always have. Killing is as much of a part of this as eating and fucking are, and it wasn't until just before she hurt me for the last time that I fully accepted who I am.

And she's no longer mouthy without a tongue.

The meat fits perfectly on my countertop. I turn her on her side, then begin rubbing the oil onto her back and ass crack. As I reach her neck, I wrap my hands around her throat, my mind racing with ideas.

What if I cut off her head?

I can keep it as a centerpiece for the dining table. I can marvel at her beauty as I eat other women who will always be *lesser* than her. I can keep my one true love with me forever.

I pinch her cheek. Her nostrils huff. I let the skin go. Even though I like the decapitation idea, there's not much flesh on her head, and if I want her to truly experience everything I have to offer her, then that requires her brain. Maybe I'll decapitate the other women.

"We really could have been something, you know?" I say. I shake the garlic powder all over her until she's covered in yellow dust. Next, I season her with ground white pepper and onion powder. I'm craving something savory for her torso. "But you had to ruin it with your fucked-up lies."

She blinks slowly, and I know she heard me. It irritates me though, her lack of reaction. The urge to stab her stomach so she finally makes a noise burns inside of me, but she'll scream soon. She won't be able to deny her terror when faced with the higher temperatures.

Maybe it isn't her fault we ended up like this. Even when I told myself I didn't want her to die, I don't know if I could have kept her alive for as long as I had planned. My hunger probably would've taken over.

I pick her up and place her seasoned body in the roasting pan. Luckily for me, she's short and small. With her body trussed, only her head sticks out of the pan. Still, I'll have to maneuver her into the oven. I'll make her fit.

Blood rushes to my groin. There's no point in keeping her now. But I can fuck her one last time, and I can season the inside of her cunt too.

I pick up the pan. Instead of carrying her to the oven, I place her on the dining table. I unzip my pants. My weighty cock flops out. I rub the oil and spices on my shaft. She scrunches her face, and the anticipation shudders through her torso.

My dick slides inside of her. The spices add to the friction of her textured pussy. My eyes roll to the back of my head. She squeezes me hard. Tears wash over the edges of her face, leaving empty streams in their wake. I slap her cheeks. She flinches, her cunt constricting tighter around me.

"Careful," I murmur. "You'll ruin your seasoning."

A wail rips from her throat, garbled and malformed, and I swear, my dick grows twice its size, my balls contracting with the need for release.

"Fuck, that feels good," I say. "Keep squeezing me, little morsel. Give me a reason to keep you alive."

Panic flutters in her stumps, wrestling with the twine, her will to live edging to the surface. Then the defiant little morsel relaxes her cunt and drops her eyes to the side.

So the meat thinks it can loosen its pussy, denying me pleasure?

I'll fix that.

I cover her mouth and pinch her nose with my hand, and though her pussy muscles tighten for me once, the meat forces itself to relax and lets go of that pressure.

I lick my lips. "I guess it's time for you to get in the oven then, huh?"

A desperate cry finally erupts from her throat, and it fuels me, that pressure finally boiling over her body and into mine. The orgasm shoots out of me and fills her cunt.

I pull out. The white liquid mixes with the yellow oil, dribbling over her blue stitches. And with all of her pussy lips and clit removed just last night, my mouth waters, marveling at her battered cunt. Using the olive oil like *this* is so much better than when I fucked her with her head shoved inside of the meat grinder.

I lift the roasting pan again. The moaning resumes, which quickly morphs into cries, but the bitch can't even argue now, and besides, meat doesn't speak. Her body twitches, and she gives a surprisingly strong thrust to the side, an attempt to avoid the final meal. But her torso merely dances in the pan like a rocking chair. I adjust her position and keep my hand fixed firmly on what's left of her cunt. She stays stuck in the pan after that.

I open the oven. It's cold, and I didn't preheat it on purpose. Maybe it'll fuck with the meat, but eating is only half of the fun. The other part is listening to her come to terms with her death as the oven's temperature rises.

I move the oven shelf to the lowest rack. Then, as I place the roasting pan inside of the oven, her head bangs into the side. I slant her body at an angle, and though her black hair spills over the edge of the oven, she fits well enough. I'm lucky it's a deep oven; only her forehead is touching the side now. I'm not sure if the contact with the walls will sear her flesh, but I suppose that if it does, it'll give the meat more texture.

I wonder how long it'll take before I can smell her cooking flesh.

I crouch down beside the oven's opening, then fix her hair so that every part of her fits inside of her final cage. Her sniffles echo between the metal walls.

"Don't worry, my sweet morsel," I say. "I'll always keep a part of you with me."

I close the door and twist the dial up to four hundred degrees Fahrenheit. I sit on the countertop. The spices and oil stain my pants; I don't mind it though. Right now, I'm the one looking into her cage, watching *her* squirm around like an animal, and it's so fucking right.

I can't help it; I stroke my cock, gently this time. Her dried pussy juices and the leftover cooking ingredients flake off of my skin, like I'm a snake or some other molting beast, but I keep going. I'll have to edge myself while she cooks. I don't want to come yet.

I'll have to leave this mobile home soon and move onto the next destination. But maybe it doesn't matter if you live in a state with open-minded, sexually adventurous women. Maybe you can live anywhere; you just need sedatives, restraints, and a sharp cleaver.

Soon, the wailing starts, and it's muffled by the oven. I jerk myself harder, memorizing the moment. The temperature rises even more, the heat seeping through the cracks in misty puffs of steam, and her cries grow quiet. Eventually, she's silent again. She may be unconscious from the heat, or she may be dead.

The smoke of her burned flesh—probably her scalp and hair touching the oven's wall—caresses the kitchen. I stare at the oven and clutch the crown of my shaft, imagining my little morsel slowly dying inside of the metal walls, cooking just for me. The savory scent of roasting meat fills the mobile home, and I accidentally come again.

I keep my dick out and continue stroking myself. I stay in the kitchen while she cooks. I don't leave her.

I'll never leave her.

Epilogue

one year later

CICADAS HUM THROUGH THE TREES, WHISTLING THROUGH THE branches. Sometimes, their song gives me a headache, but I like cooking outside when I can. Working like this feels natural to me.

A carcass is slung over my lap. I slide a metal rod into the spine, lining it up with the woman's nervous system. It's a fucking bitch to do, but it helps to paralyze the tissue, keeping the body from rigor mortis a little while longer, *and* it helps with roasting. The fishermen like to insert the rod straight into the fish's spine. Personally, I enjoy sliding it into the woman's asshole first, *then* pushing it through the spine and up out of the mouth. I like gutting them like that. It's my favorite kind of spit roast.

It takes some effort, but after a while, I get the woman over the open fire and hook her to the oversized rotisserie. Her brown hair dangles down like feathers each time the machine rotates her meat. I marvel at her skin; this one is speckled with freckles, and I like the way it looks in the fire's flickering light.

The truck camper glows behind me, surrounded by swaying pine trees. By saving up from odd jobs and from emptying the women's wallets over the last year, I was able to buy the camper outright with cash.

I climb up the steps and make my way to the closet.

Down at the bottom, where most people keep their shoes, cheap duffel bags line the floor; each contains various bones and Artemis's decaying head. Maybe I'm sentimental, but I can't let any piece of them go, and eventually, I'll find a way to use the rest. And on the top shelf, where folded clothes usually go, four decapitated heads are propped up, like filet mignons in a cold display case. Each head has a different skin tone and a different hair color. With salt and other organic material, their faces have stayed intact, like ancient mummies in a museum, and once I'm done roasting the woman outside, her head will join the display too.

The heads won't last forever; they will eventually decay. Still, I like looking at them. Mona taught me that I don't care for face meat anyway, and I don't think of their decapitations as wasting; I think of them as trophies to remind me of how far I've come.

It feels good to be a self-made man surrounded by women who will never leave me. I had to survive, so I ate my mother, and eventually, I ate my lover too. When it comes down to it, I never had a choice.

And now, they don't have a choice either.

Propped up on the floor behind a few duffel bags, I pick up the only corpse with its head intact. No legs. No arms. Just a torso. The skin is browned and dried like leather to the touch, and slices have been shaved off of the cheeks and stomach. Layers of skin flake off of the corpse, and a cockroach crawls out from a hole in the breast area. I swat it away, then pick up the skin flakes from the ground. Nothing will ever be wasted when it comes to her.

My little morsel.

I take Mona to the folding table. Her pussy is like fucking the scaly skin of a pineapple now, but I do it because I owe everything to her. After all, she's the one who helped me embrace my true self. Her eye sockets are actually hollow caverns now, her hair is burned off in patches, but she's still beautiful to me: a symbol of everything I've accomplished. I hammer inside of her, and the dry interior scrapes my dick. A patch of skin sloshes off her thigh stump. She stinks like a sewer, but no matter how many women I fuck, rape, kill, and eat, *no one* will ever feel as good as her.

She's the only one who ever came close to understanding me.

I pick a piece of her waist, then toss the scrap and the other flakes into my mouth. The texture is similar to beef jerky, though it's slightly bitter, with a garlicky aftertaste.

In the background, I hear the news on the television.

It's been one year since we lost such a strong female artist, a professor says to the reporter. *She was a total icon. And her influence shows that she was a nationwide role model for all of us. It's only right that we dedicate the university's new art studio to her.*

Another voice cuts in: *Thank you for that. The story of Mona Milk's disappearance has touched us all. But now, we leave California and head to our home state of Florida, where there's been another disappearance. Lindsey Jones was last seen a week ago outside of Panhandle Elite Community College.*

Another woman's voice cracks as she adds: *We just want our daughter back.*

I turn over my shoulder and watch the screen while idly thrusting into Mona's dry cunt. On the screen, the father wraps his arm around the mother's shoulder. The mother has the same freckles as the woman on the roast. I laugh. If they wanted her so badly, then they shouldn't have let her walk home by herself. Maybe they should've taught their daughter better than to get in the car with a handsome stranger who claims to be in her classes.

The mother cries, and with that noise, my dick explodes inside of Mona. I pull out, then leave her decaying torso on the table.

I power off the television and head back outside to check the rotisserie. Lindsey's skin is a golden brown now, her freckles darkening under the fire's heat. With each woman, I perfect my craft. And if you only count the women—not Artemis or the mobile home's previous occupant—then Lindsey is my seventh kill. My mother was my first. Mona was my second. Then there's the five additional women since then, and that's only the beginning of my legacy. After all of this careful control, I finally have everything I've ever dreamed of.

The trees are thick in every direction. If you go back far

enough, you'll find swampland, and the locals are rightfully afraid of alligators out here. That's why I stay away from the water myself. Florida is funny like that; you can be close to the interstate, but when it comes to the woods, no one goes into the dense trees to find the monsters creeping around and feeding on flesh, like me.

If I stay here any longer, they'll find me. So instead, I'll keep moving in search of an abandoned farm where I can keep a woman like a pig. Where I can raise her, kill her, then eat her. And even then, I won't stay there for long.

I didn't need Mona to love me like I thought I did. I just needed her to give me that final push into self acceptance. And with each passing day, I grow stronger because of everything she did for me. That's why she's on the folding table. I like keeping her by my side.

Most days, I feel invincible, but sometimes, the clarity rings through the hunger and for a few seconds, I know I'm *not* unstoppable. Meiwes had one, Fish had at least three, and Dahmer had sixteen. We all have our weaknesses, especially when it comes to our pride, but I'm better than *them*. They got caught, but me? I'm smarter. Stronger. Faster. I've avoided the government before, and I can do it again.

Mona showed me that all it takes is cutting off someone's legs to make them stay with you. So, I'll keep this going for as long as I can, maybe even into old age. And when the police find me—no, *if* they find me—they'll know how powerful I am. How many women I've eaten. How many cunts I've slaughtered. And there won't be any leftovers. I'm not wasteful like that.

These women are the source of my nutrients, and their heads are my collectibles. I'll keep them all. Especially Mona.

After all, food is more satisfying than love.

ALSO BY AUDREY RUSH

HORROR

Body Horror

Standalone

Skin

Psychological

Standalone

My Girl

DARK ROMANCE

Stalker

Standalone

Crawl

Dead Love

Grave Love

Hitch

Mafia

The Adler Brothers Series

Dangerous Deviance

Dangerous Silence

Dangerous Command

Assassin

The Feldman Brothers Duet

His Brutal Game

His Twisted Game

Secret Society

The Marked Blooms Syndicate Series

Broken Surrender

Broken Discipline

Broken Queen

Secret Club

The Dahlia District Series

Ruined

Shattered

Crushed

Ravaged

Devoured

The Afterglow Series

His Toy

His Pet

His Pain

Billionaire

Standalone

Dreams of Glass

ACKNOWLEDGMENTS

I want to start off by thanking Barbie, Cyran Faringray, and Nish. Barbie and Nish, I love your book reviews so much, and it's because of your content that I realized readers would be open to (and possibly even enjoy) reading about cannibalism. Cyran, your books and posts on vore encouraged me to finally get this story out there. (And if you're a reader reading this, check out all of Cyran Faringray's books, but especially *Love Like Gilded Bones*, for some delightful vore!) I appreciate all three of you so much!

Thank you to my awesome beta readers: Andrea, Becky, Chelsea, Deena, Jackie, JR, Kaila, and Lesli. You are all freaking geniuses, but let's make it personal: Andrea, thank you for helping me with pacing and confusion, as well as always having thoughtful responses any time I ask follow up questions. Becky, thank you for making sure that Kent's feelings were actually on the page. He's a hard one to read, but because of your questions, he finally opened up! Chelsea, thank you for your feedback about the book being not as spicy as my other books, which I totally agreed with, and thus, the infamous toast scene was born! Deena, thank you for your thorough and thoughtful comments to the whole novel, which helped to clear up sections and make the story more realistic. And speaking of toast, thank you for suggesting period blood eating! Jackie, thank you for helping me to solidify Kent's motives and clear up any confusion. And as always, thank you for your copy editing feedback too! Not only do you make sure my writing is squeaky clean, but your suggestions on how to make the book subtly creepier were freaking awesome! JR, thank you for making sure Artemis got a proper death and for the suggestion about adding gross moments to help with the potentially slow pace. And thank you for hyping up the book so much! I was happy and grateful to see how much you want to help the book succeed. Kaila, thank you for helping to make sure the smut was smutting and clarifying certain character interactions! And thank you for shouting your love for this story from the rooftops; your encouragement makes me blush every time! Lesli, thank you for truly helping to shape the characters into their best (or worst!) selves. I tend to feel a bit overwhelmed by our beta conversations, but once I process our discussion, I always feel like I know how to truly conquer the story, and I thank you for that! All of my beta readers are amazing, and I am so grateful that each of you helped me with this project.

Thank you to Ashley Michele, Chelsea, Little Sister, Mom, and Nish for letting me send you endless versions of the cover, especially when it came to voting on the subtitle's font. And an extra thanks to Chelsea for the final push I needed when I ended up with a tied vote: "Just pick the one *you* like!"

Thank you to Riggs and Silent Twin for giving me feedback on the blurb! Riggs, you helped to make sure the blurb was ominously ambiguous. Silent Twin, you didn't like that one line, and I didn't like it either, so talking with you about it helped me figure out how to fix it. Thank you both for your feedback!

Thank you to my ARC readers for your honest reviews; you have no idea how much you help a book launch. Seriously, word of mouth is everything in the book community, so every review, social media post, and recommendation has helped *Morsel* shine brightly! And a special thank you to Amanda Ruzsa, Amber [buzzcutbiblio], Amber [sinful.spines], Ash Redd, bookedupw_kalz, BostonianBibliophile, Brittany Genera, Chelsea Kohutek [@loser.witch], Jeska1518, Karlie Hlebak, Katelin, Kelli Briggs, Kie Miller, Kris, Kristen Resler, Lindsay Soler, Terri Seanard, and Tiffany V. for catching typos!

Another thank you to my friend, Ashley Michele. A few paragraphs ago, I mentioned the cover stuff (where I spammed your DMs with infinite graphic design questions), but I also want to thank you for your friendship. I love that we can discuss the most taboo subjects intellectually *and* smut-ily, and that you helped me brainstorm what age appropriate reaction would make the most sense for Kent's trauma. Thank you for being you, and for being my friend!

Thank you to my mentor from graduate school, who encouraged me to keep working on this story. Back then, *Morsel* was a short story called, "Fingertips," and I hope that if you read this, you're delightfully creeped out with the novel it finally became.

Thank you to my husband for talking with me about all things cannibalism, for indulging in my roleplaying desires, for brainstorming what kind of job Kent should have, and for teaching me how to use Photoshop. I am endlessly grateful to have such a kind, brilliant, and kinky husband.

Thank you to Emma for always putting a smile on my face and telling me the cover for this book is gross. (It is totally gross, I agree!)

But most of all, thank you to my readers. I've been working on this story since 2012. I never thought this book would find an audience, and I'm so freaking grateful that I was wrong. Thank you for reading my books. I'm grateful for your support. <3

About the Author

Audrey Rush writes kinky dark romance and erotic horror. She currently lives in the South with her husband and child. She writes during school.

TikTok: @audreyrushbooks
Instagram: audreyrushbooks
Reader Group: bit.ly/rushreaders
Threads: @audreyrushbooks
Reader Newsletter: audreyrush.com/newsletter
Banned Account Info: bit.ly/bannedsupport
Amazon: amazon.com/author/audreyrush
Website: audreyrush.com
Facebook: fb.me/audreyrushbooks
Goodreads: author/show/AudreyRush
Email: audreyrushbooks@gmail.com

Printed in Dunstable, United Kingdom